D1278465

THE SENTINELS

A MATTER OF
IMPORTANCE

A NOVEL

ALSO FROM GORDON ZUCKERMAN

Fortunes of War
Crude Deception

THE SENTINELS

A MATTER OF IMPORTANCE

A NOVEL

GORDON ZUCKERMAN

LIVE OAK
BOOK COMPANY

Published by Live Oak Book Company
Austin, TX
www.liveoakbookcompany.com

Distributed by Live Oak Book Company

For ordering information or special discounts for bulk purchases, please contact Live Oak Book Company at PO Box 91869, Austin, TX, 78709, 512.891.6100.

Design and composition by Greenleaf Book Group LLC
Cover design by Greenleaf Book Group LLC

Cataloging-in-Publication data
(Prepared by The Donohue Group, Inc.)

Zuckerman, Gordon.
     The Sentinels. A matter of importance : a novel / Gordon Zuckerman. -- 1st ed.

     p. ; cm. -- (The Sentinels ; [bk. 3])

     Issued also as an ebook.
     ISBN: 978-1-936909-52-0 (pbk.)
     ISBN: 978-1-936909-60-5 (hardcover)

     1. Industrialists--United States--Fiction. 2. Conspiracy--Fiction. 3. United States--Economic conditions--21st century. I. Title. II. Title: Matter of importance

PS3626.U266 S46 2012
813/ .6   2012937504

Printed in the United States of America on acid-free paper

12 13 14 15 16 17   10 9 8 7 6 5 4 3 2 1

First Edition

AUTHOR'S NOTE

In chapter 6, Dr. Robin Cook's character presents a slideshow that is a synopsis of "Employ American: A Matter of Importance," a winning economic doctoral thesis. The student authors of this fictional thesis divided the fifty-year postwar economic history from 1960 to 2010 into four separate phases: Age of Economic Equilibrium, Age of Consumer Products, Age of Real Estate, and The Bubble Bursts. These four phases are detailed for the reader in a chart located in the Appendix.

List of Characters

Mr. Aakil Chandakar—Owner of Chandakar, Inc., in Mumbai; a long-time friend and business partner to Jeff Mohr.

Madam Cecelia Chang Stone—Called Madam Chang; last living member of the original Six Sentinels; Chairman Emeritus of the Institute; Chairman of the Sentinel Trust; widow of Mike Stone; mother of Dr. Robin Cook and Ivan Stone.

Ivan Chang Stone—A member of the Sentinel Institute board of directors; son of Madam Chang; brother to Dr. Robin Cook.

Dr. Robin Chang Cook—Cochair, Sentinel Institute board of directors; Dean of the Sentinel Institute's International Economic Department; daughter of Madam Chang; sister of Ivan Stone; widow.

Terrance "Terry" Flynn—Director of the San Francisco branch of the FBI.

Charley Hutson—A member of the Sentinel Institute board of directors; served in the Persian Gulf with Jeff Mohr; works for U.S. Motors; boyfriend to Andi Taylor.

Jeff Mohr—A member of the Sentinel Institute board of directors; owner of Mohr Electronics; served in the Persian Gulf with Charley Hutson; husband to Meg.

Meg Mohr—Jeff's wife.

J.W. Porter—Chairman of the board of U.S. Motors; Charley Hutson's boss.

Claudia Demaureux Roth—A member of the Sentinel Institute board of directors; senior investment analyst at Lazarus & Co.

Mr. Tambour—A former Indian ambassador to China and the United States.

Dr. Andi Taylor—A practicing behavioral psychologist; Charley's girlfriend.

General Benjamin "Ben" T. Wells—A member of the Sentinel Institute board of directors; retired U.S. Army, three-star general; former student of Madam Chang; early graduate of the Sentinel Institute.

Larry Wilshire—A former military colleague to Charley Hutson and Jeff Mohr; an independent security contractor.

Nate White—A former FBI agent; founder and COO of White Security.

Sam "Mr. Sam" Walcott—Senior Director of the Sentinel Institute board of directors; U.S. Congressman, ranking member of the House Ways and Means Committee.

Cheng Yee—Owner of Yee, Inc., in China; friend and trusted business colleague to Jeff Mohr.

Monterey, California
June 11, 2010
"Ladies and gentlemen, we are locked in a new kind of war, a war of multinational corporate and sovereign nation manufacturing competition. If the United States is to survive economically, the global competitiveness of the American goods producer needs to be restored."

With these opening statements, retired three-star general Benjamin T. Wells began his commencement address to the Sentinel Institute's graduating doctoral studies class.

———

Just moments before, Madam Cecelia Chang Stone, the last living member of the original Six Sentinels and one of the founders of the Institute, had introduced the honored speaker.

The diminutive, gray-haired ninety-seven-year-old matriarch of the Sentinel Trust stood at the podium, sporting her well-known mischievous grin, with her posture perfectly erect and her emerald green eyes flashing with life.

"Ladies and gentlemen, as it has been my privilege to do for the last thirty-eight years, I have the honor of introducing this year's commencement speaker. Recently, I had the opportunity to talk to my former student—Benjamin T. Wells—a good friend, and an early graduate of the Sentinel Institute. This early pioneer of surgical aerial warfare is widely recognized for his ability to successfully adapt modern weapon technology to battleground tactical warfare. Over the years, his specially trained units have operated at the president's will all around our troubled world. Following Ben's retirement from the army after thirty years of service, he has spent the last year visiting his former officers, who in civilian life have scattered to the four corners of the world. As he traveled, people frequently asked, 'While we were busy protecting American interests abroad, how good a job have we been doing in taking care of business at home?'

"I invited Ben to address you today and share a few of his personal observations. Benjamin, if you please."

———

Having paused to let his opening remarks sink in, the general continued his speech.

"Frustrated by what I was learning, I decided to call Madam Chang, whose opinion I respect and trust. She instantly grasped the source of my concern and suggested I read this year's winning doctoral thesis, 'Employ American: A Matter of Importance.'

"Well, Madam Chang, I've read this thesis," said General Ben as he turned and smiled at his mentor. "What I can't understand is how five admittedly brilliant doctoral candidates were able to identify the source of our economic problems and devise such an exciting solution. What have the rest of us been doing?

"How, in an economy operating in a world experiencing a global industrial revolution, in an environment of accelerated wartime federal spending, can it be that one out of every five members of our civilian workforce is either out of work or can't find suitable part-time employment, and one out of every seven U.S. citizens is receiving food stamps?

"I've always believed we live in a world known for its ability to discover new technologies, develop new consumer products, mobilize its vast financial markets, and create billions of dollars of new consumption demand. Why, in an economy that suffers from so much underemployment and a shrinking tax base, have we failed to discover an alternative solution to prevent the outsourcing of manufacturing employment to lower-cost foreign labor markets?

"How proud can we be when our returning veterans and our college graduates must compete with more than 25 million other Americans to find suitable employment?

"Have we ever stopped to calculate what the real cost of the lost manufacturing employment really is?

"Now that we have learned we can no longer rely on the expansion of consumer debt to finance the growth of discretionary spending, don't we need to look back to other periods of economic prosperity for the clues we need to solve our current problems?

"We have been forced to rely on review and analysis by these five doctoral students of the ten years between 1960 and 1970 to learn that our economy grew at the compounded rate of 6.5 percent and created 12.2 million private employment jobs. Three new service-oriented jobs were required to support the creation of each new goods-producing job. During the same ten-year period, consumer debt remained relatively constant and public debt declined. Had we preserved the cost competitiveness of the American manufacturer, and preserved historical ratios of goods-producing to service jobs, today's employment rolls would include fifteen million more manufacturing jobs.

"To this old soldier, history's message is indelibly clear: We need to learn how to restore those lost jobs without further burdening the consumers and the federal government's balance sheets with additional debt.

"The question I have been asking myself lately is, Why are our global problems of economic imperialism any less menacing than the problems of military imperialism that were threatening the world order in 1938? At that time, the United States found it necessary, in less than three years, to convert its peacetime industrial complex into a wartime arsenal, the size of which exceeded the combined military production of all of our enemies.

"How can we, as a nation, expect to solve our problems at home until we learn how to fully employ our people?"

A standing ovation erupted, interrupting his remarks. Pleased with the response, the "General's General" took a few sips of water, allowing the audience members to calm down and settle into their seats.

CHAPTER 1

TROUBLE

Three days after the graduation ceremony, at three o'clock in the morning, a giant explosion destroyed the Sentinel Institute's engineering research laboratory. The shaking of the buildings from the blast's concussion and the sound of glass windows shattering woke even the deepest sleepers in the nearby neighborhoods.

Emergency alarms, sirens, and horns that hadn't sounded since the days of civil defense drills added to the cacophony. West Coast military units were instantly put on alert. Squadrons of defense fighters were prepared for takeoff. Closer to home, residents rushed out onto their front lawns, looking up in an attempt to discover what had happened. Their thoughts were filled with questions. *Has some kind of a bomb been dropped? Has a gas main exploded? Has some kind of terrorist act just occurred?*

The first firefighting brigade arrived twenty minutes after the explosion. Despite the steady streams of water the firefighters trained on the building, the fire raged until the building and its contents were no longer salvageable. What the fire hadn't destroyed was ruined by water and flame retardant.

The first responders reported that debris from the three-story brick building could be observed three blocks away. Anybody working on the lab's night-shift cleaning crew had been instantly killed. Flying bricks and other debris had pockmarked the sides of adjacent buildings.

The bombing of the engineering research laboratory quickly became front-page news. The destruction of such a large building was a newsworthy event. The press referred to the explosion as an act of terrorism and speculated about who might have been responsible and listed possible motives.

Members of the Sentinel Institute's board of directors were inundated with requests for interviews. The Institute's cochair, Robin Cook, was asked to appear on one of the leading Sunday morning talk shows.

The well-prepared host sidestepped the preliminary formalities and dove right to the key question, "Dr. Cook, what was so important about the experiments being conducted in the Institute's engineering laboratory that would provoke someone or some group to blow it up?"

"The Sentinel Institute was conducting experiments to prove the capability of a new chemical process that would make it possible to burn coal on a cost-competitive basis and would comply with recently adopted EPA clean air standards."

"Even so, why might the successful completion of those experiments encourage such a violent act?"

"The development of a lower-cost, environmentally compatible energy source represents a critical component required to reduce American manufacturing costs. At the same time, if we are able to replace higher-priced imported petroleum products with lower-cost clean burned coal, we could materially reduce our dependence on foreign oil, reduce a negative balance of payments, and provide employment for a lot of Americans!"

"Dr. Cook, for the benefit of our audience, please explain why the Institute insists that this program of such national importance must be completed within twelve months?"

"Now that we have succeeded in calculating the annual cost to the government of losing one manufacturing job at $80,000, we need to complete our work in time to prevent another wave of major U.S. manufacturers from accepting pending offers from the Chinese government and other lower-cost labor markets. Unless we can demonstrate why it is in the best interests of industrialists to manufacture their products in the United States, how can we expect to stop the continued outsourcing of employment? Any further erosion of manufacturing labor could add an additional economic burden to our wounded economy."

Experienced and usually prepared for bold answers from his guests, the host was momentarily surprised by the boldness of the petite, polite woman, conservatively dressed in a high-collared jade green Mandarin dress, with only a hint of makeup needed to accent the uniqueness of her soft Eurasian beauty and her emerald green eyes.

If the compelling nature of her argument had not succeeded in convincing the audience, the self-confident demeanor of the regally composed woman sitting patiently in the glare of the TV lights would have been more than sufficient to accomplish her mission.

CHAPTER 2

CHARLEY HUTSON

Charley Hutson had been courting Andi for several weeks before he invited her to join him in his wharf-side penthouse apartment. Stretched out on the floor in front of the fireplace, Charley and Andi sipped fifteen-year-old single-malt Scotch, served neat, while listening to Puccini's *Madame Butterfly* and watching the lights of Detroit and the boats on Lake St. Claire paint their cosmic images on the twelve-foot-high ceiling. The flickering flames in the fireplace made it appear as if angels were dancing through the heavens.

Suddenly a ringing cell phone disturbed Charley's artfully contrived moment. Annoyed, he glanced at the display—he regretfully disengaged himself from the warm embrace of promising possibilities with Andi and hit the answer button on his phone.

He was greeted by the raspy voice of "J.W." Porter, his boss and the chairman of the board of U.S. Motors. "You might want to turn on the news. Something important has happened that may interest you. Can you be at the office by 9:30 tomorrow morning? There are some people who are very anxious to talk to you."

The line went dead before Charley could reply.

Preoccupied with his thoughts, Charley crossed the room and turned on the big-screen TV. "Early this evening, William

'Wild Bill' Reedy, the flamboyant and charismatic president of U.S. Motors, unexpectedly resigned during a regularly scheduled board of directors meeting. A reliable source has informed us that a disagreement erupted between President Reedy and company chairman J.W. Porter about the planned installation of a new manufacturing facility in China."

Painfully aware of Charley's preoccupation with the eleven o'clock news, Andi stood up and began gathering her previously discarded clothing, saying, "Charley, who would have thought you would abandon a partially clothed woman to watch television? Do you mind telling me what just happened?"

"Sorry, the president of U.S. Motors just resigned. I bet the purpose of our meeting tomorrow is to come up with a way for U.S. Motors to keep its car production onshore and replicate the manufacturing costs offered by the Chinese government. I'm confused that the chairman would call me; I'm not even a member of the executive management committee."

"Maybe they need someone who is used to thinking outside the box, someone who can raise important questions and suggest possible alternatives. You certainly appear to be one of those people!"

Andi picked up their cocktail glasses and crossed the room to the bar. She sat on one of the bar stools and patted the one next to her, indicating that Charley should join her.

Still preoccupied, Charley said, "Why would they believe I can solve the same problem in a matter of months?"

Realizing he had been thinking out loud, he paused, "Surely you can't be interested in listening to me talk about work."

"Come on, Charley. Where does it say that because a woman is attractive and a former jock she doesn't have a brain? If, during our last few dates, you hadn't been so intent on impressing me and satisfying your own ego, you might have paid more attention.

"Had you done so, you might've learned I received my doctoral degree in behavioral psychology from the University of Chicago. For the last ten years I have been a practicing behavioral psychologist trying to understand why 40 percent of the turnover of management is the result of faulty hiring.

"They tell me I'm a pretty good listener and ask good questions. Now, why don't you pour me another drink and sit down and tell Dr. Taylor all about your problems at U.S. Motors."

CHAPTER 3

U.S. MOTORS

J.W. Porter and the other directors were informally gathered at the far end of the conference room when Charley entered. Several were sitting in the deep leather chairs; one was so relaxed he had draped his leg over the armrest. Three men stood in front of the floor-to-ceiling plate-glass window, quietly chatting. The remaining two were leaning against the small bar, talking about their latest round of golf and enjoying their regular Saturday morning Bloody Marys.

Accustomed to spending Saturday mornings on the golf course, the men had opted to wear cotton golf shirts, brightly colored cashmere sweaters, carefully tailored golf slacks, and highly shined loafers, the kind with tassels. Charley noticed that one of the men even wore black socks with bright pink polka dots.

Despite the relaxed atmosphere, Charley knew that the calm was only an illusion. *Why else would J.W. have called a meeting on a Saturday morning unless we are here to discuss something important?*

The chairman was the first to speak. "Charley, we assume you've read the newspaper articles or seen the television announcement of

Bill Reedy's resignation. I'm afraid Bill and I had an irresolvable difference of opinion over how U.S. Motors should be operated.

"I'm certain you understand my concern. The general public has given our company the benefit of a prepackaged bankruptcy requiring tens of billions of dollars of fresh credit to get us started building cars. The one thing we all seem to be able to agree on is that we are being given one more 'bite at the apple,' and this time we better get it right!"

J.W.'s words reminded Charley of a statement Porter had made in an interview with the *New York Times* that had attracted Charley to U.S. Motors in the first place. Then he'd said, "The time has come for us to rethink, retool, and reorganize. Consumer tastes are changing, and we are on the leading edge of a new age of exciting technological advancement. How is it that we find ourselves on the brink of a new era of expanding world demand, and all we know is where we have been, not where we should be headed?"

In reviewing his new protégé's first year of employment, J.W. thought, *Charley has to be rapidly becoming what we in Detroit have learned to call a rainmaker.* J.W. had come to appreciate that Charley, a seasoned executive, did his homework, was not afraid to take chances, and could be relied on to express his unvarnished point of view.

Returning to the issue at hand, J.W. said, "It's absolutely necessary for us to find an acceptable domestic manufacturing solution. Not only do we need to find the answer, it's also important that we provide a living example for other major manufacturers.

"Charley, I know it's asking a lot, but we need someone with your conceptual understanding of our business, someone who is not a product of the 'traditional' car school, and someone who has the ability to find new solutions. You have less than twelve months to complete the job before our option to extend our agreement with the Chinese matures.

"I don't look forward to having to choose between the economic survival of the company and the continued employment of the American labor market. We need to challenge the belief that American manufacturers need to outsource their production in order to remain profitable. There has to be a better answer—we just don't happen to know what it is!"

———

Andi was waiting for Charley at Mike's Place, the neighborhood tavern where they had first met. She chose the same bar stool she had been sitting on that night, which also gave her a clear view of the door. When Charley finally arrived, she could tell by the intense look on his face that he had a lot on his mind. Watching him walk toward her, she couldn't help but think, *Even with so much on his mind, this tall, athletic, dark-complected man with the curly black hair and piercing brown eyes reminds me of some big cat carefully stalking his prey.*

Charley smiled when he saw Andi waiting for him and what must been a Macallan served neat sitting on the bar. "Am I glad to see you! I've had one of those days. But before we get into all that, I want to talk to you about last night. The minute you left, I regretted I allowed the evening to end on such an impersonal note."

"Don't worry about me," Andi said, "I'm the least of your problems. You are clearly preoccupied with what must be a very serious problem. Maybe you better take a sip of that drink and tell Dr. Taylor what has happened."

Andi was fascinated by what Charley was telling her. Having devoted so much study to the reasons people employ other people, she was more than curious to hear about the strategic thinking going on behind the scenes. "Charley, what an opportunity! Surely, it must be a compliment to be asked to solve such a difficult problem."

"Or maybe he's setting me up to fail. My failure could represent the excuse he needs to proceed with the Chinese option."

"Shame on you, Charley! Instead of worrying about what possible motives they might have, why don't you give these men credit for their willingness to consider possible alternatives? Why not give it your best shot? What do you have to lose?"

Impressed with Andi's bold response, Charley asked, "Is there something I've missed about your professional training?"

"My professional training? Are you kidding? This is strictly personal. My father used to tell my brothers and me when we were faced with a particularly difficult situation: 'Don't let those sons-of-bitches push you around!' We always referred to it as Taylor's rule!"

"Taylor's rule, eh? Well, Charley's rule calls for another Macallan. Bartender!"

CHAPTER 4

MEET JEFF MOHR

Jeff Mohr answered Charley's call on his private phone after the first ring. After listening to Charley explain why he had called, Jeff said, "Of course I'm prepared to become involved."

Jeff paused for a moment. "Are you aware of Robin's students' doctoral treatise 'Employ American: A Matter of Importance'? As a fellow director of the Institute, you must have received a copy of it. Their thesis could very well represent the blueprint for a plan of action that could resolve U.S. Motors' domestic manufacturing problem."

Jeff continued, "Charley! I assure you, U.S. Motors isn't the only company challenged to repatriate at least a portion of its offshore manufacturing. If I thought for one moment it was economically feasible, Mohr Electronics would shift a significant portion of its offshore production back to the United States so fast it would make your head spin."

Jeff's comment surprised Charley, and he said, "If our two companies can solve critical problems by repatriating manufacturing, I wonder how many other organizations could become involved? Maybe there are more companies than we realize that share some of our problems and concerns.

"The more I think about the destruction of those research facilities at the Institute, the more convinced I am that one of the reasons behind the bombing might have been to create an inordinate delay. Failure to comply within the twelve month limitation could be as harmful as the failure to produce the right test results with clean-burning coal. Talk about a deal-breaker problem—if anyone other than Ivan Stone were looking for the solution, I'd really be concerned."

Responding emphatically, Jeff said, "That is just one of the reasons why all of us directors need to attend the emergency Sentinel board meeting. I don't know about you, but I need to learn a lot more about their idea that each new production job produces $2 of increased tax revenues for each dollar paid the worker. If they are right, when 35 percent of those savings are to be returned to the responsible employer, I can understand how this reduces direct labor costs by as much as 70 percent. We could be talking about an entirely new ball game. Talk about an assertion that will be challenged, this has to be the mother of all assertions."

"Jeff, we've a lot to talk about and not very long to do it. I'll take the red-eye and be in your office at seven tomorrow morning. That should give us an entire day before the Sentinel board meeting is scheduled to begin."

———

Although Charley and Jeff had been friends for many years, this was the first time Charley had visited the Palo Alto headquarters of the internationally renowned consumer electronics company. Two short flights of stairs took him to the top floor of the sprawling three-story building.

Jeff was waiting for him. In his early fifties, Jeff still looked the trim athlete he had been when they had served together behind enemy lines in the Iraqi Gulf War more than twenty years ago. His clear blue eyes, rugged jaw, and short hair gave him a youthful appearance. Jeff still preferred to wear cowboy boots, which made him appear taller than his natural six-foot height. Jeff showed him into the open office space that lay beyond the reception area. Charley thought it looked more like an architect's drafting room than the executive offices of one of the electronic industry's iconic leaders and true visionaries.

The room was filled with six smaller conference tables that held neat stacks of yellow pads and cylindrical containers filled with carefully sharpened wooden pencils. Walking over to the nearest table, Charley selected a pencil and sniffed the distinctive aroma of a freshly sharpened California incense-cedar pencil. He thought, *I've always enjoyed that smell!*

Six well-worn padded-leather director's chairs were neatly arranged along both sides of each table. On one end of the elliptical table sat a high-powered, state-of-the-art desktop computer and an oversized monitor. A row of plug-in computer ports ran the entire length of the table. A large easel supporting a big black board stood at the opposite end.

Sensing Charley's surprise with the unusual office, Jeff said, "We tend to look at our industry as a constantly changing world where yesterday's solutions represent potential roadblocks to tomorrow's opportunities. Managing the creative process may be one of our most important challenges.

"Those five tables represent our company's version of a creative laboratory for each of my executive management teams. The sixth table, the one over there in the corner, is my desk. This office was laid out to be a place where dynamic and creative minds can gather to discuss and analyze problems, come up with innovative solutions, and retain a certain sense of prideful authorship.

"This setup allows me to drift from one table to another and monitor what's happening and be available, if needed, to answer questions or make comments. You'd be surprised how well it works. I can remain well informed without having the employees writing, and me reading, so many reports. Most important, this process shortens the company's decision-making reaction time."

Charley couldn't help but wonder how different the situation at U.S. Motors might have been had executive management been able to divorce itself from its traditional car company operating mentality and encourage more customer-oriented creative thought. *For way too long, the bean counters and the engineers have enjoyed entirely too much influence in the design of automobiles, the planning, and operation of the business,* he mused.

"Jeff, wouldn't it be interesting to learn what could happen if the management of an automobile company learned to adopt your approach to business planning, your consumer-product development philosophies, and your management of the creative process?"

"Charley, you'd be surprised how much of it I might trade for some of your problem-solving ability!"

CHAPTER 5

MEET CASEY JONES

It was going to be a warm spring day in Monterey. The bay fog had burned off, revealing a cloudless blue sky, and there was only a hint of wind. Dr. Robin Cook, Dean of the Sentinel Institute's International Economic Department, hurried through the campus gardens, completely absorbed in her thoughts. Robin didn't want to be late for the meeting. In addition to her mother, Madam Chang, Chairman Emeritus, and herself, six of the Institute's directors and more celebrated early graduates would be attending. Knowing Congressman "Mr. Sam" Walcott and General Ben Wells would be there added even greater significance.

As she hurried along, her thoughts went back to some of the events of the last few days. *The Sentinel world has suddenly become more complicated. Calling my mother within hours of the engineering research lab bombing, I felt confused and worried. Why would anyone want to blow up an engineering facility? Could there be something going on beyond the regular presentation of a doctoral thesis?*

Her mother's normal cool and calm manner hadn't surprised her, "Robin, why don't we plan to meet for tea tomorrow afternoon. By then I should have been able to make some calls and hopefully learn more about what has happened."

Teatime meant 3:00 p.m. Robin always preferred to arrive early. She enjoyed the opportunity to accompany her mother when she walked through the different rooms of her 34th floor condominium and studied the art, pictures, reprints of newspaper articles, and personal letters that her mother displayed on the walls. In each of the four rooms, her mother had collected images describing important events and experiences of each of the four distinct phases of her remarkable life. In her bedroom were all the materials depicting the first twenty-two years of her early life before she left Hong Kong in 1935. This was the private part of her life that had meaning only for her. Besides her children, Ivan and Robin, very few other people had seen this portion of her collection.

The walls of the guest bedroom were adorned with the images and artifacts of the eight-year period when she and her future Sentinel colleagues met at the University of California, studied together, conceived and wrote their "Power Cycle" doctoral thesis, and began their professional careers.

The living room, the largest of the four rooms, had been reserved for the twenty-five years of memorabilia depicting the active phase of Six Sentinels' challenge of unbridled greed. Without Madam Chang's explanations of the images, they would not be meaningful to anyone who hadn't been involved in the Sentinels' early efforts. Who would have believed that such a small group of committed problem-solving leaders could prevent German industrialists from using their war fortunes and from financing the formation of a fourth Reich? Or succeed in preventing seven oil companies from perpetuating their control over 90 percent of the world's oil supply?

The materials displayed in the formal dining room told the early history of the Sentinel Institute. Founded in 1968, the International School of Economics and Politics represented what Madam Chang and the original Sentinels regarded as their greatest achievement. Over the thirty-five years following the Institute's opening in 1975, the paintings, the photos, and the reprints of newspaper articles detailed the international political and economic achievements of many of the Institute's more outstanding graduates.

Robin always tried to arrive early. Every time she had accompanied her mother on one of her personally conducted tours, she looked forward to learning about some new detail. After all the years, she knew her mother would, unconsciously, utter some new comment that would add additional meaning to one of her adventures.

No matter how early Robin arrived, Madam Chang would emerge from her fifth room, located behind two very large and heavily paneled, thick wooden doors. A large padlock connected two wrought-iron rings and secured the private room whenever Madam Chang wasn't inside. It was the only room in her house her daughter and son had never been allowed to enter.

What few glimpses Robin had been allowed revealed desk-height surface areas lining all four windowless walls. Computers, printers and fax machines, telephones, oversized television monitors, and banks of high-speed, state-of-the-art servers filled the horizontal space. In the center of the room, a large raised back-lit table usually held photographs that were being studied.

Fascinated by all the modern equipment, and frustrated by never being allowed to use any of it, Robin was always asking her mother to explain the purpose of all the electronics equipment. The only answer she ever received was, "Robin, my dear, without all that equipment, how would I be able to communicate with my friends?"

Surprisingly, her mother was not waiting to greet her when she arrived. At precisely three o'clock, the doors to the secret room opened, and the ninety-seven-year-old matriarch of the Chang and Stone family emerged. Dressed in a traditional high-collared, full-length Mandarin dress, without a hair out of place or a blemish in her carefully applied makeup, the universally admired woman greeted her daughter with a warm smile, a kiss on both cheeks, and a strong hug.

Robin was confused. *As they settled in with their tea, Madam Chang asked if she'd seen her friends lately. And had she renewed her security service? Was she sleeping well? Why is she asking me so many questions about my personal life? Is she concerned about my personal safety or the absence of a more complete private life? What could have happened, after all this time, to arouse her curiosity?*

Robin was pouring her mother another cup of tea when Madam Chang abruptly changed the subject. "Ever since you called, I've been busy talking to some of my friends that are still engaged in some very interesting activities. Apparently, most of their information comes from some very sensitive sources. According to my friends, these sources are so confidential that my friends were reluctant to share their identity with me."

After taking another sip from her second cup of tea, Madam Chang said, "Not only do you need to listen very carefully to what I'm about to tell you, but you better make certain Nate White and Terry Flynn are present at your scheduled Sentinel board of directors meeting.

"From what I have been able to learn, the 'Employ American' doctoral thesis written by your students has received considerable attention in some very interesting places. Not only do some people consider the plan to be most extraordinary, but they also appear to be threatened by its possible implementation. All five areas the plan addresses will leave you open to five different sets of enemies. There are industrialists, foreign and domestic, concerned about the economic consequences of American repatriation of manufacturing employment.

"Sovereign oil nations and big oil companies are worried about how the expanded use of coal and natural gas could materially alter American energy consumption habits.

"Regional power-generating utilities have to be concerned about the consequences if new sources of lower-cost, green energy were to be introduced.

"The insurance industry will be threatened by 200,000 employee insurance cooperatives capable of self-insuring and learning how to lay off the unacceptable risks with the London reinsurance market.

"It's possible that the big labor unions could become your most antagonistic adversaries or your most enthusiastic supporters. Their memberships have been sharply reduced by the affects of offshore relocation of manufacturing jobs, and the transfer of domestic production to nonunion factories located in right-to-work states. It will be interesting to learn if the union leaders see your program as a threat or possible provider of new jobs.

"Not only should you and your friends be concerned about your ability to solve your many complicated problems, you need to protect yourselves from attack by very powerful and ruthless sources of threatened economic self-interests!"

After unexpectedly standing up, Madam Chang announced, "Perhaps it would be appropriate if we looked at some of the images hanging on the walls."

They were standing in front of a photograph that had been taken when FBI agents were carrying the frail, unconscious young Cecelia Chang down the stairs that led from a second-story loft of an old steel fabricating plant in Berkeley. The engraved small bronze plate read "Berkeley 1943." The second picture had been taken from the protection of a stalled vintage train located in what appeared to be mountainous jungle terrain. The plate read, "Indonesia 1944." The third plaque read "Boston 1944." The fourth read "London 1944" and the fifth read "Cap d'Antibes, France, 1945."

"Robin, do you know what all five of these pictures share in common?" Without waiting for a response she said, "Each of these pictures was taken at the scene of a ruthless attack against Sentinels by operatives of a security organization employed by German industrialists.

"I'm trying to impress upon you the dangers that could be involved with your attempts to implement your plan."

———

As Robin continued to hurry toward the emergency meeting, she was forcing her mind to focus on the long and complicated Sentinel board of directors' agenda for the next three days. Instinctively, she knew her students would have only these three days to convince the Institute's seven directors of the wisdom of their helping her students to implement "Employ American."

One by one she began to reflect on what she remembered about her fellow directors and past graduates of the Sentinel Institute.

First was Congressman Sam Walcott, ranking member of the House Ways and Means Committee. For several years "Mr. Sam" had been one of the Institute's most active and influential directors. He had willingly lent his support to fundraising, keeping the Institute well advised on pending legislation that might affect the school, and had used his considerable influence behind the scenes to protect and enhance the Institute. He was a man who had been long appreciated for his candor, his outspoken nature, and his ability to ask the difficult questions.

Keenly aware that the implementation of the Employ American plan required the introduction and passage of tax legislation to reduce the effective costs of direct labor employment to global competitive levels, Robin understood why his support was so important.

General Wells' support of their plan was crucial to developing the kind of third-party endorsement the legitimacy of their plan depended on. In addition to his introductory work at the graduation, his continuing efforts within the military community could provide an invaluable contribution toward building the foundation of support they would require.

As she rounded the corner of the administration building, Robin's thoughts shifted to Jeff Mohr. How could there be a more iconic entrepreneurial leader than Jeff? It had been his vision that had been responsible for the early development of the semiconductor consumer products industry. What industry employed more people offshore than his?

If Jeff believed his company's interests were best served by repatriating a portion of its foreign employment, what might the effect of his decision have on his fellow employers?

Claudia Roth's contribution within the Wall Street investment community would be of crucial importance if they were to have any opportunity to recruit cooperative private investment capital. Her skills as a creative and influential investment practitioner would be thoroughly tested.

Crossing the street in front of the conference building where the meetings for the next three days were to be held, she thought of her brother, Ivan Stone. His involvement could be the most critical. *Without him and his team solving the affordable clean energy problem, how would we be able to convince employers of our ability to achieve global competitiveness with the Chinese? He may be a great problem solver, but determining the economic feasibility of converting coal, natural gas, and coal ash into environmentally compatible electricity and high-strength cement within six months would appear to be an impossible task to anyone else. For Ivan it must just be a challenge that needs to be resolved on the way to victory. I guess I will never understand why my own brother is not more intimidated by a fear of failure.*

Charley may be the most complex and difficult to understand of any of the directors. Over the last four years, I have known him, I think this intensely private man may have allowed us to see three entirely different sides to his personality.

Perhaps, his anger over being given the choice of going to jail or joining the army may be his most distinguishing characteristic. Very clearly, it had provided the internal drive that has influenced his approach to leadership and problem solving. It could be his indefatigable commitment to succeeding that proves so persuasive in motivating the people aligned with him.

I don't think I have ever known anyone more discerning about the environment in which he chooses to work. The one thing I feel I have learned about Charley is his unwillingness to remain in a job where he can no longer keep learning or have the authority needed to solve problems of importance.

I don't know whether I should be intimidated or excited about what could happen over the next three days, Robin thought.

———

Charley was waiting near the entrance to talk to her before the meeting started. He needed to make certain Robin, cochair of the Sentinel Institute's board of directors, understood the immediacy of the problem he was being asked to resolve at U.S. Motors.

———

Opening the meeting a short time later, Robin said, "Before we discuss the two operating problems on today's agenda, it has been suggested that we address possible security problems. At the suggestion of Madam Chang, I took the liberty of calling two old friends, Terrance Flynn and Nate White. Terry is the director of the San Francisco FBI office. Nate White, a former FBI agent, is the founder and chief operating officer of White Security. His company is considered by many to be the best private security company on the West Coast. Both men are waiting outside, and if there are no objections, I suggest we ask them to join us."

After the introductions, Terry reported, "For the last three days, Nate and I have done some preliminary checking and compiled a list of rich and powerful industries, sovereign governments, specific companies, and influential people who could be threatened by what you are planning. Just the fact that one or some combination of these entities has found it necessary to blow up the Sentinel lab and kill two janitors and a night watchman should be regarded as a clear indication of their seriousness and the danger you may be facing.

"At this point, we are certain of only two things: who the targets are, and what your antagonists are trying to prevent.

"We propose using the personal protection we will be assigning each of you as a means to identify people who wish to harm you or interrupt your work. Once we are able to determine who they are, I hope they will lead us to the source of your problems.

"To get started, we have already assigned the code name 'Casey Jones' to your case. Each of you should use this name to identify yourself and to communicate the presence of danger or an emergency."

Dismayed, Charley protested, "In other words, we're to be used as the bait in your trap!"

"Well, that's one way of looking at it," Terry said. "We prefer to think of what we're doing as more of a team effort."

CHAPTER 6

MATTERS OF IMPORTANCE

Unaccustomed to discussing problems of personal security, the directors focused their attention and comments on whether they were going to be used as the bait in their own trap. Robin made no effort to regain their attention until lunch had been concluded. Opening the afternoon session, she said, "We have a full agenda, and it's time we get started."

Congressman Sam Walcott, the senior director present, wasted no time in getting down to business. "Dr. Cook, as our resident economist and faculty advisor to these five remarkable doctoral candidates, I was wondering if you would be kind enough to explain how the math of Employ American enables the employer to be reimbursed for 70 percent of his incremental direct labor costs by the U.S. government on a 'make money' basis."

Anticipating the question, Robin had come well prepared. "Congressman, if you will allow me the time, I would like to provide you and the other directors with a brief synopsis of the students' economic analysis. For purposes of evaluation, they divided the fifty-year postwar economic history from 1960 to 2010 into four separate phases, each of which represents an era when distinctly different economic dynamics were operating in our economy.

"In order to appreciate their conclusions, it's important that you understand the foundation of their analysis. It is predicated on three historical observations. The rise and fall of discretionary spending represents an important influence over the country's economic condition."

Robin hit the remote to display her first PowerPoint slide on the screen.

"The ten-year period between 1960 and 1970 shown in this chart, which is titled the Age of Economic Equilibrium,* represents the last decade before the American economy began to outsource manufacturing employment and utilize the unused debt capacity of the American household to stimulate discretionary spending.

"During this ten-year period, seventeen million jobs were added to the economy, five million of which were created in the government sector. Of the remaining 12.2 million jobs, 3 million were created in the manufacturing sector, and 9.2 million jobs (three jobs for each new manufacturing job) were created in the service sector. It is interesting to note, during this period of continued growth in goods-producing jobs, the resultant average annual increase of 6.5 percent in GDP was accomplished in an economic environment where public debt declined from 58 percent to 35 percent of GDP. Discretionary spending modestly improved from 16.38 percent to 18.8 percent of GDP, and use of consumer debt only represents 4 percent of total consumptive demand.

"Take a look at this next chart and you'll see what can happen when discretionary spending stimulated by the introduction of manufacturing jobs is replaced with growth resulting from increasing consumer credit." Robin hit the button so that the next slide, Age of Consumer Products (1971–2000), appeared.

"Although the economy continued to grow at an average annual rate of 5.4 percent of GDP and the rate of unemployment dropped from 18 percent to 5 percent, the expansion of consumer

*See appendix, page 316–317.

debt increased from $6,408 to $57,202 per employed worker or from 82 percent to 151 percent of total earned income.

"The country was on a spending spree, incomes were improving, unemployment was declining, and no one was questioning the possible consequences of the decline in goods-producing employment (31.0 percent to 18.0 percent of the private employed workforce), or what might occur when the consumers' balance sheet becomes fully leveraged and he can no longer service the burden of his current debt or add additional debt.

"Next, we'll turn to the Age of Real Estate (2000–2007). Prior to the year 2000, Wall Street was responsibly learning how to bundle real estate debt, and sell participating interests in the pooled ownership to private investors. The realization of the presence of an incalculable new pool of liquid funds that could be used to fund the expansion of home ownership and related commercial development and to liquefy, heretofore trapped created equity in homes, represented an enormous financial opportunity for the financial services and business communities and a source of presidential political capital.

"Faced with the prospect of a leveling of the consumer goods economy, the real estate developer, the speculator, the home builder, the commercial developer, the mortgage lender, the financial service industry, the real estate brokerage industry, and the lower-income worker anxious to seize his share in the American dream, all saw the potential opportunity to benefit from the rapid expansion of mortgage credit availability.

"The economy grew at the annual rate of 4.8 percent and unemployment had increased to 5 percent. By December 2007, the outstanding consumer debt had grown from $57,202 to $99,040 per employed, and expressed as a percent of earned income, increased from 151 percent to 180 percent. Consumer debt, for the first time in history, had grown to $13.7 trillion, approximately equal to the country's gross domestic product (GDP).

"Why don't we take a moment to stretch and get a cup of coffee?"

———

After the short break, everyone returned to his or her seat and Robin continued her presentation. The screen displayed a slide titled The Bubble Bursts (2007–2010). Robin took a deep breath and began speaking, "No longer able to service their household debt, increasing numbers of consumers were defaulting on their mortgages and consumer debt contracts. The contraction of consumer debt was adversely infecting discretionary spending. Between 2007 and 2010, consumer debt fell by $606 billion, the GDP declined by $642 billion; 7.8 million people lost their jobs, and 4.0 million people were added to the workforce. Unemployment rose to 10.2 percent and 25 million people were either out of work or couldn't find suitable part-time employment.

"At the federal level, the growth in deficit spending continued. Reduction in tax revenues and increased spending created a negative government cash flow spread of 8.0 percent of GDP. Annual deficits exceeded $1.0 trillion. Public debt grew to more than $13 trillion and for the first time in history exceeded 100 percent of GDP."

As the next to last slide—The Bottom Line—displayed on the screen, Robin said, "The conclusion to be drawn for these four periods of economic history is that to be stable, growth must result both from the improvement in goods-producing employment and the extension of consumer debt within affordable levels.

"The problem that must be addressed is that of learning how to restore the global competitiveness of the American manufacturer and resurrect goods-producing employment without burdening the balance sheet of the consumer or the federal government with additional debt."

As the projector displayed the final slide in her presentation, Robin hoped her audience was awake. The Employ American— New Math section was very important.

"My students believe the achievement of this problem is an accomplishable task. Let's start with the Employ American plan to reduce new manufacturing direct labor costs by 70 percent. The average cost of all taxes paid to some level of government, including Social Security payments, approximates 36 percent of gross earned income. When a person stops being employed, the government not only loses the 36 percent of earned income it has been collecting, but must absorb another 30 percent in the form of unemployment benefits. For the average worker, earning $30,000 per year, the government's annual cost of each lost job is 66.0 percent of previously earned income or approximately equal to $20,000 per year.

"Since three service jobs are created for each new production job, the total new revenue collected by the government is roughly equivalent to $80,000 per year or approximately equal to 200 percent of $40,000 paid the production worker earning $20.00 per hour.

"Should the introduction of new legislation allow the responsible manufacturing employer to receive tax credits equal to 35 percent of the incremental savings he produces for each new job he produces, he will reduce his effective cost of direct labor by approximately 70 percent and become globally competitive."

After pausing to let the effect of her comments sink in, Robin Cook was bracing herself for the congressman's reaction.

Surprisingly, he only said, "I know the jobs have to come from someplace!"

CHAPTER 7

SHOULD WE BECOME INVOLVED?

It had been a long and taxing day. Charley and Jeff were driving from the Sentinel Institute in Monterey to Jeff's home in Atherton. Driving carefully, Jeff appeared to be lost in his thoughts.

Taking advantage of the silence, Charley thought about Andi and their last telephone conversation. *She had seemed eager to become better acquainted. The Carmel weekend Meg and Jeff had arranged could be the perfect opportunity.*

Charley's thoughts were suddenly interrupted when Jeff said, "I've been thinking about whether we should try to help Robin's students execute their plan. For purposes of conversation, I have assumed, if we were to divide up all the work of each of the problems raised by Employ American, we just might be able to make it happen.

"I've been doing some checking, and unfortunately the reduction in effective labor costs solves part of the problem but not the entire problem. Without the introduction of affordable clean energy, national recruitment and training of a qualified workforce, and state-of-the-art, affordable retooling, there isn't much that can be done to ensure the long-term competitiveness of the American producer.

"If, on the other hand, we can convincingly demonstrate how these problems can be reliably solved within workable time frames, why couldn't we sell this program to our respective companies and persuade a number of our friends to join us?"

Before Charley could answer, Jeff turned off the freeway and slowly made his way through the deserted side streets toward his home. As he pulled into the driveway, he said, "Charley, we've been friends for a long time, and each of us has accomplished a number of interesting things. Now, all of a sudden, we are thinking about attempting to change the future landscape of American manufacturing. Is this really something we should be considering?"

As they passed through the kitchen, Charley was already formulating a response. He was so lost in thought that he almost missed seeing Andi's note: *Charley, grab a suit, a fresh bottle of wine, and two more glasses. Meg and I are in the hot tub, and she has been telling me about your earlier life, you naughty little boy!*

In less than three minutes, Charley had changed into his bathing suit, selected an expensive bottle of white wine from Jeff's refrigerated storage cabinet, found two large plastic wine glasses, and was headed poolside.

As he passed through the outside screen door, he saw Andi standing on the end of the diving board, wearing a luminous blue and white one-piece Speedo. The pool lights illuminated her as if she were a theatrical star standing center stage.

Charley could tell she was focused entirely on the dive she was preparing to make. She had carefully placed her toes on the end of the diving board and pointed them inward. He watched as she extended her arms high over her head and arched her body. The scene reminded him of a high-speed photograph taken of someone in motion. *She looks like a magnificent cat ready to pounce, he thought.*

Charley was unprepared for what happened next. Andi

lowered her arms and dipped her knees slightly and suddenly it seemed as if she were thrust high into the air, where she exploded into a violent motion of spinning, tumbling, and twisting. At the last moment, she straightened her body and sliced into the water with barely a splash.

After swimming to the edge of the pool, Andi climbed out and walked over to Charley. Without saying a word, she wrapped her dripping arms around him, pressed her wet body into him, and gave him the kind of kiss that left no room for interpretation.

Settled in the hot tub, the three old friends and their new friend filled their glasses from the fresh bottle. Meg said, "Andi tells me she likes to play golf. Charley, how can you invite such a lovely person to California and expect her to stay busy all day waiting for you to return from your stuffy old meetings?"

Noticing the wine bottle was empty, Jeff suggested they play some kind of a game to decide who would have to get out of the hot tub and walk through the chilly night air to retrieve the next bottle of wine. Suddenly, Andi said, "No more wine! It's four o'clock in the morning Detroit time." She looked at Charley and smiled. "If you are going to take me to bed, you need to get on with it!"

CHAPTER 8

AFFORDABLE CLEAN ENERGY

The next morning, the directors were gathered in their seats at the appointed hour. Knowing the importance of developing competitive sources of lower-cost, reliable, affordable energy, they were excited to start today's discussion.

Robin opened the discussion. "Ivan tells me he and his people have been working on this problem of affordable green energy for more than three years. Even before the American rights to this new Chinese chemical formula became available, they could see the potential for an industrial park developer capable of offering his clients long-term, lower, fixed-cost energy contracts. In their opinion, the reduction of labor costs that our plan envisions will only add an additional advantage. Ivan, if you please?"

Ivan Stone, Dr. Robin Cook's brother, stood and addressed the group, "All our notes, our test results, and work product were stored in the bombed building. Those of us who were involved in the experimental tests believed we were on the verge of obtaining the positive results with the chemical process we needed to burn cost-competitive, clean coal that satisfies the new EPA standards. We concluded it's not obtaining the positive tests we're worried about; it's completing the tests within the allotted time frame that could prove to be our biggest challenge.

"Before the bombing and fire, we were becoming convinced, if all three of the recent technological advancements could be implemented at one appropriate location, the problem of offsetting the higher costs of carbon dioxide sequestration might become solvable.

"One of the many advantages of the Employ American plan is that it envisions the organization of a critical mass of employment in one location. The combined energy needs of all the employers could be large enough to support the installation of a self-contained, cleaner coal and natural-gas-burning generation plant.

"We know, when liquefied, sequestered carbon dioxide can be pumped into abandoned oil and gas fields and effectively exchanged with the remaining hydrocarbon deposits. Unfortunately we also understand the revenues generated will not be satisfactory to offset the entire costs of sequestration.

"We believe there may be commercially viable revenue-generating opportunities associated with each of the other two new technologies. The tests that were being conducted at the Sentinel Institute needed to be complete before we can determine if our new chemical process can be used to efficiently mitigate the toxic materials that have been recently discovered in coal ash, the residue created from the burning of coal. We are talking about a lot of weight. Typically, the coal ash represents approximately 11 percent of the weight of unburned coal. Our chemical process converts the coal ash into high-strength cement and avoids the release of carbon dioxide associated with the Portland cement manufacturing process.

"Unable to satisfy current EPA clean air standards, almost all the production of cement has been transferred to countries that have abundant and accessible inexpensive supplies of limestone, calcium carbonate, and more relaxed environmental standards. If it can be proven that the Chinese chemical process can be used to produce lower-cost, higher-strength cement, the potential profits could be used to offset sequestration expenses.

"Several years ago, without the benefit of testing coal ash, the government required burners of coal to make whatever upgrades were necessary to make certain that existing coal ash reservoirs complied with current containment standards. It wasn't until the TVA floods spread coal ash into environmentally sensitive areas that private organizations began testing the residue. It was the results of those tests that indicated that concentrations of heavy metals, including arsenic and lead, may exceed industrial waste standards. Subsequent to those new discoveries, it is not known whether the EPA has conducted any of its own tests.

"The bottom line is that, should it be determined that the industrial waste deposits contain toxic materials, the nation's stockpiles of coal ash must be reclassified as toxic waste dumps. The potential costs of having to find acceptable means for disposing of this problem could materially affect the economic structure of an industry that supplies 50 percent of our country's electrical production. My people and I are convinced the government is hesitant to proceed with the testing until there is an affordable means for disposing of the reclassified toxic material. It's the purveyance of such a service that could provide the missing link required to offset the higher cost of carbon dioxide sequestration."

Charley jumped in, "Aren't you overlooking one more step that needs to occur before your proposed operation can be expected to work? Don't you have to identify companies that are prepared to enter into long-term, profitable disposal contracts? Until we have generated enforceable contracts, how can we plan on the revenues?"

Finally, Jeff was able to ask, impatiently, "Aren't there two more potential profit opportunities? Since the criteria by which you select the location for our first campus must necessarily include an easement and a pipeline for transmitting natural gas, doesn't it stand to reason that the same system can be used to purchase and sell gas? Depending on prevailing market conditions, why wouldn't it be possible to use low-cost imported gas to reduce electrical generating costs over what it costs to use coal?

"Isn't there the opportunity to increase energy sales revenues to off-site third parties interested in contracting for longer-term delivery contracts? Why can't we take advantage of our known costs of coal to hedge the risk of selling longer-term forward delivery contracts?"

"Wait a minute," Ivan said. "Before everyone gets carried away, I would like to remind you that six months isn't a very long time to set up a new test facility and start over, almost from scratch, with only our personal notes to guide us."

General Ben, preoccupied and making notes, looked up before asking, "If what you are suggesting can be accomplished, what do we need to be doing in the meantime to identify an appropriate site for our first campus?"

"General, due to our prior interest in developing low-cost energy industrial parks, we have been evaluating potential sites for more than a year. Interestingly enough, our top three sites are located in the Central Valley within a hundred miles from where we are sitting. We already have obtained options to purchase any one of the three. We are only waiting for authorization before proceeding."

CHAPTER 9

ORGANIZING THE MONEY

That evening, the seven Sentinel directors were standing at the bar of San Francisco's North Beach Café. They were waiting for their table to be prepared in the room with the aging prosciuttos hanging from the ceiling. For eight hours, their minds had been saturated with technical terms, statistics, and unfamiliar chemistry jargon. Learning what was possible and why the test results were so important had ramped up everyone's adrenaline.

Jeff Mohr was standing next to Claudia Roth. He remembered, when they first met three years ago, how conscious he was of her presence. *Her warm, brown eyes acted like two magnets that drew me in, encouraging me to want to become better acquainted. Her facial features were an interesting mixture of her mother's high-cheekbone Nordic ancestry and the soft even features of her father's French heritage. Her naturally wavy light-brown hair was cut short and arranged to accentuate her eyes and further soften the look of her gentle features.* The best words Jeff could think of to describe Claudia were *soft*, *brilliant*, and *complicated*.

The two-inch heels she wore made her seem taller than five feet ten inches, but not too tall. Jeff wondered if the loose-fitting, warm earth-tone colors she wore were selected to discourage men from admiring her rather voluptuous, broad-hipped, long-legged, athletic figure.

In all the years he had known her, Jeff would describe Claudia as three different people. There was her soft, warm, gentle, and seemingly sensitive ways. Her brilliant mind, iron will, and tenacity accounted for her being regarded as such a talented and well-respected investment banker.

The people who knew the private side of Claudia's life preferred to talk about her bold, unstructured nature and her seeming disregard for many of the conventions that normally influenced people's behavior.

Jeff asked what he hoped she would regard as an intelligent question. "What did you think of the students' suggestion that we look exclusively to the private sector for the funds required to finance the Employ American plan? Don't misinterpret the meaning of my question. I love the idea that we can operate independent of government interference, but Wall Street won't regard this plan as a new revelation. It's been my experience they consciously try to avoid anything that is new and difficult to explain."

In response, she said, "Not so new and different! If you break the plan down into each of its three component pieces, it then becomes possible to relate each of the component parts with other familiar situations. Instead of thinking in terms of one complex and mammoth investment, I believe my partners will be inclined to think in terms of three related-but-separate investments.

"When you think of Employ American as a mega industrial park, a giant and complex power-generating facility, and a pool of credit-enhanced plant and equipment facilities, there are many familiar examples.

"Jeff, at this point we have a lot more questions than we have answers. Before we adjourn, I plan to quiz these students very carefully. They've had three years to think through the problem.

One of the questions I have involves why they believe the market's need for impeccable credit can be satisfied without requiring government guarantees or eliminating companies that should, for other reasons, be included."

"Claudia, Charley and I are planning to bow out during dinner. If I offered to buy you another martini, I was wondering if you would do me a favor? If there is any further discussion on this particular subject, would you mind taking notes?" Jeff asked.

———

Tommy's Joynt, a famous old San Francisco hofbrau, located nearby on Geary and Van Ness Avenue, across the street from the Opera House, was a favored meeting place for many of the city's post-performance theater crowd.

Not wanting to be late, Jeff and Charley arrived thirty minutes before the final curtain was scheduled to come down. They ordered a couple of draft beers and found a booth to sit in while waiting for the ladies.

"Jeff, I've been thinking about your question regarding our attempt to rearrange the manufacturing landscape of this country. After what we heard today, I am beginning to think the resolution of all these separate problems may be possible. I don't think it's a question of trying to access the probabilities of success. It's a question of if not us, who else can provide the leadership required to give the plan a chance, particularly within the time frame we've been handed?

"As brilliant as the Employ American plan may be, our success will be determined by obtaining the cooperation of key individuals and avoiding the possible dangers that may be involved."

Charley noticed that Jeff's attention wasn't completely focused on what he was saying. Following his friend's eyes to the door, he saw that two beautiful, exquisitely dressed women had entered and were searching for them.

Andi and Meg were barely seated when Andi, looking directly into Charley's eyes, said, "We'll make you a deal. We won't tell you about the opera if you two stop talking shop."

———

Four days later in Carmel, Charley woke from a late-afternoon nap. Even before he opened his eyes, he could sense Andi's violet eyes watching him. When she moved her muscular left thigh and covered his legs, he knew he was fully awake.

By the time they had finished dressing and made their way downstairs, the small afternoon tea and cocktail lounge was still open. Without the slightest hesitation, Andi walked over to a table where two Irish setters were lying. "What beautiful dogs you have," she said to the owners, "Do you mind if I pet them?"

Before the owners could respond the two friendly red dogs stood up and started licking Andi's hands. The red setters knew a dog lover when they saw one. Sitting down on the floor, Andi had placed herself at eye level with her two new friends. She knew where the dogs like to be petted, scratched, and rubbed.

Fully absorbed, Andi appeared startled when Charley handed her a Macallan. After patiently waiting for twenty minutes, exhibiting his best effort to retrieve his totally distracted mate, Charley said, "I know where we can find one of Carmel's better Italian restaurants. Café Fornio is located beneath the Pine Inn, the famous old hotel located just one block from here. I'll ask Meg and Jeff to meet us there."

Without saying a word, Andi stood up, said good-bye to her new furry red friends, thanked the owners, crossed the room to Charley, placed her arm through his, and then made a move toward the front door. They were simple but very intimate gestures.

Walking arm in arm with Andi, Charley was aware of her warmth and tenderness. *After I all but abandoned her in Detroit, why would such a lovely younger woman want to fly clear out to California to see me, particularly when she knew I would be preoccupied by a bunch of meetings?* he warned himself. *Charley, ole boy, I think you better pay attention!*

The intimacy of Café Fornio encouraged private conversation. Out of their concern for Charley, Meg and Jeff were anxious to learn more about Andi. It had been a long time since they had seen Charley so interested in a woman. They wasted no time engaging her in conversation.

After the first round of single malt scotch, served neat, had been placed on their table, Meg launched into a series of questions. "Andi, tell us about your work in Detroit."

When the antipasto platter had been served, Jeff shifted the subject to her education at the University of Chicago. "I've always held a great deal of respect for the school. This may be the first time I've had the opportunity to talk to someone who graduated from one of their doctoral programs."

Over the main course, Charley succeeded in encouraging her to tell them how an Olympic hopeful diver could end up pursuing an interest in behavioral psychology.

"What else would you study if you wanted to know why people do some of the things they do? Take my specialty. I advise employers how to improve their new employee selection practices. I wouldn't even know how to calculate the costs, both in dollars and human expense, associated with a 40 percent rate of new hire failure. What could be more challenging than helping both the employer and the employee benefit from an improved hiring experience?"

Watching their reaction to her answer, Andi decided, *Now it's my turn to have a little fun.*

She said, "First of all, allow me to answer the question all of you have been wanting to ask. Quite simply, Charley is the most interesting and attractive man, I have ever met! It isn't my fault that some other woman hasn't appreciated what I see and wanted to take better care of him!"

———

The next morning the four of them stood on the sixteenth tee of Monterey Peninsula's Dunes Course, waiting for the players in front of them to move on. This particular hole is one of the course's signature holes. It was a 550-yard dogleg left, uphill, par five.

As she was approaching the women's tee box, Meg announced, "In case you are interested, we broke even on the front nine and we have you two down with three holes to play. Care to press?"

Riding along in the golf cart, engrossed in conversation, Jeff and Charley had lost track of their match. "Charley, I don't mind paying for dinner, but I'll be damned if I am prepared to put up with all their smart comments. Let's press. If we can beat them, maybe we can reduce the level of their sarcastic humor during dinner."

Charley accepted the challenge and said, "Nobody has said anything about who is going to select and pay for the wine. I don't know about you, but I can think of some very expensive wines. Are you two ladies prepared for another game of chance?"

Jeff suggested, "Charley, why don't you let me hit first. If I can find the fairway, you can swing away. This is the kind of hole where your extra length could make a difference. If you can clear the bunker on the left, in the crook of the dogleg, you might be able to get home in two."

Taking his time, Jeff hit a good drive, 245 yards up the center of the fairway but more than 300 yards from the pin. He would also need two shots to get home.

Charley hit his drive right on the "screws." He had hit a career shot. The high-arching shot, with overspin, cleared the bunker, landing 285 yards up the fairway, before rolling another 20 yards, well beyond the crook of the dogleg. His ball lay 245 yards away from the green, within the extreme range of his three-metal.

After the others hit their second shots, they stood quietly aside watching Charley set up for his next shot. The second shot sounded identical to the first. All four of them watched as the ball sailed high into the air toward the green, landed in the throat between the two protective traps, and rolled toward the pin. Once the ball disappeared behind the leading edge of the elevated green, it was lost from sight.

Anxious to see where Charley's ball had stopped, all four friends walked up the incline toward the green. The ball lay pin high, not more than four feet from the cup, an almost certain eagle opportunity.

Meg, Jeff, and Charley were standing on the green waiting for Andi to hit her short chip shot from off the green. She was bent over her ball in address, when she suddenly straightened up and politely asked, "May I have my throw?"

Anxious to learn if he could make his eagle putt, Charley was annoyed by the delay. Thinking, *What the hell, I'm only lying four feet from the hole, why should I object?* Charley answered, somewhat huffily, "OK, take your throw."

Andi asked, very politely, "Are you certain you don't mind?"

"Go ahead. Let's get it over with so we can finish the hole!"

Rather than reach over and pick up her ball, Andi marched up on the green to where Charley's ball lay, picked it up, and threw it into the deep trap behind the green.

"Thank you for my throw. You now lay two in the trap, hitting three. You are away, and it's your turn."

Andi would always wonder what impressed her the most, the look of shock and disbelief on Charley's face or the sight of Jeff and Meg rolling around on the green, convulsed in laughter, tears running down their cheeks.

———

Unfortunately, their last night's dinner didn't prove to be either humorous or entertaining. The problem occurred while Meg and Andi were inspecting the wine list. Neither of the men was upset, when Meg proudly announced, "Now here is a wine we should order! I'd bet that Jeff's pilot doesn't stock this wine on the company plane. It probably costs more than what is allowed in his budget."

Without thinking, Charley suddenly asked, "Speaking of budget, did you hear any numbers regarding the cost of the Sentinel Trust's retaining Nate White's services?"

Instantly alert, Meg asked, "Isn't Nate White that ex-FBI friend of the Chang family? Isn't he the man who started his own security firm? Why does the Sentinel Trust need to employ a security company?"

Before Jeff could stop him, Charley explained. "Terry Flynn, the local director of the FBI, is concerned about future security problems for the Sentinel board of directors. The demolition of the Sentinel Engineering laboratory has to be viewed as a serious threat. Just as a precaution, Terry has suggested we retain the services of Nate's security organization."

"FBI, security organizations, what the hell is going on?" Meg asked.

Seeing that Meg was upset, Jeff tried to explain Terry Flynn's concerns as best he could. The more he talked, the more apparent it became that she didn't like the idea that Jeff, his family, and his friends were being threatened and were going to be used as "bait" in the FBI's elaborate trap.

On the verge of tears, Meg said, "It's different for you men. You go to work in offices protected by security guards, and when you leave you aren't always going to a prearranged location. It's not the same for your families. When we are at home, we live at an exposed location. When we leave, we are glorified taxi drivers for our children, following some highly predictable route. How do I know if the animals, the children, and the two of us are safe?

"Jeff, tomorrow morning, I would appreciate it if you would ask your secretary to call the hangar and make arrangements for Norm to take me and the children to my aunt's cattle ranch in New Mexico. That ranch is so large and remote, with the added benefit of Nate White's protection, it's the only place I can think of where I can feel safe."

CHAPTER 10

A DIFFICULT DILEMMA

Claudia Roth was sitting behind the big mahogany desk of her 30th floor corner office overlooking the Hudson River. She had been sequestered there since nine o'clock that morning, almost five and a half hours earlier. Her door was closed. Her shoes were lying somewhere under her desk. Her secretary had been instructed to hold all calls and cancel all appointments. The Sentinel Institute's funding for the Employ American plan was technical and complicated. Normally a quick study, Claudia was having a difficult time. *No matter how many times I've gone over their financing concept, I can't make the pieces fit. What is it that I am not seeing? What is the hidden problem?*

In the solitude of her office, Claudia had made lists, drawn diagrams, and generated computer spreadsheets to check a variety of what-if financial assumptions. To make the project easier to understand and analyze, she had divided it into three parts. The first stage, the land development portion, contained the cost of the land, the regulatory approvals, all the underground utilities, the surface roads, the rail facilities, and the airport. Although the scope of the project translated into big numbers, there was nothing about its size or the nature of the investment that created any particular difficulty. In Claudia's eyes, conceptually it was just a super-sized industrial park development.

The second stage was the largest and the most technically complicated. When viewed as a giant public utility project, however, it resembled other large and unusual public works projects her firm had previously financed in some pretty exotic locations. Although the presentation would be voluminous and detailed, given adequate time to study, it didn't appear to be any more complicated than other unique power-generating projects that Lazarus & Co., a highly respected New York investment banking firm, had successfully underwritten.

It was the third-stage financing required to fund each individual company's state-of-the-art retooling needs that appeared to be the most challenging. Credit risk analysis would depend on the quality of the balance sheet and free cash flow developed from forty-four related operations. Attempting to evaluate the individual economic performance of so many diverse companies seemed an impossible task.

As Claudia began to focus on what kind of information the insurance companies would require, the elusive problem finally appeared. *How could they limit credit requirements to AAA investment standards required by the insurance companies and not eliminate the participation of fine, entrepreneurial companies? If I could figure out how to solve that problem, then the financing would become much more accomplishable.*

———

At ten o'clock the next morning, she attached a handwritten note to her memorandum to her partners. It read, "Can we discuss this topic at your earliest convenience?"

Later that week a rested Claudia was seated in her soft executive chair, her shoeless feet propped on an open drawer. Her phone was tucked between her ear and shoulder. She was waving a hastily scribbled note to her secretary that read, "As soon as I complete this call, I need to talk to Robin."

"Robin, good news! My partners and I are working on a terms sheet for the Employ American plan. Subject to all the other stipulations being satisfied, I think we have the framework for three separate financings, two of which we can take to market. It's the industrial park piece that we need to discuss. We not only believe the land development portion needs to be privately funded but we also think there are some important reasons suggesting it should be considered for investment by the Sentinel Trust. If you have a moment, maybe I can explain."

Claudia, imagining the look of tension she must have created on the face of her dear friend and colleague, said, "Our analysts have stipulated that we must have advanced enforceable commitments from participating employers to introduce 80,000 jobs or 80 percent of the capacity of the first phase after the resolution of all our legislation and the successful conclusion of all our energy testing. Since timing problems preclude our proceeding on a sequential basis, somebody is going to be required to invest significant amounts of very high-risk capital. To make matters worse, the investor will be required to agree to predetermined land lease terms and conditions that will satisfy some very stringent limitations regarding possible internal conflicts of interest."

Following a significant pause, Robin asked, "Are you suggesting that I need to find out just how much confidence Madam Chang has in our ability to complete our mission? You realize that we will be asking her to commit the entire wealth of the Sentinel Trust?"

Not hearing any response, Robin said, "Give me a few days to discuss your suggestion with her. In the meantime, I will schedule an all-hands meeting. I'm certain she will want to look all of us straight in the eye, ask the kind of questions none of us can anticipate, and provide us with her thoughts in her own inimitable fashion before making a decision."

CHAPTER 11

CASEY JONES IS CALLING

The next morning, Jeff called his secretary before leaving for his office. "Jacque, would you mind calling the hangar and asking Norm when it would be convenient for him to fly Meg and the kids to her aunt's ranch in New Mexico?"

Later that morning Jacque approached his desk with a confused look on her face. "I called the hangar," she said, "and neither the plane nor the pilot is there. In searching my files, I found a three-day-old memo from Norm. Apparently, he received a flight directive and has flown the plane to the Citation's repair hangar in Sacramento. In all the commotion, I must have missed his message telling you about the directive. It must be something to do about those new winglets you recently had installed."

"Jacque, I want you to call Cessna's main factory in Wichita and subtly ask them if they have issued such a directive. Whatever you do, don't explain why you are calling. More important, don't say anything to anyone around here. Bring the answer directly to me."

Fifteen minutes later, Jacque, still looking confused, approached his desk. "I talked to three people at Cessna, and no one has any knowledge about a flight directive issued on your plane. It must have been issued directly from the FAA."

Thanking her for her help, he excused her. He reached for his wallet and took out Nate White's card. He carefully dialed the number. He was amazed how quickly Nate responded to his "Casey Jones" call.

"Jeff, you were absolutely right to call me! I'll assign two teams to Sacramento immediately, one to inspect the plane and one to look over the records. If you don't mind making a call to Cessna, it might speed things up a bit."

Once on the line with Cessna, Jeff's suspicions deepened as the Cessna representative explained, "Mr. Mohr, I'm the vice president of maintenance and repairs for Cessna here in Sacramento. Apparently we have a problem. Our crews have reported that they took the winglets off your plane and disassembled them. They found nothing wrong. When we didn't find anything, we were confused and checked your directive, the only one that we have received regarding those new winglets. Further checking with the FAA has revealed they have no record of that particular directive. No one involved seems to know how or why it was issued. We must assume that some unauthorized person succeeded in penetrating the FAA-Cessna system."

Jeff would never know whether it was the question or the realization that someone might be trying to kill him that upset him the most. He was hardly listening when the Cessna representative said, "On behalf of Cessna, we would like to apologize for any inconvenience we may have caused you. Naturally, you won't be charged for any expense we incurred on those winglets or any of the other electrical work that was performed on your plane."

"Other electrical work? I don't recall ordering any work. Are you certain?"

"Your pilot is in my office. Maybe you would like to talk to him?"

"Norm, are you aware of any deferred electrical maintenance?"

"No, sir. This is all new news to me."

"Listen carefully. Something is very wrong. Under no circumstance do I want you or anybody else getting on the plane or moving it until government agents have had a chance to check things out! Why don't you and your copilot sit still? I'm going to call a friend of mine and see if we can trade some airplane hours and use his plane. I think it's time for me to make certain Meg and the kids will be able to visit her family ranch in New Mexico."

Four hours later, 2:00 p.m. in Palo Alto and 9:00 a.m. the next morning in Hong Kong, Jeff received his second troubling call, from the president of Mohr Electronics' Asian operations. "Boss, we have just been notified that Mohr Electronics' Chinese-Taiwanese import-export license has been canceled, effective immediately. Do you know what this is all about?"

Jeff took a minute to sort out what was going on. *The explosion at the Institute, the problems with my plane, and now this. It's difficult to believe that all of these incidents happened by coincidence.*

Refocusing his attention on his Asian operations manager, Jeff said, "Unfortunately, I think I know exactly what this is all about. Tell everyone to sit tight. It may take us a few days, but I'll get this straightened out, even if I have to come to China."

For the second time, Jeff removed Nate White's card, dialed his number, and told the secretary answering the phone, "Please tell Nate that Jeff Mohr is calling for Casey Jones."

Nate could hardly wait for Jeff to finish his explanation. "Jeff, I need to interrupt. The game has just become much more serious. What other conclusion can you come to other than you are being drawn into a secret war? I'll ask Terry to join us. He needs to hear, firsthand, what you are telling me."

As soon as he came on the line, Terry asked, "How certain are you that the Chinese are involved? If what you are reporting is true, you may have inadvertently exposed a very sensitive nerve. No one has tested China's appetite for possible repatriation of American manufacturing. I don't believe we should proceed without informing the FBI director. He should be able to keep the White House informed and make us aware of anything we need to avoid.

"It's critical that everybody stay calm. Don't do anything rash, and most important, refrain from talking among yourselves. We have to assume that our enemy knows of your Sentinel relationships, has tapped into all your communications, and has you under surveillance. We don't want anyone knowing what we know until we are ready. Remember, not a word to anyone!"

———

First thing the next morning, a team of FBI forensic experts appeared at the Cessna's Sacramento maintenance hangar. Using instruments none of the other mechanics working there had ever seen, the agents spent the first hour walking around the plane, scanning every surface.

About the time they opened the cockpit door, a second team of four investigators arrived. Two of the men asked to see the maintenance logs of the Mohr plane and any related Cessna maintenance, telephone, e-mail, and fax records. The other two men started questioning everyone.

It only took twenty minutes for the onboard team to find the electronic detonator switch that had been placed inside the in-flight telephone. It was set up to activate when the receiver was picked up from its cradle. Ten minutes later they located the explosive charge embedded inside the owner's customary seat. It took three more days for them to complete their search of the rest of the plane.

CHAPTER 12

J.W. PORTER

There was nothing relaxed or informal about the demeanor of J.W. Porter and several of his trusted kitchen cabinet directors who were sitting around the conference table in the chairman's office on the 45th floor. The immaculately dressed businessmen in their dark suits, well-starched white shirts, and narrow ties were a sharp contrast to the same group Charley had met there just days earlier.

When Charley entered the room, J.W. immediately said, "Well, Charley, tell us what's so important that it couldn't wait until our regular monthly meeting."

In advance of this meeting with his boss, Charley had sent the chairman a copy of the "Employ American" doctoral thesis that had been presented at the Sentinel Institute. He was confident Porter and the others had used the past several days to digest the particulars of the plan.

"Bottom line, gentlemen," Charley said without preamble, "I believe the implementation of the Employ American plan represents U.S. Motors' best opportunity to profitably manufacture cars onshore. In order to implement this brilliant strategy within our limited time frame, I need you to consider two things. First, we must agree on a list of stipulations that need to be satisfied before U.S. Motors will commit to becoming part of the program. And second, the company should be prepared to devote resources to building a plant and employing, at a minimum, 10,000 new manufacturing workers on the first Employ American campus.

Porter and the directors were stunned by the boldness of Charley's request. Finally, Porter asked the obvious. "Charley, do you realize what you are asking? Ten thousand jobs! You know the numbers. You're talking about more than 10 percent of our total domestic workforce. In addition, you're suggesting we build a new plant, on an undisclosed industrial site, presumably not near Detroit, and committing us to annually produce and sell 300,000 cars within the next five years. That's a hell of a lot of cars! I can appreciate the importance of energizing your new program, but why such large numbers?"

After looking directly into the eyes of the powerful chairman, Charley said, "Because that is what you need to accomplish to be successful with your new line of cars. I also need to create an example that will make it possible to recruit a sufficient number of charter employers who will provide the remaining 70,000 jobs required to satisfy the plan's minimum stipulation."

Charley smiled and continued. "Sorry, J.W. If I'm moving too fast, let me backtrack a moment and explain. Jeff Mohr—founder and CEO of Mohr Electronics—and I believe we can facilitate the achievement of the Employ American plan if our firms, and at least two other major manufacturing friends, were to commit to a total of 32,000 jobs or 40 percent of the plan's minimum requirement. With that kind of endorsement, Jeff Mohr and I believe we should be able to convince other company CEOs of the merit of the Employ American plan.

"How committed is Jeff Mohr?"

"Like U.S. Motors, Mohr Electronics has its own set of problems, over and above reducing direct labor costs. These are the kind of problems that can best be resolved by repatriating a significant portion of its offshore production.

"After talking to some of our other friends, we have been led to believe that they were so enamored with the idea of reducing labor costs and fixing their longer-term energy costs they may have overlooked some other problems. Given the same opportunity, they would like to revisit some of those decisions and repatriate at least a portion of their offshore production."

Turning to his board members, Porter said, "This is certainly consistent with our findings. I'm not surprised to learn other major companies are becoming aware of some of the inherent advantages of producing new products closer to home. I don't know about the rest of you, but I regard Jeff Mohr and the other directors at the Sentinel Institute as some of the more accomplished entrepreneurial leaders of our time. If they believe in the merits of this plan, I'm impressed."

J.W. perceived the mixed reaction among the board members. Although several were shaking their heads or furrowing their brows, one finally was willing to speak in support of Charley's suggestion. "J.W., I don't think we have any alternative. We need to agree on the content of Charley's shopping list and turn him loose. In the meantime, we should start preparing for all the things we will need to do at our end. There's a hell of a lot riding on the implementation of this new plan."

Not surprisingly, one of the new directors who had voted for Bill Reedy's Chinese option, protested. "J.W. this is crazy! Nobody in their right mind will believe a group of independent entrepreneurial problem solvers can recruit 80,000 workers, pass new legislation, and raise that kind of money in twelve months. All you are going to do is create a lot of trouble and confusion for a plan that can't possibly work. It seems to me that U.S. Motors has a very full plate. You don't need any unnecessary distractions at such a critical time!"

Charley was somewhat confused when the chairman quietly suggested he wait for him in his private office. Excusing himself, Charley only heard Porter's opening volley, "I think it's time we get a few things straight!" as he closed the door behind him.

Whatever J.W. had to say to his directors didn't take very long. Within five minutes, the red-faced chairman entered his office, flopped down in his big chair, and called over the intercom, "Beth, would you mind bringing Charley and me a large pitcher of ice water and two tall glasses? What we have to discuss may take a while."

=====

Forty minutes later, Charley, smiling and noticeably excited, exited the chairman's office. Asking Beth in the outer office if he could use her phone, he dialed Andi at the university. Her telephone number was the only one he had ever taken the trouble to memorize.

When he heard her voice, he spoke without identifying himself, "Name three places you've always wanted to visit and never could."

Without hesitating she said, "New Zealand, Tuscany, and Provence."

"Forget New Zealand. It's winter there. How long will it take you to get ready?"

"About three hours. Where are we going, and what should I wear?"

"What difference does it make? I'll bring the green! We can purchase everything we need when we arrive."

"Okay, I'll be ready. But do you mind telling me who's calling?" she teased.

Chapter 13

CREATING NEW LABOR POLICY

The meeting that had been arranged between Robin and Claudia and the presidents of four of the country's leading national labor unions could have a definitive influence on both the future of the American labor movement and the success of the Employ American plan. There was a lot at stake.

The meeting had begun poorly. For an hour and a half, the four men dominated the conversation. For reasons they couldn't understand, Robin and Claudia were forced to listen while each of the men insisted on extolling the brilliant history of their respective unions and records of service.

Unwilling to waste any more time listening to pointless discussions that were part of the problem they were there to solve, Robin said, "Gentlemen, Claudia and I think you should understand that our willingness to continue this discussion depends on our ability to understand why including organized labor is consistent with the best interests of the Sentinel Trust.

"We came here in hopes of discussing the development of some fresh ideas that we could collectively incorporate into a new agenda, one that will make it possible for labor and management to work more cohesively together. If we have any chance to

repatriate manufacturing labor and prevent additional outsourcing, we need to find new ways to improve the competitiveness of
the American manufacturer.

"Assuming we can reach agreement on what your role should
be, we will need to discuss how each of your unions is going to
help sell our program to your members, to the public, to Congress,
and to prospective manufacturing candidates."

More used to issuing orders than being exposed to Robin's
suggestions, the four powerful leaders were confused, and uncer-
tain how to react.

Interpreting the men's collective silence as unwillingness to discuss their points, Robin rose, reached over to grab the handle of
her briefcase, and said, "Claudia, I told you we would be wasting
our time!"

The two women were walking down the wide corridor leading to the elevators, when suddenly the executive secretary came
running up behind them. "Wait, don't leave, there's been a terrible
misunderstanding."

Their host, the head of the American Automobile Workers
Union, restarted the conversation. "I am sorry we gave you the
wrong impression. Dr. Cook, as unaccustomed as we are to the
directness of your comments, that's no reason for us not to be
responsive. Each of us understands the sensitivity of the very big
problems you've come here to discuss. I speak for all of us when I
say we hope you will accept our sincerest apologies.

"Perhaps, I should begin by telling you we have studied the
Employ American plan, and we have questions. But, before we
start, on behalf of my three colleagues I would like to say that
we find the intent of your suggestions reasonably consistent with
the language we have accepted in some of our not-so-publicized
regional agreements.

"Your suggestion that we adapt some of the operative language included in the Taft-Hartley agreement as a guideline also makes a lot of sense. For the record, we are aware that this legislation was enacted during World War II to prevent unions from striking during periods of national emergency. We regard both the present unemployment situation and the declining work for our members as a national emergency.

"Times have changed and we need to change with them. The American labor movement and the American manufacturer must join forces if we are to restore competitiveness and employ our middle class. We would like to believe that our services are needed to solve a much broader set of problems. The four of us agreed to have this meeting out of the hope that you might be able to assist us in defining a new role for our respective unions. It's that topic we were hoping to discuss."

An hour later, the same executive said, "Well, if we have found common ground over your concerns regarding wages, benefits, and the no-strike clauses, why can't we move along?"

Claudia, who had been quietly listening to the discussion and watching the reaction of each of the labor leaders, asked, "Is it true that if all on-site employers' health insurance and workmen's compensation needs could be organized into one common pool, it would be possible to reduce the employers' annual premiums by as much as 50 percent?"

The Teamsters president said, "That is a question we would be interested in exploring. Interestingly enough, we have been thinking about the same possibility. It's never been attempted. But we would enjoy the opportunity to find out."

Responding to the positive invitation, Robin said, "Let's assume the information reported by my students is reasonably accurate. Once the first two phases of the Employ American plan are fully absorbed, we could be talking about 200,000 workers earning an annual average of $1 billion. If we assume the savings in premiums were to be in the 6 to 7 percent range per year, we could be talking about an annual investable savings of approximately $3,500 per worker. Compounded over a period of twenty years at an average annual rate of 7 percent, the minimum opportunity rate being suggested by competition of institutional money managers, the value of the worker's estate upon his retirement should exceed $200,000. The retiring employee could then choose to have the pretax balance transferred to his estate or he could choose to have it paid to him over whatever period he chooses. Should he select a period of fifteen years, his monthly payments would be approximately $2,500 per month. Unlike social security, upon death any remaining unlimited balance would be retained as part of his estate."

The Teamsters president, understanding the direction of Robin's comments couldn't wait to ask, "Why couldn't one of the services provided by our unions be negotiating the terms and conditions of the different insurance contracts and the administration of the private beneficiary pension plans?"

Not quite sure how to react, Claudia said, "Perhaps this would be the time to talk about national recruitment and training programs."

"Not until we take a break for lunch," their host said. The group, having lost track of time, suddenly realized it was 1:30 p.m.

Chapter 14

MEET MR. GREEN

Charley directed the cab driver to pull over in front of Andi's building, where she was waiting. She wore a light coat and clutched a small cosmetic bag. Charley stepped out of the taxi and held the door open for her. "Well, Mr. 'I'll bring the green,' I took you at your word. Now, do you mind telling me where we're going?"

"Not until we get to the airport," he said and slid onto the seat next to her.

"Why all the mystery? And how was it that you were able to leave work?"

"What work? J.W. and his pals need some time to decide how serious they are about enhancing their domestic manufacturing options. Rather than sit around and worry about what they decide, I thought it might be a good idea for me to invite my new best friend on a vacation."

"There's just one thing I want you to promise. For the next week, other than making love and drinking single malt whiskey, you won't allow us to do or discuss anything that doesn't involve you, your interests, or what you've always wanted to do. Carmel was fine, but I want to find out a whole lot more about the crazy lady who threw my golf ball in the sand trap!"

As they turned into the small private airport, Andi said, "Wait a minute! This doesn't look like any airport I've ever seen. What's going on?"

A Citation XLS, a midsize, twin-engine executive jet, was parked on the tarmac.

"Charley, now I'm really confused. You have me traveling on what is obviously a private plane, and I still don't know where we're going. Surely this plane can't fly all the way to Europe."

"Who said anything about going to Europe? This plane is headed to Alaska."

"I distinctively remember mentioning Tuscany or Provence. I don't remember mentioning Alaska. Why aren't we going to Europe?"

"Too many tourists this time of year. I couldn't take a chance on not being able to reserve rooms at the right hotels, particularly on such short notice."

"Why Alaska?"

"It's mid-September, the perfect time of the year to catch the big rainbows."

"Rainbows? That means you want to go fly-fishing. What makes you think I'd be interested in fly-fishing, particularly in Alaska?"

"Andi, one night while I was waiting for you to get dressed, I noticed one of your scrapbooks on your coffee table. Pardon me for snooping, but wanting to learn more about you, I started leafing through the pages. Do you realize how many different pictures there are of you and your father fishing in Alaska and Canada? Sadly, I found the newspaper article reporting his death. I'm certainly not your father, and I'm not trying to re-create your experience fishing with him. I like to fly-fish, and I thought you might enjoy accompanying me on a fishing trip to Alaska. If you don't appreciate my surprise, say the word, and I will have the pilot take us anywhere you would prefer to go."

"Alaska will be just fine!"

Looking out the portside windows as the XLS dipped its wing for its final approach into the small local airport at Lake Iliamna, they could see a single-engine de Havilland seaplane moored to the guest dock. It was waiting to transport them to their final destination.

———

The experienced bush pilot with a large beard and an even a bigger smile was standing next to an athletic-looking younger woman. As soon as the jet's engines shut down, she stepped forward. "Welcome to Alaska. My name is Sarah. It will be my pleasure to be your fishing guide for the next six days. This stuffy old crank is Kenny; he will be our pilot. You've come at just the right time. The sockeye salmon have laid their eggs. The big rainbows are feeding on the roe."

Sarah, noticing the absence of luggage, tackle boxes, and the usual array of expensive fly rods and assorted fishing tackle, asked, "Where's your gear? Did you leave it at the airport?"

Responding with her warmest smile, Andi said, "You will have to speak with Mr. Green. He assured me that we could purchase everything we would need for our trip to Europe after we arrived."

Confused by Andi's response, Sarah looked down at the clipboard she was carrying. "There must be a mistake. We are in Alaska, and I have your name written down on our reservation sheet as Mr. Hutson and guest. I don't have a listing for a Mr. Green."

"No mistake," Charley replied. "She likes to refer to me as 'Mr. Green' to remind me that I offered to purchase whatever she needed once we arrived. As for our location, I had always planned to visit Alaska; somehow she seems to have become confused. It must be one of those female things."

Catching the drift of the humor, Sarah took one of Andi's hands and led her to an old Suburban parked nearby. She smiled at Andi and said, "There are a couple of shops in town that should enable you to properly test the sincerity of Mr. Green."

For Andi and Charley, it was difficult to anticipate what would happen when two young, attractive people, armed with the trusty checkbook, invaded the only general store of a small Alaskan fishing village. Hurricanes in Kansas had caused less commotion.

The not-so-simple act of selecting Levi's for Andi was the start. For someone who takes great pride in her figure, the process of selecting close-fitting pants is not a simple task. Before she was prepared to start trying on the possibles, she had fully inspected every rack and shelf that displayed the limited inventory of denims. She selected a least three sizes of the four different styles and placed her finds on top of the rack closest to the small fitting room.

After trying on each pair of jeans, Andi paraded in front of the three-panel mirror to see how they fit. By the time she was inspecting the third pair, a small group of local men had entered the shop to observe what was going on. Focused on finding a proper fit, she seemed oblivious to all the attention she was attracting.

The process repeated itself as she wandered through the shirt, the sweater, and the coat departments. No one paid any particular attention to Charley as he went from area to area quietly selecting his own wardrobe.

Andi's growing entourage followed her from the general store to the sporting goods store located directly across the street. The whistling began when she was struggling to pull on the waders.

Still dressed in the waders, Andi moved over to the rack where all the different fly rods were displayed. After carefully inspecting the rods, she made her selection. Wanting to test its action, she asked the sales clerk, "Would it be possible for you to attach a suitable reel, loaded with proper weight lines?"

Rod in hand, Andi turned and walked through the front door out into the street. After stripping out nearly eighty feet of line and completing three false casts, she waited until the line of her fourth back cast lay horizontally behind her before pulling the butt of the rod downward in a deliberate but smooth motion. Her line shot forward and stretched flat, allowing the attached line and leader to fully extend before gently falling on the asphalt surface.

Turning toward the whistling and clapping crowd, she went back inside the store and said to the clerk, "This one will do!"

Looking at Charley, she smiled and said, "This rod is quite suitable. Thank you very much, Mr. Green!"

CHAPTER 15

JEFF'S TOUR

It was 10:00 a.m.; Jeff was sitting at his desk in his Palo Alto headquarters office. Recent reports from Tennessee sounded promising. Despite Ivan's progress, he was concerned that it was September, three months after the bombing. *The clock is ticking and we still need to determine the depth of interest in Employ American. Writing down the names is the easy part. Identifying the key problems that might motivate them to participate as a charter member is going to be more difficult!*

The ten companies he had selected for possible participation were scattered all over the United States. The first three companies were located in Los Angeles, Orange County, and San Diego. They were some of the most successful suppliers for the West Coast's largest aircraft manufacturers and had been important customers of Mohr Electronics for many years. What had originally started as customer-supplier relationships had matured into business friendships of mutual respect and trust.

Jeff's conversations with the company's CEOs were remarkably similar. Invariably, the CEOs would say, "Explain to us why Mohr Electronics has decided to support and participate in the

Employ American plan. Is this something we should be paying attention to?"

Given encouragement, Jeff explained some of the problems his company was facing and why he was confident participating in the plan might help his company more effectively compete for added market share.

Each of the meetings ended the same way. "Jeff, once you and your friends determine that you can solve each of the five key problems you have been describing, make sure you let us know. Fulfilling your required 80,000-job stipulation might not be such a difficult problem. If we decide to participate, we want to make certain there is space for us in your first phase."

Moving eastward, Jeff's next stop was in Dallas to meet with the CEO of one the country's largest trailer manufacturers, another longtime friend. Their meeting concluded with a word of caution from the CEO. "Jeff, I wish this Employ American plan were as simple as you describe. You need to consider the reactions of companies that either can't or don't want to qualify for inclusion in your program because they can't or won't comply with your new employment criteria. They could view your program as threatening when they consider competition from offshore sources. You could become the enemy without realizing it.

"Unless you figure out some way to include companies that don't need to add more employees, aren't you encouraging them to move offshore? What's the difference between adding jobs and preventing jobs from being shipped offshore? The effect on employment will be the same. Just remember, we could very well be one of those companies!"

Jeff considered his response carefully before saying, "Isn't the question you're really asking me is how we can distinguish between companies that are legitimately planning to move production offshore and companies that are hoping to qualify for new employee tax credits without any intention of creating new employment?"

"Jeff, I fail to see what is so complicated. Why wouldn't your people be prepared to qualify any company, independent of its employment intentions, that agrees to relocate on your campus? Surely the signing of an enforceable commitment would represent diagnostic proof of their desire to benefit from all the advantages you're offering."

It wasn't until Jeff reached St. Louis, on his return trip, when the next difficult question was asked, "Is there anything in your bill to prevent offshore companies from taking advantage of Employ American production efficiencies?"

Jeff paused before answering. "If we are trying to encourage American-owned companies to manufacture domestically, why wouldn't we want to encourage foreign-owned companies to do the same thing? Jobs are jobs!"

———

After ten meetings, Jeff was exhausted. The self-imposed stress of explaining things to respected friends and answering their questions had taken its toll. Grateful for the opportunity to be aboard his plane, headed home, Jeff didn't waste any time falling into a deep sleep.

Startled when the in-flight phone began to ring, he answered it half asleep and was having a difficult time understanding who was on the phone and what they were saying.

"It's Herb Builder calling from Seattle. We have to talk. If it wasn't so important, I wouldn't ask you to stop by on your way home. I know flying to Seattle is out of your way, but I can't stress how important it is that we meet. What we need to discuss isn't related to Employ American, and it's something we should not be discussing over the telephone. I'd appreciate it if you could adjust your flight plan and visit me here in Seattle. You won't have to leave your plane. Let my people know when your plane is on final approach and I'll make arrangements to meet you on board."

Herb was waiting on the tarmac outside the gate of the private fixed-base operator when Jeff's plane taxied to a stop at the indicated spot. As soon as the cabin door was opened and the stairs were extended, Herb Builder climbed up the stairs, entered the cabin, and shook hands with his old friend. "Thanks for coming, Jeff. I'll come right to the point. A very complex and potentially dangerous situation is developing in Taiwan and China that appears to involve both our companies and maybe the two of us personally. Are you familiar with the term *transshipment*?"

Still groggy from his in-flight nap, Jeff merely shook his head no.

"Some time ago, one of our Chinese suppliers came to me complaining about how some of his competitors were able to consistently undercut his prices. He hired a local Asian security firm to quietly investigate the problem. It didn't take long before they reported certain Chinese suppliers were transshipping their merchandise from China to Taiwan where it was stamped 'Made in Taiwan.' Then shipments were repackaged, reinvoiced, and sent on to Mohr Electronics in Palo Alto and our company here in Seattle.

"After checking, we were able to determine there's a substantial difference between tariff fees charged on products produced in Taiwan, a favored nation trading partner, and those charged on the same products made in China. According to information from our accounting reports, over the last six months, our company has suffered a loss of more than $10 million."

"Ten million dollars!" Jeff was fully awake now. "That's a hell of a lot of money! How can you be certain these transshipping problems involve Mohr Electronics?"

"Both our companies occasionally receive shipments that are meant for the other; they're the same parts from common manufacturers. Once we began to think something might be wrong, we started tracing some of your missent shipments and learned you were absorbing many of the same costs we have been forced to recognize."

"Why is this a problem? Can't we just inform the appropriate authorities at Commerce and inquire why they aren't enforcing their own trade laws?"

"If it were that simple that's exactly what we would have done. Within two weeks after our supplier hired an investigative firm, two of that firm's investigators were discovered and eventually killed. If these transshippers were prepared to kill investigative agents, it makes you think that whatever they're trying to protect must be very substantial."

Shaken by what he had just heard, Jeff said, "Obviously, the Chinese aren't going to so much trouble to protect their tariff-reduction scheme on account of our two companies. We need to determine how widespread or to what government levels in China, Taiwan, and possibly the United States this transshipment program has permeated."

"Now you're beginning to understand why we need to be careful. How can we blow the whistle on our suppliers without blowing it on everybody else?"

"Herb, why don't you give me a few days to find out what we know from our side? Then we'll get together and figure out what course of action we should be taking."

CHAPTER 16

MY NEW BEST FRIEND

The small, four-seat, single engine de Havilland seaplane plowed across the smooth surface of Lake Iliamna. The fully loaded plane with pilot, guide, two guests, and full fuel and supplies for the lodge was struggling to reach takeoff speed.

To Charley, it seemed as if the pontoons were pushing the water, not planing over the surface. The struggling plane shuddered as the engine reached full power. Glancing at Andi, he was surprised to see that she seemed preoccupied with the view of the lake. Her hands were settled in her lap. *How can she appear so relaxed? Doesn't she understand the danger?*

Charley could feel the level of his anxiety growing in direct proportion to the visibly lessening distance to the fast-approaching tree-covered shoreline. The closer they came, the more he tightened his grip on the arms of his chair, and harder he clenched his teeth. In an attempt to calm himself, he concentrated his attention on the pontoons. He was watching them lift little by little until they broke free of the surface tension of the lake. The sudden release popped the plane out of the water and it became airborne. Gaining altitude, they cleared the tops of the trees with room to spare, before turning back over the lake's unobstructed surface to gain the necessary altitude they would need to clear the ridges of the surrounding mountains.

Still not completely at ease, Charley leaned forward to study the altimeter. Remembering stories about Alaskan bush pilots flying around in the clouds below the height of the mountain peaks and ridges, he was trying to estimate what elevation was needed to clear any obstructions. *You never know when it might be important to gauge the elevation of the bottom of the clouds against the height of peaks. Flying "zero-zero" below those peaks is a risk I don't want to take.*

The main fishing lodge was situated on top of a hill overlooking the dock area of the small lake where they were lined up to land. Charley knew enough about flying to appreciate the smoothness of the landing of the overloaded plane. *Maybe I should give Kenny more credit. He certainly seems to know what he is doing!*

After unloading their precious new cargo of fishing gear and outdoor clothing, Andi and Charley started to walk up the long gravel drive that eventually led to the main sports lodge and its covey of small guest cabins. Their individual cabin was situated on top of another hill, some distance from the main lodge and the other buildings. Privacy wouldn't be an issue.

Andi, understanding the cabin would be their home for the next seven days, immediately began her inspection. She looked under the bed, pulled back the covers, and inspected the sheets. She checked to make certain there were extra blankets and towels. She opened the door to the shower, turned on the valve marked with an "H," and waited for the hot water to pour from the shower nozzle. Checking the cabinet beneath the basin she found extra toilet paper, bars of soap, and several cans of insect repellent.

She saved the clothes closet and the chest of drawers for last. After counting the wooden hangers, she ran her hand along the shelf above the rod checking for dust and bugs. Finally, she went outside to inspect outdoor brackets for hanging waders, protected shelves for storing wet boots and shoes, and benches to sit on when it was time to pull waders on and off.

Her inspection complete, she turned toward Charley and announced, "A woman could have a good time here!"

Andi was in her element. As the only woman in the middle of eleven traveled and experienced sportsmen, she was the center of attention. Whether it was over cocktails, supper, or an after-dinner drink, she made a point of taking an interest in each of the other guests.

Flattered by the attention of such a beautiful and charming woman, each of the guests would talk about their favorite fishing trips, their work, or their families. It didn't take long before all twelve fishing guests began to feel like they were becoming new, *old* friends.

Each morning, Kenny and Sarah joined them in the lodge for the day's hearty breakfast. Their host, a lifelong Alaskan fisherman and commercial guide, would assign the day's fishing destination to Andi, Charley, Sarah, and Kenny the pilot. With lunches and fishing tackle carefully stored aboard the de Havilland, the regular group of four would begin their flight toward their designated location and a new adventure in some of the world's finest clearstone river rainbow trout fishing.

Andi noticed that no matter how many times they took off in the small aircraft, Charley always grimaced and gripped the arms of his seat until his knuckles turned white. On the third day, when he still wasn't relaxed, Andi couldn't restrain herself. "Tell me, Mr. Green, how are you enjoying the flight?"

Their entire day was devoted to discovering the fishing secrets of the different waters. They fished wet, and they fished dry. They always experimented with different flies, casting locations, and methods of retrieve. They cast into the wind and they cast downwind. They fished the riffles, and they fished the eddies.

Andi and Charley were waist deep, fishing in fast-moving water. The prospect of catching a really big rainbow dominated their thoughts. Andi directed her casts downstream, Charley cast upstream. Andi fished the water immediately in front of her; Charley concentrated on fishing farther out. Andi fished with wet flies; Charley fished with dry flies.

Charley was not surprised when Andi caught the first fish. Changing his fishing tackle to duplicate what she was using, he moved closer to where she was standing, shortened his casts, and, fishing upstream, landed his fly a respectful distance from hers. Totally focused on his own futile efforts, Charley was only vaguely aware when Andi began to catch a fish or get a strike on almost every cast.

Standing within twenty feet of her, he could sense her aura of confidence. She wasn't hoping to catch a fish; she expected to catch a fish. He watched as she casually modified her casting techniques to adapt to changing conditions. He admired her concentration and her excitement when she hooked a really big fish and played it ever so gently. He enjoyed listening to the side comments she would make to Sarah while she was retrieving her catch.

By the fourth night, Charley began to realize something strange was beginning to happen. Following another delicious dinner that had been punctuated throughout with interesting conversation, he asked, "Andi, what do you say to a late-evening, stroll along the lake? There's something I would like to discuss."

They had been walking almost fifteen minutes when Charley stopped, turned to her, and said, "I guess, I will never understand. When we first met, I would have described you as an unbelievably sexy, fun woman who likes to drink single malt scotch and throw golf balls into sand traps. Then, I learned that you are an intelligent, well-educated career woman who has some very interesting ideas about the adventure of life. Now, I feel like we are becoming good friends. You're the expert; how can all this be happening?"

Putting her arms around his waist and looking directly into his eyes, Andi smiled and said, "For somebody who is supposed to be so smart, you have certainly taken your time to finally start to get it!"

"Get what? I still don't understand. I'm forty-seven years old. There has to be at least ten years' difference in our ages. Though we've only known each other for a short time, I can't recall ever being more sexually attracted to a woman. And now, when I think about you, the first thing that comes to my mind is the quiet time we spend together, doing simple things, and talking about things of personal interest. Isn't that what old friends do?"

"Charley, you're totally different from the person you have been forced to play in your professional life. I don't know why you try so hard to hide the kind and gentle person I saw when we first met. I knew that if I hung in there long enough, he would reappear. That is the person I want to become better acquainted with. No fair putting him back in the box when we go home!"

After walking about another quarter of a mile in silence, she stopped and asked, "Now, there is one question I would like to ask you! Since we have only two nights left, how are you planning to change your new best friend back into a wanton woman?"

CHAPTER 17

HAVING A GOOD DAY

Nate White's patient surveillance was beginning to produce results. His security company had organized a task force to investigate the bombing of the Sentinel Institute's engineering research lab. For weeks they had been sifting through the debris, studying campus security tapes, and trying to learn everything they could about all the different experiments that had been conducted in the building.

It wasn't until they had reviewed the campus security tapes for a third time when one of White's agents said, "Wait, can we run that tape back?

"Look, there they are in the parking lot. Do you see those two men getting out of the late-model white Chevrolet Tahoe? Did you notice anything unusual other than they were both carrying what looks like fully packed sports bags? There's no campus-parking permit on the vehicle's windshield.

"Now, let's fast forward to a few minutes after the explosion. Do you see the same two men entering the same white vehicle? It's too dark to identify the faces, but we can read the license plate."

With the benefit of the number, Nate's team was able to trace the white Chevy to a local car rental agency. The people at the agency identified the vehicle and matched the rental agreement with a Nevada driver's license.

Assuming it was probably a fake, the top-ranking agent assigned two men to follow the only lead they had, even if it meant traveling to Nevada.

Two days later, Nate received their report via phone and then he called Director Flynn to give him the play-by-play.

"We ran the photograph through the Nevada Motor Vehicle records and found that another license had been issued to a man with the same facial characteristics. With very little extra effort, we were able to determine that he and the second man live in the small residential town of Minden, Nevada, one of the state's early Mormon communities.

"Our check with Social Security indicated that neither man is presently employed, collecting unemployment benefits, or receiving disability or Social Security benefits. For several days, the local agents assigned to stake out the two men reported that the first one and then the other were regularly observed entering the Minden post office. It seemed obvious they were expecting some kind of letter or package.

"Two days ago, when two priority mail envelopes arrived, our agents were waiting. They carefully opened them and discovered that each contained $50,000 in used $100 bills. The code concealed in the cancellation marks indicated the post office from which the envelopes had been mailed, the time, and the date.

"We assumed the large quantities of cash was obtained from a bank near the post office of origin. We drew concentric circles on the subject city map, in quarter-mile radial increments, around the indicated post office.

"A separate team of agents called on the innermost banks and then worked outward. They were looking for records indicating the cashing of one check in the approximate amount of $100,000 or two checks for $50,000 within a few days of the delivery at the Minden post office.

"After two days of meticulous checking, and three concentric rings later, they found the bank and a photocopy of the wire transfer used to create the funds. Following the trail of the wire back through four levels of banks and three levels of blind companies, our agents were finally able to determine the money came from a small company owned by major West Coast public utility companies."

"Thanks Nate, I'll take it from here," Director Flynn said. "FBI records in Washington indicate that both men are freelance private investigators who can be hired to perform the 'more sensitive' work.

"While we have sufficient evidence to approach a grand jury and seek an indictment, we think it might be best if we considered a more direct approach. By confronting the executive management of the West Coast utility companies with our evidence, we might find a way to dissuade them from initiating any future attacks and convince them to help accelerate the implementation of Employ American."

CHAPTER 18

HEADED HOME

After seven days and six nights, Andi and Charley were anxious to return home. A thick fog had settled over the lake, the lodge, and each of the small cabins. Looking out their cabin window, Andi was having a difficult time seeing the nearby lodge. A view of the lake and the parked seaplanes was impossible. When Charley looked up, all he could see was thick fog, dense clouds, and no ridge tops.

After following the well-marked path to the main lodge, they entered the building and discovered Kenny talking on the short-wave radio. Other pilots were reporting a 1,200-foot bottom on the clouds. Checking his notes Charley saw that he had written the peak elevation to be 1,400 feet. If they were to take off, this indicated to Charley that they would have to fly blind on a directed course before they could hope to break into the clear only 200 feet below the ridgeline that protected the small lake.

While he was taking his time to think through the problem, he noticed that Andi was sitting very still and very quiet. *Obviously she understands the problem and is relying on me to work it out.*

Kenny was trying to explain that conditions appeared worse than they really were. "Not to worry, for those of us who are accustomed to flying in these local conditions, we know the headings and the altitude we need to achieve, even if we don't have a visual. I've taken off in a lot worse conditions than these. Piece of cake!"

Charley had made up his mind. *No point in taking a risk that I don't need to take.* Turning toward Andi, he announced, "Maybe it's best if we don't leave until the weather improves. How would you like to spend another day with your new best friend in a fishing cabin surrounded by white fog?"

Two not-very-rested old friends were enjoying their last fisherman's second cup of coffee and a quiet conversation when Kenny and Sarah marched through the door leading to the kitchen. Kenny proudly announced, "It's a perfect day for flying, we've got a full load of fuel aboard, and your gear has been stored. Since you are on your own schedule, how would you like to join Sarah and me for a little sightseeing trip of western Alaska?"

——

Four hours later when they returned to the airstrip at Lake Iliamna, they found that Charley's chartered plane was fully fueled, the flight plan had been filed, the ordered catering was stored on board, and they were ready to take off.

Once the plane had reached the desired altitude and leveled off, Charley asked, "Listen, my new-old best friend and my wanton woman, I've organized a little surprise for you. I had some of your favorite champagne put on board. I was hoping two old friends could drink a celebratory cocktail to a great vacation and to the future day when you'll answer my 'best friend' question. May I interest you in a glass of champagne and a bit of caviar?"

The copilot understood the owner's preflight instructions. As soon as the plane had reached the desired cruising altitude, he released himself from his seat and began to assemble the champagne, the chilled flutes, napkins, the iced tin of osetra caviar, the box of toast points, and a small container of sour cream.

Standing in front of the two passengers, a concerned copilot said, "Excuse me, Mr. Hutson, we may have problem."

Holding out the two bottles of champagne, the copilot said, "Look closely at these bottles. The one in my left hand is the one we put on board before we left Detroit. The one in my right hand was put on board by the local catering company. Why should two identical bottles of champagne have slightly different colored tin-foil covers covering the wired champagne corks? I have never noticed any difference with any of the other bottles of the same champagne we frequently serve on this plane."

Some instinctive feeling made Charley take both bottles from the copilot. He held each up to the light, trying to inspect the contents. He could see nothing strange or unusual through the opaque green glass. As he was about to set the two bottles on the extended game table he thought the bottle in his right hand seemed a bit heavier than the one in his left.

"Andi, lift these two bottles and tell me what you think. Does one weigh more than the other?"

She lifted the bottles in her hands. "The right one is definitely heavier."

Speaking slowly and with a calm voice, Charley turned to the copilot and calmly said, "I think we need to turn this plane around and put it on the ground as quickly as possible."

The local sheriff was waiting on the tarmac when the XLS rolled to a stop in front of the same hangar from which it had departed less than ten minutes before. He motioned for the pilots and the passengers to disembark. A clearly shaken Andi and Charley and the two pilots were escorted off the plane and into the relative safety of the lobby of the fixed-base operator.

After placing the two bottles on the edge of the runway, the sheriff withdrew his service revolver, and using the hood of his car as a brace, fired his first shot into the apparently "normal" bottle. Other than the expected pop of the suddenly released gas that followed and the sound of shattering glass, nothing unusual occurred.

The sudden explosion that followed his next shot left absolutely no doubt that a bomb had been hidden inside the second bottle. Charley felt a sense of invisible danger flood his mind; it was a feeling he hadn't felt since he had been in Iraq almost twenty years ago. Intuitively, he knew it was time for him to take charge. Trying not to further alarm a noticeably frightened Andi, he said, "Do you mind if I call my office? Maybe, they can figure out how to get us out of here. I don't mind telling you I'm not too enthusiastic about getting back on the XLS."

J.W.'s secretary picked up the phone on the first ring. "Oh. Mr. Hutson, the chairman has been trying to reach you for the last three days. If you don't mind, I'll put you right through."

J.W.'s familiar strong voice immediately came on the line. "Charley, I wanted to be the first to tell you, but by this time, I assume you've read about it in the newspapers."

"Read about what? I've been in Alaska fly-fishing."

"U.S. Motors has announced that it intends to exercise the clause in our Chinese agreement allowing us to delay making our production location decision for one year. You'd think we had just shot the pope! We're catching heat from every possible direction. The patience of the public, the government, and Organized Labor has been thoroughly tested. We need you back here. The clock is definitely ticking!"

"J.W., we've just experienced some problems of our own. Let me take a minute to fill you in—"

After Charley told J.W. about the champagne bottle, J.W. said, "Charley, no matter what you do, don't get back on your plane.

For all we know, there could be a second explosive device hidden somewhere on board. I will send one of the company's private planes to pick you up. In the meantime, keep your eyes open, your head down, and don't talk to anyone. If someone is prepared to organize such an elaborate scheme, there is no telling what else they have decided to do."

Disregarding his boss's order, Charley called Jeff Mohr. After Charley briefly described the recent events in Alaska to Jeff, Jeff said, "It appears we're being targeted. I should inform the rest of the board."

CHAPTER 19

TARGET ANDI

Sitting back in his seat, en route to Detroit, Charley thought about his tour in Iraq in the early nineties and how survival had become an instinctive process. *How different the situation must be for Andi. Other than being my friend, what has she done to be part of any of this? Somehow I need to move Andi to a safe location.*

Lost in thought, he was startled by the ringing of his in-flight telephone. The call was from Nate White. "Charley, it's important you listen carefully and do exactly what I tell you. Both you and Andi could be in real danger. As soon as you arrive in Detroit, we need to get her out of town as quickly as possible."

Nate didn't have to repeat himself. Charley understood what he had to do. Leaning forward and taking one of Andi's hands in his, in an effort to impress her, Charley said, "Andi, it's very important that you listen very carefully to what I am about to say. That phone call was from Nate White; apparently they have identified the two operatives responsible for bombing the Institute's building. They've left Nevada and are headed toward Chicago and possibly Detroit. Once we land, I need to drop you at your apartment and ask that you meet me at Mike's Place no later than 4:30 p.m."

———

By the time the FBI agent's Sacramento report reached Director Flynn, the final Alaskan report was already sitting in the same basket. Flynn couldn't believe what he was reading. After placing the two reports side by side, he couldn't help noticing that the instrumentation used in the exploded bomb on Jeff's plane was similar to the unexploded bomb that had been found on Charley's plane. The switches, the explosives, even the wiring techniques were identical.

———

The bar was almost deserted when Andi walked through the front door. Her favorite bar stool, the sixth from the end, was empty. So were most of the other stools. She looked around the room nervously, still confused that Charley had asked her to have a drink so early after their arrival in Detroit. She was surprised when Charley emerged from the back room.

"Charley, when you said 4:30, I never expected you'd be on time! Whatever happened to Charley Hutson's mean standard time?"

He smiled. "Actually, I've been standing in the alley since 4:15. I wanted to make certain no one was following me, and I wanted to see if anyone was following you."

Noticing the frightened look flash into her eyes he understood. *I guess I have just scared the hell out of this sweet, sheltered woman. I wish I could tell her more about what's really happening.*

"Andi, let's order a couple of drinks and take them over to that corner table. There are some things I need to explain."

At ten minutes after five, Charley looked at his watch and said, "In five minutes a cab is going to pull up in front of the main entrance. I want you to walk out that door to the cab and ask the cabby if his name is Casey Jones. If he says yes, it's important that you get into the cab and follow his exact instructions. Casey Jones is a code name the security company we have hired uses to identify themselves in the event there is perceived danger.

"Jones is going to give you an envelope full of money and some detailed instructions. They describe how you are to proceed to Raton, New Mexico, via a series of connecting trains. Once you arrive, you will be escorted to the Davis ranch. It's a 400,000-acre cattle station that occupies most of the northeastern part of the state. You may recall that Meg's maiden name was Davis. You will be joining her and her children. Oh, there is one more thing. You are going to be taken directly to Union Station, no going home, no packing a suitcase, no changing clothes. I will call your employer and explain that you had an emergency in your family."

"Charley, what the hell is going on? First the problems in Alaska and now this. Is the introduction of the Employ American plan so threatening?"

"That's the problem. We don't know. Until we can learn more about what's happening, we can't afford to take any chances."

———

Charley had been wrong. He had been followed from the minute he left his office building. The "Charley team" was experienced in following their prey. They understood how to keep from being discovered. Using two different operatives, they could switch off and work from both sides of the street. A backup car that could handle any unexpected movements trailed them.

Forty-five minutes later, when she abruptly exited the bar and entered the waiting cab, they were prepared. One of the agents and the driver of the backup car followed the cab as it made its way through traffic to Union Station. They were even prepared when the cab drove past the depot, the public parking lot, through an open gate, and pulled to a stop along the tracks, next to the waiting train. From a respectful distance they watched as the woman passenger stepped from the cab and climbed the three stairs leading to the last car of the train.

Waiting to observe whether anyone else boarded the train before it departed, Casey Jones of the yellow cab watched as the train began to move, picked up speed, and left the station.

The train had made three stops before the gong was rung for the first seating in the dining car. Following her instructions, the woman in the rear car began to make her way forward through the four cars separating the last car from the dining car. As she walked along the corridor of the third car, she observed that the door to the third compartment had been left ajar. After she passed, a man entered the corridor behind her and began to follow her. Entering the dining car at almost the same moment, it was only natural they would both be seated at the same and last open table.

Without trying to be too obvious, she began studying the man sitting across the table from her. *He seems to be a nice-looking man. Judging by his lively eyes and warm smile, I wouldn't be surprised to learn that he is just another friendly, lonely man trying to make a long trip not seem so long.*

Two martinis and a bottle of wine later, the two were well satiated by a surprisingly good meal. The man asked his new dinner companion if she would join him in the bar car for a final-final.

Passing back through the train, he mentioned he needed to retrieve something from his compartment. While she was waiting in front of the open door, the woman stealthily slipped her hand into her open purse.

Anybody standing in the passageway would have seen a man's arm suddenly reach out, offer her his hand, and gently pull her into his compartment. They would have been even more surprised by the sound of what was obviously a pistol shot. Holding his leg, with the oozing blood, he said, "Andi, you shot me! What's the big idea? You have a funny way of accepting a man's invitation for an after-dinner cocktail!"

"You have a strange way of inviting a girl into your compartment. By the way, the name's not Andi! Reaching into her purse for the second time, she pulled out her badge. "FBI agent, Abigail Simpson at your service! Andi stayed in the cab when I got out at the train station."

CHAPTER 20

TAKING CHARGE

After one more red-eye, Charley walked into Jeff's office ready to resume their conversation. Before he could say anything, Jeff put his finger to his lips, signaling for silence. Next he rose out of his chair and motioned for him to follow. As they headed past Jeff's desk in the direction of the elevator, he heard Jeff say, "Hold my calls. Cancel my appointments. Charley and I are going out for a drink, and we could be a while."

The two men were walking through the public park located across the street from the Mohr headquarters, well out of earshot of anyone who may have been interested in their conversation, when Jeff said, "Charley, these attacks could be the work of two different organizations. Nate and Terry have decided to delay arresting the two men in Nevada in hopes they will make a mistake and provide them with more tangible evidence.

"This morning I received an e-mail from Larry Wilshire. His people have picked up rumors indicating that some sort of powerful Chinese are asking questions about you, me, and our two companies.

"When I told him about your situation in Alaska, he mentioned that he knew of other similar situations that had been previously executed by any one of several Asian security companies.

"Before you say anything, I should warn you I've already made arrangements to charter a private plane. No one knows about our trip but the two of us."

"Private charter, our trip? Where are we going?" Charley asked.

"Just keep walking. When we reach the hotel located on the other side of the park, we will hail a cab that will take us to Madam Chang's apartment. She has requested we join Robin, Claudia, and Ivan for a brief meeting. Following the meeting I have a privately chartered jet standing by. We are headed to London to meet with Larry Wilshire and his team."

Following a forty-minute cab ride, the doorman at Madam Chang's high-rise residence announced their arrival. Judging by the way they were seated around the table in front of the big picture window facing the Golden Gate Bridge, sipping tea, an always-suspicious Charley began to assume they had been invited for a social visit. When they sat around and talked of whatever seemed of interest to Madam Chang, he began to relax. Later she rose from her chair and walked over to one of the living room walls, saying, "I want to show you some new pictures."

Charley had to admit, *How can you not be impressed when a ninety-seven-year-old woman wants to show you fifty-year-old pictures that only she can explain?*

After they had returned to their seats and accepted a second cup of tea, Madam Chang said, "Thank you for coming on such short notice. For several weeks, I have been thinking about the suggestion that the Sentinel Trust consider funding the land development segment of the Employ American plan. Knowing all that is involved, what questions do I need to be able to answer before I make my decision to commit the Sentinel Trust?"

Twenty minutes later, settled back in a cab headed toward Butler Aviation at the San Francisco airport, Charley couldn't contain himself. "Jeff, one minute I think we are having a pleasant cup of tea with a grand old lady, and the next minute I learn that the Sentinel Trust's money has been designated to be invested in whatever program we regard to be in the best interests of protecting the American people from unbridled greed and avarice. As long as I live I guess I will never understand how anyone can put such importance on the pursuit of mission without regard to the practical consequences of failure."

A smile and silence was the only response Charley received, at least until they were airborne and were enjoying their second Macallan.

Jeff broke the silence. "After I informed Larry about our various problems, he implied that exposure of an internal corruption problem, although embarrassing, can be easily handled. But the entire situation becomes much more serious when the issue includes the repatriation of manufacturing jobs. The Chinese business community—and government, and its major exporters—will be left with no choice but to regard our Employ American efforts as a direct threat to their long-term national manufacturing strategies. Put the two problems together, and their reaction could be inestimable."

"Jeff, this is one of those times when I find myself agreeing with Larry. How certain are you? Is this really something we should pursue? I have that feeling once we start, there will be no turning back."

Jeff replied, "After listening to Madam Chang, I started to rethink Mohr Electronics' manufacturing strategy. Five Asian contractors provided more than 90 percent of Mohr Electronics' current production. After we leave London, I have made arrangements to visit my old friend Aakil Chandakar in Mumbai and our four contract manufacturers in China. If you think U.S. Motors' revelation about its Chinese option caused a stir, can you imagine what could happen if we were to announce our decision to repatriate 50 percent or 20,000 of our consumer electrical manufacturing jobs?

"I know that 20,000 jobs doesn't sound like much when you look at the total scale of the Chinese manufacturing complex, but when you begin to think in terms of the threat a longer-term erosion of employment might represent, the problem takes on an entirely different cast."

"Do you know how many people are employed, offshore, in the electrical consumer products industry? There are individual companies that employ more than 500,000 people."

Taking the advantage of an opportunity to take more than a regular sip from his glass, Charley said, "If they are willing to kidnap Andi and prepared to blow your plane out of the air without knowing whether you, your family, your pilots, or any of your guests might be on board, then there can be no mistaking their intentions. They want us killed or stopped!"

"Charley, there is absolutely no doubt that you are right. What's bothering me is how we're going to develop a better understanding of how widespread and to what government levels—Chinese, Taiwanese, and possibly American—this scheme has spread. Until we can identify our enemy, how can we expect to solve our problems?"

Charley responded, "This may be one of those times when we don't have the luxury of delaying any longer. We need to assume the worst and take charge.

"Jeff, don't forget, after Larry received his field promotion to lieutenant, he served in my command. I distinctly remember if I wanted a job done but didn't want any questions asked, I asked for his help! If we choose to include Larry and his team, make no mistake, it will be understood that we have decided to take charge."

CHAPTER 21

LARRY WILSHIRE

The jet carrying Jeff and Charley taxied to a stop inside a private hangar located a considerable distance from the main terminal of Heathrow International Airport. Larry Wilshire, along with three of his most trusted lieutenants, was waiting to greet their much loved and respected former military colleagues, Captain Charles Hutson and Lieutenant Jeff Mohr.

Fifteen years can materially change some men's appearance, but not Larry's. Although he had gained a few pounds, appeared to be more buff, and his sandy blond hair possessed a few gray flecks, he still resembled an NFL middle linebacker who was used to attacking any strange person who ventured into his space. Charley could still remember worrying about what fascinated him most, the cold, calculating way Larry went about his job or the maniacal way he reacted toward anyone or anything that he perceived was preventing him from completing his mission.

Larry wasted no time breaking the ice. "Jeff, once we learned you and one of your competitors had stumbled into the Chinese transshipment racket, we did some checking. Apparently, Herb Builder's investigative efforts succeeded in stirring up a real hornet's nest. The Chinese are concerned that any further investigations could expose the seriously lucrative practices of some very large Chinese companies and the incomes of a few high-ranking government officials. Public disclosure of the documented damages incurred by American importers could expose the Chinese government to serious financial consequences and reveal its poor-faith operations. These are risks Beijing would like to avoid.

"These secret Asian security companies used by Chinese manufacturers are as ruthless and cold-blooded as they come. They operate in a world totally different from anything we can relate to. Don't forget that multinational companies, international drug cartels, terrorist organizations, revolutionary sponsored kidnappers, international arms dealers, and political revolutionaries operate in an opaque world, well beyond the laws and law enforcement organizations of any sovereign country. If there were no need for counter-security companies, the need for companies like mine would not exist."

"Larry, let me ask you a question," Charley said. "What's the worst thing that can happen if we indicate that we wish to continue to pursue the transshipment problem?"

"Other than getting yourselves killed, I can't think of a thing!"

"I'm being serious. Shouldn't we assume that the bigger the threat we represent, the greater the leverage we might be able to exert on the Chinese? Without the extra leverage, how can we convince people who only understand strength and power to change their attitudes?

"For more than thirty years, they have been pursuing their 'Build It in China' manufacturing policies. Do you really believe they are willing to tolerate anything that might materially interfere?

"Why wouldn't we want the Chinese to believe we are totally committed to implementing our Employ American agenda and exposing their transshipment practices?"

"Captain, it's really important that you are quite clear in your own mind that this is what you want to do. I'm sure that I don't have to remind you why we made such a great team in Iraq. You gave the orders and never asked embarrassing questions. My teams finished their assignments and moved on. Once we start, there will be no turning back! Assuming you want to proceed, for a case of this nature, I need to remain personally involved. I need to be in a position where I can be maximally effective.

"Jeff, I want you and Charley to listen very carefully! You need to send your plane back to Detroit, remain here, and cancel all your plans. We want to be absolutely certain we are starting with a clean slate. No calls to your family, offices, the FBI, or Nate White's organization. Casey Jones is on vacation. For the next few days, we need to keep you off the world's radar screen while we make our arrangements."

———

September was a perfect time for Larry, Jeff, and Charley to investigate some of Ireland's great trout fishing streams and rivers, frequent local pubs, and enjoy a drink with some of Ireland's greatest characters.

During the day, as they traveled from one region of Ireland to the next, they took advantage of the invitations Larry had been able to organize to fish on some of Ireland's oldest and most aristocratic estates. Accompanying them as their guide was Father Pat, a longtime pastor from County Cork, a local charity country-and-western singer, and part-time fishing guide. Father Pat was a forty-five-year-old short, lean, energetic man. He was a big personality and was used to charming anybody who came near him.

On the first morning, Charley was having difficulty attracting fish. Noticing his frustration, Father Pat walked over and stood on Charley's left and watched him fish. Using his own smaller leader material, Pat attached one of his personally tied flies to what Charley estimated to be at least twelve feet of monofilament. Next, he walked upstream to where the slow-moving water seemed to curl around a point on the opposite bank. He cast well upstream, landing the fly well above his intended target. Mending the line upstream, twice with a quick flick of his wrist, Pat patiently waited while his fly, moving on top of the water, drifted in front of the point. Just as the fly was beginning to enter the small eddy, the big fish hit.

Turning toward his pupil, the proud teacher said, "Charley, every stream has its secrets. Part of the charm of fishing in Ireland is that it requires the angler to master so many different waters, insect conditions, and fishing techniques."

Unaccustomed as they were to having seven days of free unscheduled time, Jeff, Charley, Larry, and their trusty guide were attempting to fish as many different waters as possible and at night to make a tour of every pub.

No matter which pub they entered, nobody was a stranger to Father Pat. They all wanted to be remembered and ask him to sing his latest songs. The personable priest would place his hat on the bar, pick up the guitar invariably stored behind the bar, and sing his songs. Whenever customers asked for another drink, they put something in the hat.

CHAPTER 22

ALTERNATIVE COLLATERAL

The day had arrived when Claudia and Robin were expected to present their financing plan for Employ American to the senior-most members of New York's investment analyst community. Even before she entered the room, Claudia could sense the New York meeting with the securities analysts was going to be difficult. Judging by the standing-room-only attendance, the animated pre-meeting talk, and the presence of the most senior investment officials, she knew this meeting wasn't going to be another drab discussion of technical issues and quantitative analysis.

Following Claudia's opening remarks, a long-time, well-regarded senior investment analyst asked, "Ms. Roth, why do you and your partners consider providing industrial plant and equipment financing to be such a critical element in your Employ American plan?"

Robin was impressed. *These people don't waste any time in asking the tough questions!*

Claudia smiled at her old friend out of respect and used the moment to collect her thoughts.

"For a long time, I've been concerned that there have been too many instances when capital-intensive, longer-term investment proposals have been required to give way to higher-return, shorter-term investment alternatives. In accessing America's relative competitiveness, Dr. Cook's study group was able to ascertain that improved production efficiency, resulting from the introduction of these state-of-the-art capital improvements, is needed before manufacturers can be expected to effectively compete in a global marketplace.

"Sixty-five years ago, following the conclusion of World War II, many American factories were vulnerable to problems of technological obsolescence and even more to the efficient production equipment being installed in Europe and Japan. The U.S. factories that had so admirably supplied the wartime demand were old and well worn.

"According to our calculations, the beneficial effects of installing modern equipment would provide American manufacturers with many of the same advantages that were previously enjoyed by Japan and Europe during the postwar era."

Another senior analyst asked, "Ms. Roth, why do you think it's necessary for us to fund the costs of a new power generation plant when there is sufficient regional capacity to satisfy your needs?"

"Your observation may be accurate in today's terms, but our analysts believe the demand for electrical energy is going to increase by 50 percent by the year 2030 and may be fraught with costly environmental compliance problems. The combination of rising costs and depleting available capacity will make it increasingly difficult to arm the American manufacturer with reliable supplies of competitively priced electrical power comparable to what the Chinese are prepared to provide incoming employers."

"Ms. Roth, how can we distinguish between the questionable attributes contained in previously pooled residential mortgage securities and this effort where you are proposing to pool industrial mortgages?"

Responding to the question, Claudia said, "I congratulate you on asking the key question my partners and I felt we had to satisfy before we could consider sponsoring such an offering. The real question you are asking is: How can we satisfy the most demanding of financial criteria and not discriminate against smaller more entrepreneurial companies? This becomes a particularly sensitive issue when you consider that, historically, these companies are responsible for more than 50 percent of this country's new job formation.

"Before I answer your question, we have been asked a corollary question: If we are going to permit credit-worthy companies to supply their own debt, then how do we protect the investor from a fund primarily made up of smaller, less credit-worthy manufacturers?"

A strange silence settled over the room. Even Robin was amazed by Claudia's boldness.

Taking her time, Claudia finally said, "First of all, the size of a company or its balance sheet provides no conclusive guarantee of credit quality. When you have had the opportunity to study the small print in our underwriting agreement, you will discover that we have addressed this problem. Any otherwise qualified new employment company that cannot fulfill the most exacting credit-rating requirements may introduce alternate third-party collateral or credit capacity."

"Wait a minute!" the same credit analyst said. "Are you suggesting that a credit-worthy company with no intention of employing additional people can acquire the tax credits and use them to shelter its own earnings?"

After making certain that everyone understood the question, Claudia responded, "That is exactly what I am suggesting. By definition, Company A's ability to receive new employment tax credits will be determined by its certifiable ability to move people off the rolls of the unemployed or to prevent people from being transferred to the ranks of the unemployed. Should company A need to sell off some of its credits to supplement its credit application, we fail to understand why the government would be harmed. Doesn't the economy benefit from the same addition of jobs? The only change is how the tax benefits are divided between the source of the new employment and the source of credit support."

Robin was never quite certain whether the standing applause Claudia received was meant to indicate the audience's approval or if it was a signal that the meeting should be adjourned. When it became convenient for the two friends to leave, Robin said, "Oh, no, you don't. You aren't going anywhere until I take you into that bar across the street where I can buy you a congratulatory cocktail and you can explain how you came up with that conclusion."

CHAPTER 23

MEETING IN MUMBAI

Mr. Chandakar and his personal security attachment watched the plane carrying Jeff, Charley, and Larry line up for its final approach to Mumbai's international airport. They were waiting to take charge as soon as the pilot taxied the plane into the industrialist's private hangar.

This was not going to be an ordinary meeting. Anybody who had the privilege of working close to Mr. Chandakar understood the respect, affection, and trust he had for his longtime friend and business partner, Mr. Jeff Mohr. Stories describing what these two men had been able to accomplish were legendary throughout Asia's emerging industrial economy. The merging of their respective skills and resources located half a world apart had long represented a working example for much-copied successful business models.

Aakil Chandakar was a tall, light-skinned man who moved with the smoothness and agility that reminded people of his previous life as a talented and promising member of India's national volleyball team. He was handsome in the classic way, wore gold-rimmed glasses, spoke English flawlessly, appeared to be a man who carefully listened to what he was being told, and always chose to express himself in his uniquely soft and gentle manner.

The two men greeted each other with vigorous handshakes and big bear hugs. After stepping back, Jeff said, "Aakil, I want to introduce my longtime friend and most respected colleague, Charles Hutson. Charley works for U.S. Motors and is responsible for finding a solution that will enable his company to competitively manufacture cars in America.

"I gather that Larry Wilshire requires no introduction. I understand you have been a client of his for quite some time. He certainly enjoys using you for a reference."

For the next three days they visited each of Chandakar, Inc.'s, manufacturing and assembly plants. The first plant was the environmentally controlled cavernous building where the microchips were being manufactured. The second plant, and perhaps the most interesting, was where the chips were inspected and fitted to the connections of all the different sub-assemblies.

The third building, the one most carefully guarded, housed the long assembly lines where the sub-assembled components were attached to the main storyboards, before being inserted into the housings of the different main servers.

The work being performed in each of the buildings was technical and microscopic in detail and required frequent quality control inspections.

During the day, well-briefed plant managers accompanied Mohr Electronics' local director of operations, Jeff, Charley, and their host through each of the plants and discussed and resolved operational problems. When Mr. Chandakar inquired about Larry's absence, Jeff said, "Larry has asked that he be excused to concentrate on other issues."

Consistent with tradition, the last night of their visit had been reserved for one of Mr. Chandakar's traditional dinners in the luxury of his palatial home located inside one of Mumbai's oldest English-family estates. The magnificent home had been built in the late nineteenth century by one of India's early British industrialists.

"Jeff, I have invited another old friend to join us for dinner. I think you, Larry, and Charley will enjoy meeting India's former ambassador to the United States and China. Mr. Tambour is officially retired, but don't let that fool you. Free of the burdens of official office, my friend has been asked to become involved in some very interesting 'special' projects by the Indian government. He remains a highly respected and trusted member of the inner circle of the world's diplomatic corps."

The dinner had been carefully orchestrated to showcase many of India's greatest delicacies. Each of the courses was complemented with a special wine selected from the private cellars of some of the world's finest vintners. The quality and remarkable origins of the wines stored in Mr. Chandakar's cellar, for decades, had been the topic of serious conversation by some of the world's great wine connoisseurs.

Jeff, for Larry and Charley's benefit, asked Aakil and Mr. Tambour to tell them about some of their great experiences and whenever possible talk about new current events that were taking place on the Indian and Asian continents.

An accomplished asker of questions, Jeff was able to keep his host and Mr. Tambour fully engaged in telling stories over seven courses and countless bottles of fine wine. Sensing they were nearing the end of the dinner, Jeff rose from his chair to make the customary toast expected of the guest of honor. "My dear friend, Aakil, I can't remember when I have been included in a more enlightening dinner party. If your magnificent hospitality weren't enough, the opportunity to hear you and your honored friend discuss some of the world's more complicated problems will always make tonight a special memory."

Once the servant had served the vintage French cognac and

offered a selection of some of the finest Cuban cigars, Jeff said, "My friend, the time has come for us to talk of business. There are changes that are about to occur in the United States. These could bring structural manufacturing modifications to our industry. These changes will require Mohr Electronics and other companies like ours to look forward to a different kind of future."

"Are you are referring to your proposed Employ American plan we have been reading about in the American newspapers? We are not certain how to interpret what you are suggesting. Should we be threatened by America's desire to repatriate a portion of its out-sourced manufacturing or should we see it as a new opportunity?"

"My friend, as usual, you are very perceptive. Now that our overburdened service-oriented economy has been scraped away, we can see what a mistake it has been for us not to preserve a better balance between our service and our manufacturing work-forces. Current economic circumstances dictate we must immediately revisit that policy.

"Among other things, the work of those five Sentinel Institute doctoral candidates has helped us to better understand the true value of manufacturing jobs. For the first time, we can see how the use of an American labor force can become competitive with the lower labor costs of offshore markets.

"Consistent with this thought, I think it would be prudent for you to assume Mohr Electronics will wish to recover at least 50 percent of its offshore manufacturing and in the future will be outsourcing fewer jobs.

"Charley and I happen to believe the Employ American plan might possibly work, but a variety of problems will need to be solved before we can proceed. The most important part of my making this trip is to ask you for your cooperation."

"Wait a minute, Jeff, you announce you want to take work away from us and you want my cooperation? Did I miss something?" Aakil asked.

"While it's true we need to transfer a portion of our manufacturing back to the United States, I haven't said anything about taking any work away from your company. Quite the contrary, if we are successful, the total demand for your company's services should expand, not contract. We will propose that your company be asked to remain responsible, at a minimum, for all the production you currently provide. The only thing we need to discuss is how much of the production we plan to recall from two of our Chinese contractors would you be willing to fulfill from a new plant in our Employ American campus."

"Jeff, we have been friends for too long not to be totally direct with each other. As much as I appreciate your personal loyalty and goodwill, there has to be some other overriding reason why you want us to follow you back to the United States. It's not as if you couldn't resume the management responsibilities we currently perform for you."

"As usual, you are very perceptive. Actually, there are two. Changing manufacturing locations could create an incredible number of production management problems. Why would we want to compound the problems of geographic relocation by having to introduce and train an entirely new production management organization when we can continue to utilize yours?

"The second reason affects the plan. It's critical that manufacturers conclude that global demand for 'produced goods' can be more economically supplied from an Employ American campus. By shifting a portion of your production to one of our campuses, you would be sending a clear message regarding competitiveness to the rest of the world."

Charley was having a difficult time comprehending what he had just heard. *Had Jeff really flown halfway around the world to inform his old friend of his desire to move his manufacturing operations back to the United States, ask for his cooperation, and invite him to become a charter member of the first Employ American campus?*

Taking his time to collect his thoughts, Aakil finally responded in his soft-spoken, articulate Indian manner. "Do you mind if I rephrase your question? Aren't you asking me if our company would be motivated to help you preserve and enhance its manufacturing profits even if it requires working in a different country and employing American personnel? My answer is the same as it was fifteen years ago when we started our journey. How can I help you? We have prospered together, enjoyed a rare friendship, and accomplished some very remarkable things. I would like for our partnership to continue. Of course, I am willing to help you."

Charley, Larry, and Mr. Tambour had just witnessed a rare moment in the history of Indian-American industrial relations. Cigars were relit, and cognac snifters were refilled.

Finally, Aakil suggested, "If we can continue, I have another subject we need to discuss. It pertains to China's recent cancellation of your import-export license or, as we refer to it, the erection of the 'Chinese Bamboo Barricade.' We interpret their action to be a very clear expression of their desire to perpetuate their influence over world manufacturing.

"Left unattended, their failure to remove the Bamboo Barricade could trigger a global trade war we could all come to regret. Waves created in China have a habit of washing up on the shores of India. By the time the Chinese government understands that the threat of U.S. labor restoration is minimal compared to the possible repercussions of trade wars, an unbelievable amount of damage could occur.

"As an Indian industrialist, I should warn you, nothing can be more complicated than dealing with the Chinese. They view our emerging economy as a direct threat to their continued high growth rate."

"Mr. Tambour, said Jeff, "Ever since we learned about the Chinese transshipping practices, we have been considering how much leverage the disclosure of these fraudulent tariff practices could create. It might be interesting to test the extent of their sensitivity."

"Mr. Mohr, aren't you talking about, on an admittedly sophisticated basis, blackmailing the Chinese government? Is that a wise thing for us to attempt?" asked Mr. Tambour.

Wanting to continue the point of the conversation, Larry said, "Our meeting here tonight can't be a secret. I have uncovered the fact that, since our arrival in Mumbai, we've been followed, our phones have been tapped, and all our written and electrical correspondence has been intercepted. Mr. Tambour, I wouldn't be very surprised to learn our loyal opposition is already working overtime in an attempt to determine what your presence here tonight might mean."

CHAPTER **24**

ORGANIZED LABOR

Sponsored by four national labor unions, the second town meeting was scheduled to be held in the largest of the now defunct Eastern Air Lines hangars on Long Island. Leaders of each of the four unions and their locals had been spreading the word that something of vital interest was going to be discussed. The employed, the unemployed, the underemployed, graduating college seniors, and recently discharged military personnel were encouraged to attend. The cavernous space of the deserted hangar was filled with concerned people. The overflow was standing along both sides and in the rear of the arranged seating.

The host, the president of the American Aircraft Worker's Union, opened the meeting. "Ladies and gentlemen, together with the leaders of all the other unions represented here tonight, I welcome you. In a minute, I am going to introduce two very unusual women. Recently, the leaders of each of the host unions represented here tonight had the opportunity to meet with Ms. Claudia Roth and Robin Cook. These ladies are going to tell you about a new and very exciting plan that has been designed to restore the cost competitiveness of the American manufacturer and resurrect lost goods-producing jobs in this country.

"Previously unaware of the true consequence of relying on the expansion of consumer credit rather than systematic introduction of goods-producing jobs to stimulate economic growth, we are left no choice. The restoration of manufacturing employment must occur before we can expect to materially improve our economy.

"For forty years, our economy had been forced to endure the consequences of failing to find workable solutions to prevent the outsourcing of goods-producing jobs. At the same time we have been increasing the annual cost of our growing debt burden. In the year 2007 the debt bubble burst. Over the last three years, we have been experienced a $600 billion decrease in discretionary spending and consumer debt and a loss of eight million jobs.

"Resurrecting manufacturing employment won't be easy. Bold solutions to big problems must become the order of the day. The first step of the Employ American plan calls for reducing the cost of goods-producing employment to global competitive levels. Their plan is based upon their observation that each new manufacturing job creates three additional service jobs and $2.00 of additional government tax revenues for each dollar paid by the responsible employer of the new production worker. If the government were to enable the employer to participate in 35 percent of the incremental tax revenues he creates, his direct labor costs would decline by 70 percent. Should Congress pass the pending legislation, the employer of new manufacturing workers will be able to reduce his direct labor costs to internationally competitive levels.

"Unfortunately, the reduction of direct labor costs won't solve the entire problem. Before an American manufacturer can be expected to successfully compete with his foreign competitor, he must be able to reduce his costs of green energy to long-term affordable levels. That subject will be the subject of another town meeting. Tonight we are gathered here to hear of their plan for providing each of the more than eighty manufacturers, employing 200,000 workers on our first Employ American campus in Northern California, with a reliable and suitably trained and motivated workforce.

"I would like to introduce Dr. Robin Cook. A nationally recognized economist, Dr. Cook is a regular guest on many of the Sunday morning news talk shows and a guest lecturer on a college tour series. Dr. Cook, if you please?"

Dr. Cook took the podium and began her speech. "By concentrating so much diversified employment at one location, the Employ American plan can materially change the recruiting and training problem. Job fairs can be conducted in population centers located all over the United States to recruit qualified and motivated people who will be attracted by the magnitude and the diversity of the job training opportunities to be conducted on-site in California.

"For those who apply and qualify, all the educational and living expenses will be paid. In addition you will be paid a salary, commensurate with the level of your designated qualifying skill. This is money that can be sent home. Each employee and his dependents will receive full medical coverage during the time of attendance. Graduates will be eligible for employment by any one of the more than eighty companies expected to locate on our first campus.

"You might want to question if this can be done.

"Have you ever considered how Israel, currently a nation of six million people, was able to absorb two million Jews from all Eastern European countries? Most of these people didn't speak Hebrew or any other common language, or possess marketable employment skills.

"Or how developing countries are able to develop the necessary skills required to fill all the jobs that are being outsourced? It's all about contractual arrangements that pay people a living wage while they attend vocational and apprentice training schools."

The effect of thousands of people spontaneously rising to their feet in applause would make an interesting impression in any sports stadium. When it occurs in an enclosed aircraft hangar, it is overpowering.

After the standing ovation finally subsided, a strange thing happened. Instead of orderly filing out of the hangar, people feeling new hope turned to talk to the people standing beside them. Strangers were talking to strangers. The working press would report, "Not since World War II have we witnessed such a demonstration of national excitement!"

———

Exhausted from several days of meetings, Claudia and Robin had wandered into one of New York's SoHo restaurants in search of some good Italian cooking, a strong Chianti, and a lot of good-friend girl talk.

A basket of warm bread and a dish of herbed olive oil had been set on the table. After the waiter had finished his ritual of having Claudia test the wine and poured the first glass, Robin said, "This is the first time I have had the privilege of working with a true partner. Ever since our first meeting, I have felt as if our respective background and skills fit together like a hand in a glove. I've given a lot of talks and received favorable reactions, but never have I sensed what we have been able to accomplish."

Claudia, without taking her eyes off Robin, said, "I've been experiencing the same sensation. There were moments when I thought we were operating on some special frequency. It was as if you and I are the left and right side of the same brain."

Having lived alone since her husband died, Robin now found herself in strange territory. "With all the exposure I have to people at the Institute and the contact I enjoy on my touring lecture series, I find myself repeatedly returning to an empty house. For a long time, I have been living a very secluded and private life. My Sunday meetings with my mother represent a bigger part of my personal life than I am comfortable admitting. Working with you is very different. Could it have something to do with the fact that our families have been friends for two generations, that we share a common heritage, or that we are well-educated and experienced professionals? My instincts tell me there is something more!"

Smiling at Robin's sincere sharing, Claudia said, "While you've been living alone, I've gone through three marriages and more affairs than I care to admit. You have no idea how appealing working with you has been. Knowing I can depend on you, not having to worry about pleasing someone else, and being able to do whatever I want could become a habit."

Robin, lost in her thoughts, was surprised when the waiter placed the steaming plate of veal scaloppini in front of her. Thankful for the interruption, she smiled at Claudia. "I'm sorry. I hope my silence hasn't confused you. Something you said started me thinking. I'm so used to living in my private world, inside my own mind, that the sharing of personal feelings is a new experience."

CHAPTER **25**

ATTACK IN MUMBAI

Once Jeff, Aakil, and Mr. Tambour had shifted to discussing international trade issues, Larry and Charley excused themselves. The two old war buddies were quietly sitting in deep, cushioned heavy wooden chairs in the darkened recesses of the rear garden's large open-air veranda. They were sipping a second snifter of Napoleon brandy and enjoying the aroma of the fine cigars.

They never knew if it was their highly trained instincts, something unusual that they heard, or movement they were able to sense in the darkness, but they both moved at the same time. Automatically, they tipped over the big chairs. Assuming a crouched, defensive position, Larry pulled his 9 mm Beretta automatic from his shoulder holster. In the next moment, he reached for his ankle piece and tossed it to Charley.

The concussion from bombs exploding in front of the dining room picture window cracked the bulletproof, laminated plate glass. Large pieces of glass remained connected by the inner layer of material that bonded the sheets to the outer layer. The specially designed window had served its purpose. Other than being showered by flying splintered glass, Mr. Chandakar, his guests, and his servants had been protected from the main force of the blast.

In the next moment, Charley could see the servants tipping over the heavy dining room table and taking sanctuary behind it. Together with Chandakar, Mr. Tambour, and Jeff, they were busily pulling weapons off the underside of the capsized table.

Although everything seemed to be happening in slow motion, Charley, temporarily frozen by the shock of the blast, watched the enemy operatives. With drawn weapons, they moved forward from the recesses of the dark garden toward the illuminated dining room. One at a time, they moved from the protection of one large ceramic planter to the next, firing as they advanced.

With each shot, the picture window disintegrated a little more. It was only a question of time before the attackers would be able to rush into the still-lit dining room and overcome their prey.

Moving undetected in the dark recesses of the covered patio near the side entrance to the house, Larry and Charley were able to take cover behind a low stone planter.

Well within Charley's and Larry's handgun range, the advancing members of the attacking force were no match for the very accurate fire from two invisible enemies. A few men had been killed and two more lay wounded before the enemy attackers retreated into the protective darkness of the rear garden.

Taking advantage of the momentary pause, Charley and Larry were halfway between the planter and the side entrance when another, more powerful blast came from the front of the house. All the lights went out. Realizing the attack could be coming from both sides, Charley and Larry rushed through the darkened dining room, past the overturned table, and knelt on both sides of the entrance that led to the front part of the dark house.

Out of the corner of his eye, with the help of the moonlight shining through the shattered picture window, Charley saw two of the guard-servants rolling up the magnificent Persian rug that only minutes before had lain under the dining room table. Another helper was pulling on what appeared to be a heavy wrought-iron ring attached to a large wooden trapdoor. Chandakar and his guests, each now armed, wasted no time disappearing through the opened door.

Charley and Larry shifted their gaze into the opaque darkness of the grand saloon. Streetlights shining through an uncurtained portion of the tall rectangular window allowed them to see dark silhouettes approaching their position. Well trained in the art of up-close, night fighting, the seasoned veterans waited until the last possible moment before firing. The sounds of pain and surprise assured them their shots had hit their marks.

Taking advantage of their attackers' shock and surprise, they hurried to the overturned table and disappeared through the trapdoor.

Charley was impressed with how quickly the servant-guards closed the trapdoor and secured it with a heavy beam that neatly fit over the cast-iron brackets and under the beams supporting the dining room floor. Almost immediately, the darkness of the cellar was suddenly illuminated by a series of small electrical lights. They were standing in the middle of what appeared to be a very large wine cellar.

Two of the servant-guards began to roll one of the floor-to-ceiling wine racks away from the wall, revealing a big heavy iron door. A couple of men struggled to open the door. As the iron door swung open, Charley could see the entrance to a long cave-like tunnel.

Aakil signaled for everybody to follow him. When the last of them had passed into the tunnel, two of the guards took up defensive positions behind the narrow slotted door and closed and locked it in place. Mr. Chandakar, his guests, and his other guards continued their retreat into the relative safety of the tunnel.

Charley estimated they had progressed less than a hundred

yards when they approached a turn in the tunnel and another iron door. This time he noticed two different sets of locking pins on each side of the door. Before securing their protective position behind this second door, their host calmly signaled for the two men protecting the first door to retreat.

At each turn they passed another slotted iron door, and the two servants guarding the previous door would retreat to the next protective position.

When they had made their fourth turn and passed through their fifth door, Charley asked his host. "Why the two separate locking systems, one on each side of the door? Surely, only the inside locks are all that is required to prevent our attackers from proceeding."

"Ah, my respected guest, you assume we will always be retreating in the same direction. Have you considered the possibility that our attackers could also be advancing from the other end of the tunnel? It's entirely possible we might have to retreat in the opposite direction."

When they had passed through the sixth door, Chandakar said, "I think it's best if we remain here in the sixth compartment, midway through the tunnel, until we are able to ascertain if our attackers have entered the other end of the tunnel. I'll send two of my most trusted men ahead to ensure we don't have problems."

"Mr. Chandakar," Larry asked, "is there any way you can turn the lights out in the rest of the tunnel? If there is anyone at the other end, it would be better if we could proceed in the dark."

"Good thinking. There is an electrical box with a switch in each of the segmented parts of the tunnel. Unfortunately, from inside the tunnel we can only turn the light off and on, one compartment at a time. The one for this portion is located right above your head."

"If you don't mind, I would like to accompany your men," Larry said as he turned off the lights in the next compartment.

Moving along in the darkened tunnel, Larry noted that they had changed direction five times. Before they approached the twelfth compartment and the thirteenth door, he hesitated before turning off the last system of lights, thinking, *If there is someone at the other end, we don't want to alert them of our presence.*

"If we can get to that last door without being discovered, we should be able to see if anyone is waiting for us," Larry whispered.

Arriving undetected at the last door, with the benefit of his trusty credit card, Larry was able to check the sliding bolts. The door remained unlocked. Habit caused him to hesitate and think, *If there is someone waiting for us on the other side, wouldn't they lock the door and trap us in here? Or maybe they are waiting for us to emerge from the cave. Talk about being easy targets!*

CHAPTER 26

THE COCKTAIL NAPKIN GAME

Overnight, when Robin and Claudia's tour required them to leave New York, Nate White's surveillance problems increased exponentially. Provided with a written itinerary of each day's speaking events, press receptions, and private invitations, Nate's surveillance teams had sufficient time to plan ahead and to make any necessary preparations. Team members were required to report hourly. With each successive gathering, audiences were becoming larger, and the security problems were becoming more complex.

Additional teams were assigned to protect the two ladies. Travel schedules were checked. Advanced teams were assigned to cover the hotels where they would be staying and any restaurants or theaters they would be entering. Their commercially ticketed airline flights were canceled and replaced with flights on privately chartered aircraft. Public airports were avoided. Ingress to and egress from the private airports and terminals were arranged through side entrances.

Sitting in the back of the chartered plane en route to Cleveland, beyond hearing range of the agents, sitting forward, the two friends were engaged in deep conversation. "Claudia, are you aware that more than eighty million people or more than 25 percent of the

American workforce lives within a two-hundred-mile radius of Cleveland? We are going to be talking to a lot of people in the traditional manufacturing world with some of the biggest concentrations of underemployment. I think it's best to assume we are visiting one of the most concentrated groups of victims of outsourced, offshore manufacturing jobs. These people are truly part of our nation's disenfranchised population. I think we should be prepared to deal with a lot of personal frustration and anger."

The two ladies didn't know whether they should be pleased or concerned by the size of the security escort that was waiting to transport them to their hotel. A second group of agents was waiting to escort them through the main lobby, up the elevator, and down the hall and to each of their rooms.

Later, the same detachment was waiting to accompany them to the auditorium and remain with them until it was time for them to appear on stage.

Nervous and distracted by the possible threat from the audience, Robin was able to complete her opening remarks without interruptions or people raising their hands. The audience was strangely quiet.

Claudia, standing in the wings, was confused. From her position she could see some of the people who were standing in the aisle. At first she didn't notice anything strange or unusual. Then she noticed a number of angry-looking men standing with their hands on their hips glaring with what she interpreted as a "show-me" look on their faces. Unfamiliar with what she was seeing, Claudia began to feel afraid for her own and Robin's safety.

Shortly after that, things began to heat up. A noticeably angry member of the audience asked, "Why should we support legislation designed to create jobs in another state? Even worse, how do we know that these new campuses won't encourage the few employers that still remain in our community to transfer their companies to one of your campuses?"

Robin sensed the angry nature of the audience. She told herself, *Robin, the audience's reaction to your answer could determine the outcome of this entire meeting.*

After taking several seconds to organize her thoughts, she said, "As difficult as it may sound, the objective of this new program is to assist American-based employers in becoming more efficient, more competitive, and to create more jobs, not to solve local employment problems. When added to an employer's new virtual cost of labor, the inherent advantages in one of these Employ American campuses can make a material difference. Lower costs mean more new jobs for more Americans. The problem is that they just won't be here, at least, not initially! The particular combination of factors that create the most cost-competitive advantage can only be found in a certain places. The selected site in California is one of those places."

After pausing to allow the audience to absorb the new information, she said, "It's important that I remind you there is nothing new about geographic shifts in employment. For many years, young people have been moving from the Rust Belt to the Sun Belt. Let me explain what is different. We are prepared to establish a number of recruiting centers here in Cleveland to introduce our new employment opportunities. People of all backgrounds, ages, experience, and training can apply."

Surprisingly, a calm began to settle over the audience. They may not have liked the message but they respected the messenger. For years, members of the audience had listened as too many politicians made too many empty promises. They were able to recognize when someone was shooting straight.

Another member of the audience asked, "Do you think your program will bring back offshore jobs?"

"We hope so," Robin said. "Think about an American company that has both domestic and offshore manufacturing capabilities. In this economic environment, the ability to add domestic employment could be a long and slow process.

"On the other hand, if they conclude that the retrieval of offshore employment is consistent with their best interests, the employers are relieved of having to expand their markets. They only have to decide to supply the same market from a different location."

The next question came from a female member of the audience. "How can you be certain that employers are willing to shift the location of their manufacturing facilities to take advantage of lower perceived production costs?"

"For years, local chambers of commerce, government officials, and industrial realtors have understood the economic benefits that occur when their efforts to create added employment are successful. It is that perception that has motivated them to encourage employers in higher-cost areas to move to their cities. Conceptually, there isn't much difference between what growth-oriented communities have been doing for a long time and what we are proposing."

Hands that had been placed on hips were busy clapping. "Show-me" looks of anger were becoming looks of hope. The mood of the audience was beginning to change. The audience facing Claudia was different from the one that had confronted Robin. Although the meeting had ended on a positive note, both women were clearly disturbed by what they had experienced.

Over the protests of their security detachment, an emotionally wound up Claudia and Robin weren't quite ready to return to their rooms. Insisting on a late-night cocktail, both women were determined to stop at the hotel bar.

They were sitting at a small table, in the far corner, enjoying their after-meeting, late-evening cocktail, when Claudia said, "I don't know how you do it. I'm sure you sensed the mood of the audience. There were a lot of angry people who were waiting to take their frustration out on you. When that man asked his first question, the entire evening could have gone up in smoke.

"I was fascinated and scared as I watched you calmly and bravely answer question after question. Isn't it interesting to see how people react to what they regard as honest information? I'm sure you noticed that from that point on people began to ask more positive questions and trust your answers.

"Robin, I don't recall you ever using the local industrial recruiting example. I think that argument marked the point when the mood of the audience seemed to change." Raising her glass, Claudia said, "Here's to our team. In the future I hope there will be many times when we will be able to look back and remember how much we treasured these moments."

"That may be asking a lot," Robin said. "Right now, I am having a very difficult time understanding what is so enjoyable about talking to angry people expressing their fear!

"On the other hand, have you noticed that we have two free days before we are expected to be in Indianapolis? Maybe we have earned some free time and a bit of distraction?"

"I was wondering when you would bring that up. I have an idea," Claudia said, and she asked the waitress for two fresh cocktail napkins and a pen. "Here we are, just the two of us, and we are free to do whatever we want. Well, almost. We still have to inform our security people. Even so, we have nobody to please but ourselves. On one side of this cocktail napkin, I'm going to write one of the things I would most enjoy doing. Then I want you to write what you want to do on one side of the other napkin.

We will take turns adding to our lists until we either run out of ideas or space on our cocktail napkin."

Robin was impressed. "What an interesting idea! I think another drink would improve my imagination. I wouldn't want to learn that your ideas were better than mine."

Half an hour later, after two more drinks, the excitement of seeing each other's ideas became overwhelming. Without warning Claudia reached over and grabbed Robin's napkin and began to read the top item on the list aloud. Not to be outdone, Robin reciprocated.

As if the suspense of learning about each other's secret wishes weren't enough, the humorous side comments produced enough laughter that the other patrons were beginning to take notice and were trying to understand what was so funny.

"You want to do what?" Claudia exclaimed. "God help our security guards. I hope they'll be able to keep up with us!"

"At least we won't be arrested. That last idea of yours sounds like some of the things we used to do in college. How would we explain to the folks in Indianapolis why their two scheduled speakers are in jail in Cleveland?"

CHAPTER 27

LEARNING TO COMMUNICATE

Larry and two of the guards had been gone for a long time. Those who were nervously waiting near door number seven definitely thought sufficient time had passed for Larry and the guards to have reached the far end of the tunnel and return. With the passage of each minute, anxiety levels grew. The strain of peering into the dark tunnel only aggravated the situation for the impatient few by the door.

Under enough stress, a man's mind can play strange tricks. Jeff's thoughts were working overtime. *How can I end up down here in a tunnel beneath a strange city, cornered between two sets of vicious enemies whose only desire is the kill us and prevent Employ American from happening? Will anybody ever know what has happened? What about Meg and the kids? How long does it take for somebody to walk past five doors and return?*

Finally, soundlessly, Larry and his two companions emerged from the tunnel. Their sudden appearance startled the same people who had been straining to look for them through the darkness. Putting his finger to his lips to signal silence, Larry locked door number seven, left the lights on, and ushered the people back into the lit compartment between doors six and five.

Totally bewildered, Charley asked, "What the hell is going on?"

Larry began to explain. "When I approached the far end of the tunnel, I was able to see the lights in another wine cellar in a different house. Call it intuition, but it just seemed to me that I was looking at an invitation to emerge from the protection of the far end of the tunnel. After working into a position where I could peer through those slots without being seen or heard, I saw one of the wine racks slightly move. When I inspected it more thoroughly, I saw the tip of a rifle barrel resting between two wine bottles. Knowing what I was looking for, I inspected the other wine racks. There were three more rifles pointed at the opening of the tunnel. After I used my trusty credit card to determine the open position of the locking bolts, I concluded my original suspicion must be correct. They will be waiting for us when we emerge from the other end. Even worse, when we don't appear, I wouldn't be surprised if they come looking for us."

Confused by Larry's calmness, Charley asked, "So, what are we supposed to do? Are we going to sit here, less than 400 yards from a ruthless enemy, and wait for them to arrive?"

"That might be more difficult than you imagine. Each time we retreated back through one of those doors, we were very careful to slide the locking bolts into place. If they are going to approach from that direction, they will have a lot of work to do first. It could take hours."

"What about from the other direction?" Mr. Chandakar asked. "How do we know our attackers haven't entered the tunnel behind us?"

Before anyone could answer, Jeff jumped in, "Mr. Chandakar, would you mind answering two questions? Those two explosions on both sides of your home were big enough to attract a lot of attention. What kind of a response would you normally expect?"

"For explosions of that magnitude, in our kind of neighborhood, at a home like mine, with a former Indian ambassador in residence, I have to assume, in addition to the regular response from the fire department and the local police, we could expect a maximum response from the government's secret service, and India's antiterror units. By now, the street has to be filled with responders and a command center is being set up."

"Wouldn't it be reasonable to assume that whoever was attacking would anticipate their arrival and want to disappear before the cavalry arrived? If this attack was authorized by the Chinese, the transshippers, or some other industrial concern opposed to our program, the last thing they would want is to have their presence discovered."

"Maybe we should consider the purpose of the first attack was to drive us into the tunnel, toward a hidden enemy approaching from the other direction? Doesn't Larry's discovery confirm this possibility?"

Larry said, "If they are out there, my security team here will know. While we were trying to catch all those defenseless trout in Ireland, my team was working with Mr. Chandakar's security company. Once our presence in Mumbai had been reported, we realized that the enemy might anticipate that Mr. Chandakar would host one of his famous dinner parties. If they wanted to attack, it seemed to us that would be the natural place they would choose. Taking up positions at both ends of the tunnel may have been a possibility, but I'd bet our assailants at the front are long gone and the balance of their attack is concentrated on the other end."

Larry said, "Breaking through those heavy iron doors will generate a lot of noise. The sound of the explosions should indicate from which direction they are attacking. My people have been trained to delay their attack until they hear the sound of the next explosion. At that point, my men will take control of the outer perimeter and drive any external forces back into the houses, from there through the wine cellars and into the tunnel. They have instructions to force them toward us. The plan is for us to trap them between opposing fields of fire."

After waiting twenty minutes and not hearing a blast, Larry decided he would return to the far end of the tunnel and try to learn what was happening. Charley decided to inspect what was happening at the front end of the tunnel. They turned off the lights, removed their shoes, tested their flashlights, and pulled up their socks before disappearing into the darkness in the opposite directions.

Within minutes both men had returned. Larry spoke first. "They aren't trying to blow those doors off their hinges. They have torches and tanks of acetylene. They are cutting their way around the locking mechanisms. They must be worried that a blast large enough to blow the doors might bring down the ceiling of the tunnel or alert people to their presence.

"Without the sound of the explosions, our forces have no way of knowing what is happening down here and won't know when and where to attack. Somehow, we need to find a way to establish communications with them."

Charley reported, "Things are not quite so clear at the front end. Like Larry, I was able to move back through the dark and approach the last door leading to the front-end wine cellar. Unfortunately, there was no light and I couldn't take the risk of unlocking the first door. If the wrong people were waiting, they would have a clear and unobstructed path right to us. Rather than take the risk, I decided to retreat and lock each of the doors behind me. We may not know what is going on in the tunnel's front end, but if they are out there we should have plenty of time to prepare."

Jeff had only been half listening to the reports. His attention was focused on the different electrical circuits that ran along one side of the tunnel. "Does anyone know where these circuits lead or where they get their source of power? How were we able to turn off the lights in the remaining portions of the tunnel without turning off the lights where we are now?"

One of the guards, whose daytime duties included electrical system maintenance, responded. "Perhaps it would be best if you think of the lighting in the tunnel as consisting of a master circuit and separate connecting circuits that provide light in each of the separate compartments."

After inspecting the electrical panel and the conduits that ran through it, Jeff asked, "Tell me about the master circuit. What else is connected to it? Where is its power source located?"

"For security purposes, the power source is a transformer located in an underground vault that is independent of the main house supply. As far as I know, the only other attachments are the air conditioners and air handlers that are used to ventilate the tunnels and maintain the constant temperatures in the wine cellars."

"Do you remember where the compressors and the air handlers are located?"

"Yes, sir. They are located inside the perimeter wall not very far from the rear service entrance to the second house."

"Very good. Now, do you remember how much noise that equipment makes when it turns on and off?"

"The motors that drive the air compressors make very little noise. The air handlers make all the racket. The metal propeller blades make a sound like they're hitting something metallic every time they slow down when the system is turned off or speed up when the system is turned on. It's a very distinctive sound, one that is hard to ignore."

"If we were able to temporarily short-circuit the master circuit, would the compressors and the air handlers stop running?"

"Yes, sir. The disruption of power would be sensed the same as if the main power switch were shut down. You are describing safety precautions we regularly use as part of our routine inspections."

"And once the compressors shut down, how do you restart them?"

"We just restore power. There are circuit breakers that automatically re-engage."

"So if one of Larry's men happened to be standing near the air-conditioning equipment, he would hear the equipment when it began to shut down and when it started up?"

"If he were standing within thirty feet, there is no way he could not hear what was happening."

Turning to the rest of his colleagues, Jeff announced, "Gentlemen, I think we have just learned how we can communicate with the outside world and how they can communicate with us, provided one of us remembers his Morse code training."

"I must have missed something," Larry said. "How does turning an air conditioner on and off have anything to do with Morse code?"

Jeff responded, "If we cause the air conditioners to turn off and on at irregular intervals we can send Morse coded messages. The question is, how will we know if one of Larry's men is receiving and understanding our message?"

"That's the easy part," Larry answered. "Once they figure out what we are doing, they will realize all they have to do is turn the master circuit on and off and our tunnels lights can be used to send signals, the same way we are using the ventilation equipment."

Jeff went to work. Using the sharp tip of the sight on the end of one of the automatic weapons, he peeled the insulation off the master circuit wires. Holding the same weapon by its wooden grip, he placed the metal barrel against each of the exposed wires. Instantly the lights in their segment of the tunnel went black. Sensing Jeff had removed the barrel from the two wires, everybody held their breath in anticipation of the lights turning back on. In less time than they imagined, the tunnel lights illuminated again.

Charley, always the warrior, asked, "How long do you think it will take before someone up there notices what we are doing? Maybe the better question is, how long do we have before we have to worry about these attackers who are cutting their way toward us?"

Larry said, "We know there are only five doors separating us from them. If two of the doors have already been breached, then only three more are separating us.

"When I think about it, maybe we should be thinking in terms of only two doors. Surely, they aren't planning to use their acetylene torch to cut their way through the last door. Knowing we are waiting on the other side, they must be planning some other way to blow out the door and not collapse the tunnel."

"What if they have some sort of armor-piercing weapon, like an anti-tank gun?" Jeff asked.

"Exactly," Charley said. "Once they know which door separates them from us, what can we do to stop them, unless they don't know which door it is?"

"Which door? Once they see our lights, they will know we are in the next compartment," Jeff said. "When they see light penetrating through those two slots in the door, wouldn't it be reasonable to assume they would think we are in the next compartment and fire away with whatever they have?"

"Not if we were to retreat one compartment back and leave this one lit," Larry commented. "Not only would we buy more time, but we would also be able to see them emerge into the illuminated compartment. They could become the easy targets."

CHAPTER 28

IVAN AND MADAM CHANG

For years, Ivan had looked forward to the occasional and casual conversational encounters he enjoyed with his mother. No matter how complicated or technical his descriptions of his most recent adventures were, his mother's nimble mind seemed to be able to follow his explanations and ask difficult questions.

As she listened to her son talk about his most recent exciting experience, she was frequently reminded of how this highly energetic, intensely imaginative, and analytical young man seemed to have inherited from both of his parents their most aggressive tendencies.

What do I really know about my only son? For years I have had to remain content knowing what little information he would pass along, newspaper accounts of his developmental exploits, and the occasional reports from my friends.

Today's conversation was no exception. If it hadn't been so important that the managing trustee of the Sentinel Trust understand exactly what they were up against in replicating the destroyed experiments, I wonder how much I might have learned about his three-year-old program to develop a reliable source of affordable green energy.

As chairman of the Sentinel Trust, I retain the authority, under my sole signature, to approve or deny any request for funds. Not only will the test results determine our ability to proceed with the Employ American plan, but they could encourage the Trust to make additional investments and further jeopardize Sentinel Trust investment capital.

The tone of Ivan's voice, his techniques in distilling the problems, his intensity, and his indefatigable commitment to complete the task at hand reminded Madam Chang of his father, her husband, the always proud and determined Mike Stone. Sometimes when her mind wandered, she thought it was her beloved husband who was talking to her.

After listening carefully to what Ivan was explaining, Madam Chang said, "I've heard you describe some pretty wild and seemingly unfathomable problems, but this cleaner coal problem is totally different. What makes you believe it's a solvable problem under any circumstances, much less the six-month time frame you have been provided?"

Responding to the question, Ivan said, "Actually, there are two reasons. The first one involves our successfully solving the chemical processing issue. I have selected a site on the Tennessee River that was inundated with coal ash from that recent flood at the Tennessee Valley Authority coal-generating electrical site. Enormous deposits of the coal-ash residue created from the burning of multiple sources of raw coal are accessible at a variety of locations.

"To facilitate working on this problem, we have purchased six concrete transit mixers, installed state-of-the-art scales, and rented weight-sensitive cranes to load measured quantities of chemicals. Water tanks have been installed to store the large quantities of seawater we will truck in from the Atlantic coast. State-of-the-art testing equipment has been installed in the trailer we're using for an office. Piles of coal ash have been trucked in from three separate locations. Our site looks more like a construction project than a highly sophisticated testing laboratory, but we are progressing."

"Ivan, I have been talking to some of my old friends in Washington. They tell me that the government may be much more motivated to assist you than you might believe. According to them, they have their own problems with the untested coal-ash residue. The absence of a cost-effective disposal solution is only going to delay additional testing for so long. If they are forced to reclassify all those deposits without a workable cost-effective disposal solution in hand, power rates on 50 percent of the country's electrical generation could be dramatically increased.

"You might be pleasantly surprised to learn, subject to your satisfactorily completing your tests, how motivated the federal government is to help you solve your problem."

———

Recollecting his mother's words played a significant role in holding up Ivan's and John Paul's spirits. One of the five contributing Sentinel doctoral scholars, John Paul had used his Chinese experimental and working experience with the new chemical process to develop the "coal ash to high-strength cement" technology. His original notes had been the foundation for their test work at the Sentinel Institute, and his private diary containing his reflections on their preliminary test results had formed the basis for their Tennessee tests.

John Paul was the son of the great Venezuelan Minister of Petroleum Juan Pablo Perez. His efforts, together with Ivan's vision and creative problem-solving ability, had represented the driving source behind the more recent testing. The two men along with the other members of their team had been in Tennessee for more than a month. The tests weren't going well. When one test failed to produce the desired results, they would change their chemical formulas and start over.

After a particularly long and frustrating day, they were sitting in the local bar. They had just ordered their second round of the local bourbon and branch water when Ivan, almost as an afterthought, said, "I wonder if we're even using the right ingredients, much less the proper proportions. Working from memory and our notes, we could be leaving something out and not even know it."

Without thinking, John Paul said, "That can't be so difficult to figure out. Why don't I contact our former suppliers? Surely, they must have copies of our old invoices. Not only will we be able to identify all the different ingredients we were using, but we should also be able to determine the approximate quantities."

By three o'clock the next afternoon they had received the final fax transmissions of their old invoices. The sun was coming up the next morning when John Paul and Ivan had finished the last of their calculations. By eight o'clock they were back on-site, making changes to their formulas, when Ivan suggested, "Instead of treating three separate samples, why don't we concentrate our efforts on one source of coal ash and repeat the tests using six different formulas? Once we find the solution for one strain, it shouldn't be so difficult for us to learn how to modify the chemical formulations to meet the challenges of the other strains."

Four days and twenty-four transit mixer batches later, they sensed they were getting close. The heavy-metal content in the finished batches was beginning to decline. It took two more days to repeat the experiments and make minor adjustments. The measurable content of the heavy metals in the green cement tested to 2.25 parts per million, well within the EPA's industrial waste standards. The industrial strength of the resultant cement was testing well above minimum acceptable levels.

They were seated at the same bar, where six days ago, they had allowed their feelings of doom and defeat to dominate the atmosphere. Their mood had dramatically changed. Their feelings of fear of failure had been replaced with hope and anticipation.

Ivan interrupted their excited chatter by saying, "Now that we have the right formula, we need to go back and determine what the cost of converting large volumes of coal ash to 'green cement' really is. We will need to compare those numbers with the cost of purchasing competitive imported cement products. Once we know what our relative cost advantage may be, we'll be able to generate the calculations required to compute the available income contribution for offsetting the high cost of carbon sequestration. Assuming the results are favorable, maybe I should schedule an inspection for the EPA administrator and her staff. She may be as anxious to see our results as we have been to produce them."

CHAPTER 29

LIFE ABOVE GROUND

Consistent with their carefully rehearsed plan, Larry's two senior lieutenants and their teams had been stationed in concealed positions near each of the Chandakar homes. The team outside the main mansion, as instructed, watched as the explosions were detonated, the six attacking operatives entered the burning building, and only four came out. The cessation of small arms fire was followed by four of the operatives dragging their two dead or wounded comrades to a waiting van. As soon as the entire team was on board, the van departed.

Entering the vacated, still smoking house, Larry's team found no trace of Mr. Chandakar, his guests, or his servant. The team commander surmised that Chandakar and guests must have retreated into the sanctuary of the wine cellar, below the closed and relocked trapdoor. If they made it that far, they must have made their way into the lockable system of compartmented tunnels that form the underground passage between the two homes.

In the meantime, unaware of what had happened at the main house, a second enemy operative strike force was preoccupied with efforts to enter the second house, cover the other end of the tunnel, and stop the escaping Mr. Chandakar and guests.

Following instructions, Larry's team remained hidden in the shadows surrounding the second home. Their orders called for them to wait for the sound of the first underground explosion (indicating the enemy operatives had entered the tunnel) before attacking. Waiting as instructed, Larry's team watched the enemy operatives unload and carry their precious cargo of weapons through the house and down into the wine cellar. When the last of the weapons had disappeared into the house, four operatives remained outside, guarding the entrance.

Larry's team emerged from the shadows and eliminated the four guards before entering the house. Moving from room to room, they quickly and quietly used their silenced automatic weapons to dispose of any remaining operatives who had not passed into the cellar. With the house secure, and all operatives driven into the cellar or the underground tunnels, the unit waited.

Attempting to listen for the sound of muffled explosions, small arms gunfire, anything that would provide some indication that contact with Chandakar's party had been established, Larry's team was annoyed by the interruption of the clattering metallic sound each time the nearby air compressor and its air handlers shut down and started up. The metallic noises were making it impossible for them to hear any telling sounds that might be coming from the tunnel.

Finally, one of Larry's men noticed the different time intervals between the starting and shutting down operations of the air-handling equipment. He said, "When you listen to the varying intervals between the noise of that air handler starting and stopping, it makes you wonder if someone is trying to communicate with us. What else could explain why this airshaft ventilation equipment would be turning off and on at such irregular intervals? Maybe someone is trying to communicate with us in Morse code?"

After listening to the sequencing of the equipment, one of

Larry's lieutenants took out a stub of a pencil and started to record the series of dots and dashes that conformed to the short and long intervals between the off and on cycles. When the equipment appeared to settle down to its normal steady performance, the leader studied what he had written. Showing his notes to the others, he said, "My God! This is Morse code. I'm a bit rusty, but aren't those dots and dashes signaling an SOS? If I'm right, we need to find a way to communicate with Larry and his friends. By now, we have to assume the approaching forces could be reaching their target."

"Boss, if they have figured out how to short-circuit the ventilation equipment, there must be a source of electrical power around here that is separate from the one supplying the main house. If we can locate the power source, by turning it on and off, we should be able to communicate with them as they are communicating with us."

While Larry's commanders, assisted by Mr. Chandakar's security force, were busy developing their own contingency plan, the city police, the fire department, the Indian secret service, and the country's antiterror force were arriving on the scene of Mr. Chandakar's burning home. In accordance with trained procedure, they were setting up a central command center, securing their communication lines, and reporting in to their supervisors. First response teams were sent in to the still-burning portions of what remained of the once proud structure.

The alerted press, the TV vans with their up-link data transmission facilities, photographers and their cameras, and the newscasters were arriving on the scene. Their initial reports suggested that the bombing of Mr. Chandakar's home occurred while he was hosting a dinner with two American industrialists, the founder of British Security, Inc., and India's former ambassador to China.

When the first response team emerged from the smoldering

and smoky debris, aggressive reporters were waiting to ask them for a report of what they had seen.

The seasoned reporters were confused to hear that no bodies had been found. Repeating his answer, the spokesman for the team said, "We found evidence of gunfire, substances on the floor that looked like blood, overturned and shattered furniture, but no bodies. Someone must have removed the dead, the wounded, and the captured before we arrived."

Not one of the reporters realized they were standing within a few hundred feet of an ongoing life-and-death underground struggle.

———

A courier from the far end of the tunnel arrived with Larry's most recent message. "Door number nine breeched, only two doors left. Please proceed."

A rucksack containing an enormous explosive device was hurled through the second house's cellar doorway at the head of the stairs. The explosion was so strong it destroyed the contents of the wine cellar and killed anybody who might have been stationed in the cellar.

Protected from the blast by the three directional changes of the tunnel, the members of the attacking unit were unprepared for the sound of the explosion, the rush of air, the sudden illumination, and the small bits of debris that blew along the tunnel's path.

Believing elite members of their own team were protecting their rear position, the confused enemy operatives were trying to decide whether to proceed with their mission or shift their attention to fending off a possible attack from the rear.

After only briefly hesitating, they had the antitank weapon brought forward and trained it on what they assumed was the last door separating them from their intended prey. Signs of illumination were visible through the two slots.

In the confined tunnel, the loud flash of the antitank round exploding the door exceeded anything they were expecting. Temporarily stunned, the attacking enemy force hesitated before the following the blast into the next lit compartment. Entering the illuminated tunnel compartment before them, they were surprised not to discover the presence of dead or wounded prey. The sound of the heavy door slamming shut, one compartment behind them, added to their confusion.

Any surprise at finding themselves trapped in an illuminated tunnel, between two locked cast-iron doors located within four hundred feet of each other, disappeared when they began to take incoming small arms fire from behind the locked door in front of them. Exposed and vulnerable, they began to retreat only to be greeted by small arms fire coming from the tunnel behind them. Sensing the hopelessness of their situation, they dropped their weapons and raised their arms in surrender.

The first responder arriving on the scene at the second house heard, "Hold your fire. We are coming out!"

As all the different government agencies and press teams arrived at the second location, all they could do was stand back and watch as Mr. Tambour, Larry, Charley, Jeff, and Chandakar and his personal staff were loaded into a waiting van and driven away. Larry's team and the remaining unwounded captives entered the second waiting van, which followed the first.

Within the next few minutes, the security forces entering the tunnel from the second end would discover the dead and wounded operatives who had been left behind.

CNN newscasts reported the event in every major television market in the world. The names of Aakil Chandakar, the celebrated Indian industrialist; Mr. Tambour; Jeff Mohr, the iconic American electronics business leader; Charles Hutson, U.S. Motors' director of long-range planning; and Larry Wilshire, president of British Security, were prominently mentioned. It had been a long time since the press had the opportunity to report a very vicious attack and daring rescue of five such prominent, high-profile personalities.

CHAPTER 30

SOMEONE FINALLY UNDERSTANDS

The message waiting at the front desk of their Cleveland Hotel destroyed any possible chance that the two ladies would be able to spend some relaxing time together before leaving for Indianapolis. Claudia opened the message, read it, and showed it to Robin.

Robin and Claudia,

Returning detachments from Afghanistan, Iraq, Korea, Germany, and Kosovo are arriving at Fort Campbell, Kentucky, within the next thirty-six hours. The army is going all out to organize a suitable homecoming to express the country's appreciation for their service. Gen. Ben has made tentative arrangements with the camp commanders for the two of you to be part of the entertainment program. He has also offered his services to introduce you.

We both agree your presence will be an excellent opportunity to expose your Employ American program to the returning veterans and the large contingent of the working press scheduled to attend.

Please advise!

Mr. Sam

Robin and Claudia were standing in the wings of the enormous outdoor stage. Hidden behind the side curtains, they could see the politicians and the entertainers as they performed on stage. They were also standing close enough to the audience to be able to study the faces of those seated in the front rows.

Nudging Claudia, Robin asked, "Have you noticed how mixed the audience's reactions seems to be? It's hard to believe that so many of the veterans don't appear more excited about being here."

Claudia shifted her gaze from the stage to the audience. It took her a few seconds to identify what Robin was describing.

"You're right! What can they be thinking? I've seen that look of boredom, but never in this kind of setting."

Despite the fact that Wells had retired from active duty more than two years before, the military's affection and respect for him was still clearly evident. For those few in the audience who were not familiar with his reputation as the "General's General," they could hear people say, "Talk about someone who really is respected. I've heard people remark, 'Whatever the general says, you can believe!'"

Standing at the lectern, General Ben began his opening remarks. "I know many of you are concerned about what kind of country you have been defending and, now that your military obligation has been completed, what kind of country is waiting to greet you.

"The United States is still the great country you left, but it is not without its own problems; first, we find ourselves in a seriously overleveraged and underemployed situation. Unfortunately, in a limited job-creation environment, you will be competing for employment with 25 million people who are either out of work or unable to find suitable part-time work.

"The two exceptional ladies who are waiting to address you are deeply committed to solving this problem. They are hoping to gain your support to implement a plan they call 'Employ American.' It is a complex program which, if successful, speaks to the problem of improving employment without subjecting our households or our country to increasing levels of debt. Dr. Cook, if you please?"

As Robin took the stage, Claudia continued examining the faces of the impassive veterans in the first few rows. During Robin's opening comments, rather than trying to watch all the faces, she decided to observe the reactions of no more than two or three of the more passive soldiers. *I would describe the look on their faces as disinterested and bored*, she thought.

Robin didn't waste any time cutting to the chase. Almost immediately she focused her comments on the training schools and recruiting programs. "While the underemployed in our country are staggering under the yoke of declining manufacturing, there are those of us who believe the problem can be solved. Ms. Roth and I have come here to invite you to become part of the solution.

"The implementation of the plan requires that we recruit and train a contemporary labor force to fill the 200,000 jobs we plan to create in the first Employ American industrial campus."

Claudia observed to herself, *Robin's done it again. With those first few opening remarks, she succeeded in capturing the attention of this big audience, even the bored ones I have been watching.*

"Once we succeed in creating an environment where the American manufacturer's competitiveness can be restored, we believe goods-producing jobs will be returned to our shores.

"Now, let's talk about recruiting and training. Working in close cooperation with the employer, the appropriate labor union, and the Sentinel Institute faculty, we are planning to introduce an entirely new approach to regional job fairs and job qualification schools. For those who apply and are accepted, we plan to provide the centralized vocational and apprentice training required to fill those 200,000 jobs. Much of the model we will be using has been adopted from Israeli government programs, military vocational training programs, and the G.I. Bill of Rights.

"Each of you already possesses the qualities we're going to need to make this new experiment successful in recruiting, qualifying, and training. Where else can we hope to find a finer system of team leaders, instructors, and applicants for all the training programs we will be required to offer? For any of you receiving an honorable discharge, the need to attend 'Q' school will be waived. In exchange, you will be asked to take a test to determine your fields of interest, areas of personal proficiency, your qualifications and experience for instruction assignments, and your interest in leadership responsibilities."

As Robin waited for the essence of her comments to sink in, she motioned to the man standing behind the curtain stage left. Almost immediately a big curtain resembling an American flag began to descend. It was followed by another sign that descended from stage right. The "Uncle Sam" character pointing at the crowd, which was the same one that had been used on recruiting posters, filled one side. On the other side, the words, "Employ American Needs You" were printed in big bold letters.

Claudia noticed that tentative interest seemed to be slowly replacing impatient boredom. Robin had deliberately tried to speak in terms familiar to service personnel.

"Specific industry vocational training, team building, and developing leadership skills will be the primary focus of this effort. From the minute you arrive until you graduate, you will be organized into eight-person teams under the supervision of a team leader. You will be responsible for your own growth and learning as well as the progress of other members of your team."

After pausing for a moment, Robin asked, "Does any of this sound familiar?"

"Since you will need a place to live, your first assignment will be that of designing, obtaining regulatory approvals, obtaining a construction loan and a building permit, and the actual construction of your new house. Some of you will be trained to become masons, carpenters, electricians, plumbers, cabinetmakers, drywallers, painters, and roofers. All of you will learn how to work as a team.

"Once completed, the house will be yours, and you will be expected to live there. After your group of eight graduates, the program will purchase the house from you at the then appraised value. Any profits will be evenly distributed among you. It is our expectation that each of you will be leaving with new skills, money in your pocket, and the opportunity to apply for construction jobs or enter the next level of training."

A woman sitting in the fourth row asked the first question. "How will you determine the makeup of each eight-person team?"

Smiling, Robin said, "By the order of your arrival. Each of you will be assigned your own bedroom and bath. Personal privacy should not be an issue."

Someone else asked, "How do we know that we will be able to get along? Won't you be mixing old with young, male with female, whites with blacks, Latinos with Asians?"

"You have just answered my favorite question. You will learn to treasure your experience as a great opportunity to learn what's required to get along with people of different backgrounds. You will develop an appreciation for group dynamics and you will experience firsthand how the system of independent free enterprise works.

A young man stood, raised his hand, and asked, "And, if we fail to get along, then what?"

"Three strikes and all eight of you will be sent home. We suggest that you learn how to pull together!"

Tentative interest turned into smiling comprehension.

People in the audience could be seen turning to one other. Someone was overheard to say, "Finally, someone is starting to understand!"

CHAPTER 31

BACK-CHANNEL COMMUNICATIONS

News of the Mumbai attack was being carefully managed. Over the protests of the press, the Chinese, Indian, and Taiwanese governments, and big manufacturers, no additional information was provided, no interviews were granted, and no government or medical reports were forthcoming.

Special Indian secret service personnel had taken any dead or wounded enemy operatives to secure military hospitals and secret detainment camps. Any interrogation results were handled with extreme care and consistent with top-secret confidential procedures. A total shroud of secrecy had been placed over the entire operation.

What wasn't kept a secret was Mr. Jeff Mohr's and Mr. Aakil Chandakar's earlier press conference where they announced their decision to continue their long-standing relationship in India and expand it to include participation in the first Employ American campus in Northern California.

A confused press had no difficulty in speculating about what the real story behind the attack on Aakil Chandakar and his guests might have been. One reporter asked, "Is there a possible connection between Mr. Chandakar's earlier announcement and the attack at his home?"

The growing question of why no dead or wounded had been found at the site of such a ferocious attack was prominently reported. Readers and audience members were beginning to ask, "Who was trying to hide what?"

In China, Taiwan, and the United States, after the initial reporting, there were no further newspaper or television reports of the incident. No one wanted to prevent or interfere with possible establishment of a back-channel communications network and possible negotiations.

———

The second morning following their rescue and receipt of sanctuary at the American embassy, Larry's plane was being made ready to depart from Mumbai's international airport for its designated flight to Hong Kong. The fuel tanks had been topped off. The pilot and copilot had completed their preflight inspection, the catering had been placed on board, and the plane had been moved outside the Chandakar hangar. The flight plan had been filed. All that was missing were the passengers.

Six hours earlier, the Indian government's plane carrying Jeff, Charley, Larry, Mr. Tambour, and Mr. Chandakar had taken off from a military base located a considerable distance from Mumbai's international airport. The flight would terminate at a highly restricted Indian military air base outside New Delhi.

They were flying eastward across the Indian continent when Mr. Tambour received his first secure communiqué from the Indian State Department. "Mr. Tambour, when we finished interrogating the remaining captured operatives, we discovered four members of the attacking force were members of the Chinese secret service. Four others are members of a particularly ruthless Taiwanese security company.

"We are interpreting their presence and what limited information we were able to obtain to suggest that the attack was a carefully coordinated effort of senior members of China's National Security Agency, central government, and the security company regularly employed by a number of China's largest export manufacturers. Most of the captured have mentioned that they were totally unprepared for the counterattack by Larry and his men."

Mr. Tambour, sitting quietly, was thinking about the significance of what he had just been told. He was having a difficult time comprehending the full extent of what it might mean. Thinking out loud, Mr. Tambour said, "I wonder if whoever planned this attack considered what might be involved when a supposedly friendly government attacks a government official and private citizens of other friendly countries."

Fifteen minutes later a second communiqué arrived. "I've been asked to inquire what recommendations Mr. Tambour might suggest regarding a possible response."

Mr. Tambour wrote, "Please convey my appreciation to my colleagues regarding their understanding of the sensitivity and seriousness of the present situation. My friends and I are working on a plan of our own. I would appreciate it if you would agree to delay any response until we have had a chance to discuss what we believe the best course of action may be."

Having completed the transmission, Mr. Tambour addressed his friends. "Gentlemen, while you complete your meetings in China, I might use the opportunity to talk to some of my old friends in the Chinese government. As long as we can keep the real facts about the attack out of the newspapers, I think we should be able to test the Chinese government's appetite for a back-channel negotiated solution."

Jeff asked, "Mr. Tambour, do I need to be concerned about

what the effect of my forthcoming discussion with Mohr's Chinese contractors might have on your discussions?"

"Initially, I thought about asking you to delay those meetings until I was able to complete my talks. Now that I've had some time to think about it, I believe your putting maximum pressure on your Chinese contractors should help me make our case."

The next call, twenty minutes later, over the secure military line, was for Larry. After listening carefully to what he was being told, he explained to the others, "We've been advised not to make any advanced plans to schedule Jeff's meetings. Each of your flights will originate on a random schedule from the same military base, outside New Delhi, where we will be landing in a few minutes. When you are ready to make your calls, no flight plans will be filed. You will land at an unspecified airport, and your meetings are not to be scheduled until your plane is on final approach.

"Prior to your departure from each of those four Chinese bases, arrangements will be made in accordance with the same operational diversion we used in Mumbai. Under the circumstances we can't be too careful."

Early the next morning, well before their presence could be reported, an unmarked plane departed, without a passenger manifest, for an unreported destination.

CHAPTER 32

THE SUNBELT TOUR

Robin and Claudia's swing through the Sunbelt states was scheduled to begin in Charleston, South Carolina. Organized labor, the security industry, the military, local colleges and universities, church groups, and the local elected representatives of both parties had planned separate local events. They had a lot of ground to cover if they hoped to expose their plan to the broadest possible cross section of the population.

Public interest had been growing. Senators and congressmen were beginning to conclude that any hope of their being able to remain obscure on the "New Employment" tax bill was rapidly disappearing. Transparency and voter accountability were becoming the order of the day. What could have turned into weeks of drudgery, frustration, and hard work was taking on the feel of positive momentum and excitement.

Antagonists of the Employ American plan were beginning to reassess their position. Their chatter behind closed doors was forceful. "Clearly, something needs to be done! We need to discredit these two ladies on a personal level and disrupt their momentum."

Adversaries to the plan employed and carefully prepared

remonstrators to ask difficult and confusing questions. Opposing congressmen, local politicians, and conservative, high-profile local personalities used local press conferences, newspaper editorials, club membership lunches, and their presence at cocktail parties and other social gatherings to present their points of view. Unsupported statements were becoming quite common. Questions without proper foundation were being asked. Rumors about the two ladies' personal conduct were being spread. Even at their own scheduled town meetings, carefully prepared people were paid to attend and interrupt with disturbing questions.

Casey Jones doubled its security. The FBI assigned new agents to identify the remonstrators, check their backgrounds, and keep the director informed. The battle lines were being transferred from the implicit to the explicit.

Robin and Claudia were learning how to handle the tough questions and the heckling. When confronted with unfounded allegations, they would calmly answer, "That's an interesting question. Would you mind sharing with us the information you used to prepare it?"

The local press in each of the cities was learning to respect Robin and Claudia and their mission. Antagonists with their threatening questions had learned that they had better be prepared to back up whatever they were asking or suggesting.

The two ladies were becoming overnight celebrities. Photographers waited to take their picture in the restaurants, at the ball games, at the theater, and at any social functions the women had been invited to attend. Pictures and articles appeared regularly in local newspapers, weekly magazines, and on the eleven o'clock news.

The trouble started in Charleston, South Carolina. Well known for "dirty tricks," the local newspapers were skilled in fabricating incriminating stories. The first morning following the two ladies' presentation to the local investment community, the headline read "Who Are These Two Carpetbaggers? What Have They Come Here to Sell?" A picture of Robin and Claudia sitting close to each other, talking in an intimate manner at a local restaurant, appeared in the next morning's newspaper. The following afternoon's paper featured another picture of them entering a hotel. A clock in the background of the photograph read 12:30 a.m.

It was becoming difficult for them to make presentations or grant interviews without having to respond to not so cleverly posed questions regarding their personal relationship. Robin and Claudia, two nationally recognized career professionals and very proud women, were shocked and embarrassed by some of the innuendos.

Mr. Sam was waiting in the hotel coffee shop when they appeared for breakfast a few days later. "I've read the tabloids. I have seen the television reports and heard the speculative comments of talk show hosts. I've even received calls from concerned Washington reporters covering your tour. They all tell me you two are being forced to endure the worst kind of public abuse. I'm sure I don't have to remind you what's at stake. I thought we should talk about it."

What started out as a very sensitive conversation with two hurt and deeply upset women became a discussion of renewed determination. Robin said, "Sam, I believe you when you say we should regard this personal attack as a compliment. If someone wasn't really threatened by what we're attempting, why would they be trying to personalize our campaign?

Claudia spoke up. "You are asking a lot of us to let all these accusations flow off our backs like so much water. We understand why we need to rise above this controversy, proceed with our mission, and let the public make up its own mind. Even so, I'm not so certain that we don't need to fight back. The only way they can beat us is if we beat ourselves. We just can't allow that to happen!"

———

In Atlanta, traditionally one of the South's more progressive cities, the questions became ugly. The innuendos became more severe, and the intent of the comments and questions made by reporters and interviewers were becoming more obvious.

Robin and Claudia were learning that silence followed by a winning smile no longer represented an effective defense. They were not able to keep things under control by relying on their wit, their style, and their grace.

A freelance reporter who was paid to ask particularly ugly questions began to needle Robin. His tactics, which employed baseless information, were well known by many of the more responsible and experienced members of the press who were present, but not by either of the speakers.

Robin was concentrating on answering a previous question, when the unfamiliar reporter rose, interrupted what she was saying, and asked, "Is it true you and Ms. Roth are lesbian lovers?" Robin smiled and attempted to move on, but the reporter persisted. "Not so fast. I've asked you a direct question. I expect a direct answer."

When a hush settled over the room, Robin immediately realized she was left with no room to retreat. Sensing that the more polite members of the press were embarrassed by the question, but nonetheless curious to hear her response, she stared directly at the reporter and said, "Excuse me, sir, but I don't seem to recognize you. May I ask your name and what organization you represent?"

The reporter, said, "I don't understand what my name and the name of my employer have to do with your answer. I'm still waiting!"

"Excuse me, sir, but prior to our meeting I was apprised that an antagonistic reporter might be attending who has been paid to ask questions that are neither relevant nor supported by accurate information. I was trying to determine if you are him."

The spontaneous outbreak of laughter shattered whatever tension had been building. Robin was not about to back off. "Mr. whatever your name is, I'm certain as a responsible member of the press that you understand the courtesy of identifying yourself and telling us which news organization you represent. To start things off, my name is Dr. Robin Cook and I represent the Sentinel Institute of Monterey, California."

Another embarrassing silence settled over the room. The other reporters' attentions were focused on the reporter whom many of them had long ago learned to disrespect. They were interested in learning how "the worm" would answer Robin's question. Following a significant pause, he finally responded. "My name is Ralph Black. I'm a freelance reporter in the employ of the law firm, Harris, Bramwell, and Duncan. I have been asked by my clients to report on your background and personal character."

"Mr. Black, normally I wouldn't wish to answer a personal question formulated by a group of attorneys without having council present. But since you have asked me a question about my personal life, I'm going to answer your question. Before I do, may I inquire about the foundation for your question? Ms. Roth's and

my careers, our personal histories, and our professional creden-
tials are well known."

"Dr. Cook, it's no secret. The newspapers, television, and magazines have been full of pictures of the two of you entering a local
hotel late in the evening. Would you mind explaining the nature
of the relationship between you?"

"Mr. Black, I would like to compliment you on the accuracy
of your information. Let's talk about the picture of the two of
us entering a hotel. I'm not certain why you would choose that
particular picture. You could have selected other pictures of our
attending the ball game, the symphony, or any one of the several
restaurants we have frequented.

"Atlanta can be a very interesting city to visit. What you might
surmise from those pictures was two professional colleagues,
traveling together, taking some time out for a little entertainment
and returning to the hotel in which we are both registered in
separate rooms.

"So you're asking me if we're lesbians, involved in a homo-
sexual relationship."

Noticeably, the reporter began to squirm. Finally, he said,
"Yeah, I guess that pretty well sums it up!"

"Thank you, Mr. Black. I appreciate your candor. You can
report to your employers my answer. Ms. Roth and I are longtime
friends of respect and affection; we're not lovers. We have been
traveling and presenting our program to a variety of audiences in
a series of large cities in an effort to garner grassroots support for
some very important pending legislation.

"Now, having answered your question, I would like to ask you
a question. Rather than be concerned about how our personal
lives might affect what is a serious economic issue, shouldn't your
legal employers be more concerned about how they are going to
advise their clients? In case you've missed it, people are becoming

informed and concerned about the growing levels of underemployment in this country. We are here to speak in favor of certain pending tax legislation designed to improve the American manufacturers' ability to compete in both domestic and foreign markets. Perhaps you should be asking your employer if it's in our best interest to resurrect manufacturing employment in this country. If you would like to ask me any questions about this topic, I would be pleased to answer them."

It was hard to tell which of the reporters were clapping, whistling, or laughing, but they were clearly in favor of Robin's response.

———

By the time Claudia and Robin reached New Orleans, a strange thing was beginning to happen. Reporters who had been accompanying them on their tour were beginning to resent any further abuse of them by audience members or press. People in the audiences were starting to become incensed. Further attempts to embarrass or discredit the two ladies were being met with growing crowd resistance.

In Houston, members of the audience asked good penetrating questions that concentrated on the core causes and the possible positive effects of the Employ American plan. Their clear, positive answers were followed by appreciative applause.

On the night following their last public appearance, long-time friends of Claudia's had scheduled a reception in their River Oaks home for the two ladies and forty of their closest friends. In Houston, a southern city long known for its heritage of entrepreneurial enterprise, its hospitality, and its progressive frontier attitude, an invitation to attend an intimately planned event to meet a visiting friend was considered a great compliment. Invitations were quickly answered and rarely refused.

It had been a long time since two such exciting women had been invited to be the guests of honor. From the outset, the evening was turning into one of those unusual events that occur when the guests are sincerely interested in learning more about the subject topic, and the guests of honor are interested in learning from whatever feedback is being offered. Claudia and Robin asked at least half the questions. The spirit of conversational reciprocity continued through the cocktail hour, over dinner, and into dessert and after-dinner drinks.

It was 12:30 a.m. when Robin and Claudia politely excused themselves, thanked their hosts, and got into the limousine waiting to transport them back to their hotel. Exhausted, leaning back in the soft, overstuffed rear seats, her shoeless feet propped on the nearby ottoman, and holding her final-final scotch of the evening, Claudia was excited and wanted to talk. "If every one of our tours could end like tonight's, I think I could become accustomed to this kind of life. When have we had the opportunity to answer so many thought-provoking questions asked by so many exciting people who are used to making things happen?"

Raising her glass as if to make a toast, Robin said, "I could never make up my mind whether it was the questions or the opinions they were expressing that I found more interesting. In any event the bed is going to feel pretty good. Maybe the best thing that is going to happen is that nothing is planned for tomorrow. I'm looking forward to sleeping in, having a leisurely breakfast, and reading all the newspapers before we have to board our flight to Phoenix."

CHAPTER **33**

THE CHINESE DILEMMA

Despite the unorthodox last-minute announcement of Jeff Mohr's arrival, the business owner in Guong Zhou was more than eager to make whatever adjustments were needed to accommodate the chairman of his largest American customer.

Normally, Mohr's periodic inspections were made by one of the company's quality-control teams. Flattered by Jeff's willingness to come such a long way, particularly after the reported attack in Mumbai, the local owner immediately tried to make whatever arrangements he needed to appropriately greet his honored guest.

Once operations inspections were completed, over the traditional, not-so-ceremonial, hastily arranged, late-afternoon dinner party, Jeff's local contractor wasted no time explaining. "Times are changing in China. Costs of labor, energy, and raw materials are inching higher and higher. Shrinking margins are pressuring the Chinese manufacturers to raise prices. Since we are your lowest-cost manufacturers, we believe you and our other clients should be willing to renegotiate our contracts and pass along any increased costs to your customers."

Charley sat quietly watching the strange scenario unfold. Any discussion involving technical problems of the production lines had been handled on a give-and-take basis. Clearly, both sides had been using the less complex operating issues to establish a constructive working atmosphere for the more sensitive discussions that would undoubtedly follow.

Charley couldn't help but notice that the atmosphere was entirely different from what he had witnessed in Mumbai. This was not a gathering of old, caring friends trying to find mutually acceptable solutions to big problems. The dinner agenda and the social atmosphere were more characteristic of two adversaries trying to negotiate a deal.

When the host-supplier started to list their company's concerns and complaints, Charley focused on Jeff's reaction. After listening to the one-sided discussion, Jeff politely said, "Let me make certain I understand what you have been telling me. Can I assume this list of items you have raised represents the changes you wish to see made in our working agreement? If my board ratifies these changes, are you willing to enter into another ten-year contract?"

Charley was having a difficult time comprehending what he was hearing or more accurately what he wasn't hearing. Nowhere in any of the discussions had there been any mention of repatriating production back to the United States. Looking down at the list of major points he had been making, he was only able to observe their host's requests. There was not a single entry regarding any problem Jeff might have been interested in discussing.

Over the next few days, as they met with two more of the Chinese contractors, Charley started to form the suspicion that Jeff was up to something. He watched Jeff respond to similar treatment in the same manner. Unless he was asked, the iconic leader made no effort to insert any of his own concerns or views into any of the conversations.

Over dinner, the night before they would visit Mohr's long-term

Chinese contractor in Taen Jen, Jeff said, "Charley, I'd appreciate it if you would pay particularly close attention to what may happen tomorrow. Depending on my feel for the situation, I may decide to play my 'China hole-card.' I think it's time for me to put them on notice that we could be playing in a different arena!"

Within minutes of entering the Taen Jen production plant, Jeff sensed something was different. The owner, Cheng Yee, was not present. The factory managers were unusually restrained and formal when they responded to the simplest operating questions. Even the conversations at lunch between Jeff and the different plant managers provided no clue as to what was wrong.

At four o'clock, a senior plant official said, "Cheng Yee just called. He has received an urgent call from the Chinese prime minister and is expected to fill in at a state dinner in Beijing. He apologizes for having to cancel your dinner engagement. He hopes, however, that he can briefly meet with you here at the factory before he has to leave."

Jeff was confused. *Something has gone wrong. Obviously Cheng doesn't want to be trapped into discussing an awkward issue over a long dinner. I've known Cheng for years. Our contract with his company was the first one we executed when we initially came to China. Our working relationship has been excellent, probably the best we have in this country. This meeting could prove enlightening.*

A copy of the Cleveland newspaper was lying faceup on the plant manager's desk. The article, "Bringing Our Jobs Home," was prominently displayed on the front page. Jeff now understood the problem.

When Cheng Yee appeared, he made a deliberate effort to act in his most reserved and stern manner. Jeff knew this was the persona Cheng assumed when he spoke at formal occasions. *This is not the man I have become accustomed to. The Cheng Yee I know is a man with an inquisitive mind and a warm and sensitive personality.*

Sensing Cheng's controlled anger, Jeff was still trying to figure out how to act when Cheng Yee said, "We have been friends and trusted business colleagues for a very long time. Three days ago when I received this article, I began to call the other owners you have been visiting. They all have said the same thing. You have been drawing them out regarding their thoughts of a future relationship, and you refrained from making any suggestions or expressing any ideas of your own. Were you trying to build a list of excuses you could offer your board explaining why you aren't willing to recommend the extension of their contracts?

"I think you owe me an explanation! What's going on?"

"Cheng, the content of that article represents an accurate reflection of the changing mood in the United States and the growing support for a new program designed to improve domestic employment. It also happens to be a program in which I'm personally involved. If you will permit me, I would like to give you a more detailed description."

Having listened carefully to Jeff's explanation, Cheng Yee asked, "Over the next ten years, how many manufacturing jobs does the American government wish to repatriate?"

"The magic number appears to be about five million jobs, or the equivalent of one-third of the net loss of manufacturing jobs the United States believes it has endured over the last thirty-seven years. We expect to create the other ten million jobs from internally generated sources."

"Are you telling me the United States plans to compete in the international marketplace with goods produced from these new campuses you are planning to install? Do you really believe you can replicate all the advantages we are able to offer an incoming manufacturer?"

"Cheng, it's important that you hear me out!"

Ten minutes later, Cheng said, "Jeff, I really believe you believe all these new programs you have explained can be made to work. Even so, are you certain that you are prepared to bet your entire production capacity on a new, unproven, and untested program?"

"No, but I am willing to make a calculated bet on half of my production!

"Cheng, I'm prepared to make you a proposition that I may not offer your other Chinese colleagues. As I have previously announced, subject to the completion of the Employ American plan, I'm considering repatriating approximately 50 percent of our Asian production. I think it will work best if we agree to leave your production here in Taen Jen and Aakil's production in Mumbai relatively undisturbed, provided each of you would be willing to construct a new plant on the campus in California to produce the other 50 percent."

"For whatever reasons, Jeff, if you believe that new campus can perform, I'm not about to question your judgment. Unfortunately, the Chinese government must approve the decision you are requesting. Obtaining their consent may not be so easy. I am sure you can understand how a government committed to adding 25 million jobs per year to its economy could be threatened by your proposal.

"On the other hand, maybe refusing your offer isn't so easy. Should China choose not to participate, how would we be able to explain our decision to other customers? Unless we have a very good reason, how do we justify our decision that China's manufacturing policy is a one-way street? We could end up sacrificing a lot of future production we don't have to lose.

"While I'm thinking about that problem, let me ask you another question. The newspapers have been suggesting you and

Charley Hutson have been busy talking to your friends. How many jobs are we discussing?"

"Probably more than the 100,000 we need to energize the first phase of our campus!"

CHAPTER **34**

A MEXICAN VACATION

Claudia and Robin's road shows weren't the only meetings being conducted in Houston that week. The results of the most recent Texas public polls on the Employ American plan had been published. Public approval had risen to 67 percent. Informal polling of Congress indicated a small plurality favored passage in the House. The positive, filibuster-proof vote in the Senate was still in doubt. The votes of the senators in the seven western states would determine the outcome.

There was another much smaller and more exclusive meeting being held in a private suite at Remington's, a much-favored Houston restaurant. There was no smiling, humorous conversation, and most assuredly, no laughing. The men gathered in that room were there for one reason, to put a stop to the Claudia's and Robin's efforts to arouse public support before things got totally out of control.

Very early the next morning, more than two hours before Robin and Claudia would normally expect to receive their wake-up calls, the bedside phones in each of their rooms started to ring. Still half asleep, Robin was groping for the clanging instrument, when she heard a firm knocking on her door.

Ignoring the no longer ringing phone, she got out of bed, grabbed her dressing grown, and struggled to put it on, as she slowly made her way to her hotel room door and the continuing rapping.

When she finally was able to undo all the safety catches and open the door, an unfamiliar man who introduced himself as a member of the next morning's security shift greeted her. Still groggy, she briefly looked at his offered identification and badge.

"Dr. Cook, there has been a change in plans. For security purposes we will be leaving from an alternate airport. A different plane is waiting for us at Hobby Airport. May I help you gather your things and pack your suitcase? Coffee and a catered breakfast have already been placed on board."

"What about Claudia?" she asked. "Has seen been told?" A quick glance at the open door across the hall answered her question.

The car carrying the two women, who were still half asleep, entered the Hobby air terminal through an electric gate in front of what appeared to be a Cyclone-fenced drive leading to the airstrip arrival area of the private jet terminal. The car stopped directly next to the waiting aircraft's open cabin door. Two security guards were waiting to escort the two women up the stairs and into the airplane. The uniformed copilot loaded their luggage in the rear compartment.

From the minute they met downstairs in front of the hotel, the two sleep-deprived women had began a serious conversation. They were still talking as they climbed aboard the waiting plane.

Still absorbed in conversation, enjoying their first cups of coffee and the warmed croissants, neither of the two women noticed anything unusual as the plane gradually climbed to its 33,000-feet cruising altitude. They had passed over San Antonio, when the plane failed to make its customary northwest course adjustment. Seeing the approaching Rio Grande River, and sensing a loss in altitude, Claudia knew something was wrong.

Absorbed in a book, Robin was unaware of what was happening, until, startled, she heard Claudia fire a series of questions at the two security guards riding in the front of the plane. "What's happening? Why aren't we flying toward Phoenix? Why are we headed into Mexico? Why are we losing altitude? Who are you? Where are the regular guards?"

Before either woman could react, the bigger man stood up, drew his gun from his waistband holster, and trained the menacing-looking 9 mm Beretta directly at the two women, who were still belted into their seats.

The other man with drew a roll of duct tape from his small travel bag and quickly made several passes with it around Claudia and the seat in which she was sitting. Next, he did the same thing to Robin. After standing back to admire his handiwork, he tore two eight-inch strips from the roll and pasted one over each of their mouths.

As he was holstering his pistol, the large man said, "I hope you enjoy your Mexican vacation."

Other than looking out the windows, there wasn't anything Robin and Claudia could do but wonder what was going to happen next.

Robin, whose mind was cluttered with justifiable feelings of fear, regarded the desolate high mountains and the arid desert regions as one big, sparsely vegetated wasteland.

Not so for Claudia. At one time or another, she had traveled through more remote areas of Mexico than she cared to admit. If she and one of her former husbands weren't hunting for trophy mule deer in the mountains north of Hermosillo or big-horned sheep on Tiburon Island, they were shooting ducks at Culiacan, doves and quail near Hermosillo, and fishing for small-mouth and large-mouth bass at Lake Hidalgo.

Claudia was no stranger to the Sea of Cortes, Baja California, or the west coast of Mexico. Her bold, active mind was working overtime. *We must be flying below or between the radar detection screens of regional airports. Maybe I should be looking for familiar landmarks. Who knows, if we're able to get ourselves out of this mess, it might be handy if we know where we are.*

The plane they were riding in was flying below the radar screen when it turned to make its final approach to a deserted airstrip. Immobilized like mummies, Claudia and Robin were finding it hard to breathe, much less make any mental note of any recognizable landmarks.

Before the plane taxied to a stop, they were blindfolded, the tape binding them to their seats was cut away, and more tape was used to bind their hands behind their backs. No effort was made to remove the tape from their mouths. They were lost; they were scared; they were stiff, hungry, and thirsty; they were alone in a primitive strange country; and they were desperately in need of a bathroom.

They weren't given any time to think about their plight. As soon as they had half fallen and stumbled out of the plane, they were pushed into the back of some old vehicle and immediately driven at high speed along bumpy dirt roads away from the airport. Over the road noise, the wind, and the unmuffled engine, they were able hear the plane, with engines at full throttle, accelerating along the short runway.

Within minutes, the sleepy abandoned dirt strip had returned to its natural state. Cows resumed grazing, dogs barked, and chickens scratched at the graveled edges. All the strange and grim-faced people had departed.

CHAPTER **35**

UNFINISHED BUSINESS

Clearly upset by Larry Wilshire's report about Robin and Claudia's kidnapping, Nate White thought it necessary to immediately convene one of his weekly task force meetings. Almost immediately, he was interrupted by a member of his staff, who had abruptly entered the meeting, saying, "Our agent, monitoring the in-flight phone of the executive jet headed to Hawaii with Mr. Mohr and Mr. Hutson aboard, has reported that Mr. Hutson had just completed a very lengthy call to a Madam Chang in San Francisco.

"Apparently, before they left India, Mr. Mohr and Mr. Hutson were handed Wilshire's British Securities' final transshipment report. Their brief indicates that the transshipment practice of tariff avoidance is widespread and involves high-up government officials in China and Taiwan and an enormous amount of money."

No longer able to accept new news calmly, Nate reacted, "Don't they realize if we can pick up their telephone transmissions, so can anybody else who knows the frequency of that particular in-flight telephone?

"I don't know what upsets me the most, the confirmation of the magnitude of this transshipment problem or knowing that Mr.

Hutson has used an unsecured transmission. Either could cause us a lot of trouble and expose our friends to more danger!

"What the hell is happening? A week ago I received a confidential memorandum describing what must have been a high-level planned attack in Mumbai. Has some kind of a secret war been declared against these Sentinel directors? Do I need to inform Terry Flynn?"

———

About the same time in Detroit, J.W. Porter was announcing to his "kitchen directors" the contents of the intercepted call. "Charley Hutson claims he possesses certain information concerning high-level Chinese and Taiwanese government involvement in a fraudulent tariff-avoidance operation. He refers to the process as a 'transshipment' operation."

Obviously upset, one of the new directors said, "J.W., you need to see what's in those reports. Can you talk to Charley before he does anything with that information? I'm sure you realize some of U.S. Motors' suppliers are companies that have important subcontractor relationships with Chinese companies and the Chinese government. If we aren't very careful, you might be surprised how much trouble those reports could create!"

———

Several hours later, when the government plane landed in Cimarron, New Mexico, Charley saw a U.S. Motors' plane, parked alongside the Cimarron Cattle Company hangar. As they deplaned, Jeff heard the hired hand announce, "The new hands are busy branding calves. I've been instructed to take you there. If we hurry, I'm sure we can make it before they finish today's herd."

Charley said, "Not before we take a few minutes and talk to the gentleman standing inside the hangar. From the angry look on his face, I wouldn't be surprised to learn he has been waiting here for a very long time."

The meeting between Charley and his boss was neither pleasant nor long. J.W. wanted a copy of the transshipment report and to know why the investigation had been authorized in the first place.

Twenty minutes later, Jeff and Charley were sitting in the rear seat of the Suburban as it hurtled down the rutted and dusty ranch road at sixty miles per hour. Charley was eager to discuss his brief meeting with J.W.

"Jeff, did you notice how anxious J.W. was to get his hands on that report? Learning that he may have a conflict of interest within his directorship must have come as quite a revelation. Can you imagine what might happen to U.S. Motors, its directors, executive management, and suppliers should their conflicts of interest become public knowledge?"

"Charley, once you handed J.W. that report, you may have just dropped a rather large rock in the water. It'll be interesting to see if the waves reach Beijing."

———

Both Jeff and Charley were relieved when the Suburban swung to a stop near the working corrals. As soon as their driver departed, Jeff said, "The next time someone suggests that he give us a ride, remind me to say no. There were moments when I thought the chance of our being killed was far greater than anything we faced in the Mumbai tunnel."

Not wanting to interrupt the work in progress, Jeff and Charley started walking in the general direction of the working pens. It was impossible for them not to notice all the construction that was involved in the erection of what appeared to be an equipment storage shed and a new hay storage barn. Glancing at all the activity, Charley thought, *There have to be more than twenty men working here. But how come they don't have the regulation construction worker's tan?*

Long before they approached the "processing area," they could hear the noise. Calves were bawling, horses were snorting, and people were yelling. Finding a spot where they could sit on the top rail of the corral fence, they were ready to observe a real old-fashioned, Western calf branding.

Andi and Meg and four others were covered in perspiration, fine dust, and occasional spots of splattered blood. The team was so preoccupied with their work that they didn't notice the new arrivals.

Jeff and Charley watched as one of the hands released the next calf from the narrow chute. Meg's aunt roped the head of the calf and as soon as the line had pulled tight, her cousin Annie roped its back legs. Utilizing the pulling strength of the two horses at either end of the ropes, they stretched out the struggling animal. Another worker reached over the back of the calf, grabbed some loose skin beneath its midriff, lifted the bawling animal into the air, and deposited it on the ground before placing his left knee on the animal's rib cage and applying enough weight to immobilize it.

Meg was holding what appeared to be a long-handled tubular set of clipping shears. She approached the struggling calf, fit the open end of the shears over the small nub of the horn, and with one quick spreading of the handle nipped off the beginnings of the young horn. One of her sons stood aside, waiting to apply a thick black paste used to stop any bleeding, keep the flies away, and prevent infection. The matching horn on the other side was quickly dealt with as well.

Next, Andi reached under the midriff of the bull calf, grabbed its testicles with her left hand, and worked them down to the bottom of its scrotum. Using a crimping tool, she severed the testicles and their connecting cords, applying enough hand pressure to seal the exposed edges. Meg's son applied more of the black goop.

Hand number six pressed a white-hot branding iron firmly against the calf's right flank. When he pulled the iron back, it was his signal to the riders to release the branded animal.

Seeing Charley and Jeff sitting patiently on the top rail of the corral fence, well out of the way, Jiggs, the cowboy boss, said, "Come on, we only have a few left to go. Let's get the lead out. We wouldn't want the cold beer to get warm!"

As soon as the team finished, Jiggs motioned for the new arrivals to join him and the rest of his crew at the back of his pickup. Jiggs opened a cooler and pulled out several ice-cold beers. "I think we earned them today," he said as he handed the cans around. "There are even a couple of Cokes for our younger hands."

The younger of the two boys walked over to the branding oven and used his pocketknife to scrape off a new batch of well-cooked prairie oysters into a metal dish. It had been his job to gather the severed testicles, wash them off, and place them on the heated upper surface of the branding iron oven. "Guests first," he said, as he extended the platter to Jeff and Charley.

"Charley, you really need to try these," Jeff said as he reached out and helped himself. "They are a real delicacy!"

"Don't mind if I do," Andi said as she selected one of the morsels from the plate. Sensing Charley's hesitation, she said, "What's the matter, Charley? Don't tell me you are one of those guys who will eat raw bluepoint oysters but is afraid of a well-cooked prairie oyster."

Jeff and the boys broke out in laughter. Charley hesitantly reached forward and selected one of the particularly well-cooked, smaller morsels. Tentatively, he took his first bite. Surprised at how tasty it was, he ate the remaining portion in two bites. "Well, I'll be damned, that was really good! May I have another?"

Dinner was delayed twice. After two weeks of separation, Charley and Andi, and Jeff and Meg, discovered that showers and naps can take a very long time. Once everyone was assembled in front of the big fireplace and the single malt scotches had been served all around, Meg and Andi were interested in talking about their accomplishments on each of the four separate ranch round-ups. Finally, at the appropriate moment, Andi reached down to grip her new silver belt buckle, and gesture toward Meg's before she said, "Take a look at these. You're talking to the 2010 Davis Ranch Domino Champions."

"Wait a minute!" Jeff said. "Dominoes are a San Francisco game, how is it that you have to come clear out here to find a bunch of 'pigeons' to take advantage of?"

"Pigeons, my ass," Meg said. Jiggs, the cowboy boss you met today, teaches the kids on the ranch how to play dominoes every year during roundup. Those kids have had years to play dominoes. Around here, each year's championship is a very coveted award."

Andi added, "Wait until you play them! You'll learn!"

Her last sarcastic comment caught Charley's attention. "Jeff, you understand the game of dominoes. Don't you think, after dinner, we should challenge the champs to a little game of chance?"

———

After stirring the dominoes, Meg said, "Choose for set."

"Not before we settle the stakes!" Andi said. "Around here we get up early in the morning, and it's always so cold. Why don't we say that the losers have to get up first, close the windows, and sing 'Good Morning Mary Sunshine'?"

At five o'clock the next morning, Andi awoke to Meg's laughing and Jeff's swearing, "Goddamn it, these floors are cold! Who left the window open?"

She didn't have to wait very long before she was forced to listen to two of the worst voices she had ever heard, singing their rendition of "Good Morning Mary Sunshine."

Jeff's mood hadn't improved much by the time Meg announced over breakfast, "If you two are going to hang around here, you better be prepared to earn your keep! There are two horses being saddled for you. We have a lot of open country to cover today, and we could use your help."

That night when he got out of the shower, Charley couldn't decide what hurt more—his chapped inner thighs, rubbed raw from all the riding, or any one of a dozen bruises he had managed to collect when he was trying to flank the roped calves.

CHAPTER 36

MEANWHILE, BACK AT THE RANCH

Judging from the serious look on Jeff's face, Charley knew something had gone wrong in China. Jeff was motioning for him to pick up the second phone. The unmistakable soft, British-accented voice of former ambassador Tambour was instantly recognizable. "Jeff, I was recently informed that the first scheduled back-channel meeting needs to be delayed. Apparently, something is happening and the Chinese government is not ready to talk.

"There was something different in the tone of their voices and the brevity of the conversation that seemed strange. I don't mean to be the bearer of ill tidings, but you might wish to alert your friends that trouble may be headed your direction."

Jeff reached for his wallet with one hand as he replaced the telephone receiver with the other. He took out his Casey Jones card, double-checked the number, and dialed carefully, thinking, *I don't need to make any mistakes, Robin and Claudia could be in a lot of trouble and not know it!*

At the same time, Charley remembered that Andi, Meg, and her two sons had announced they were planning to ride their horses along the river to "that big hole" where they had seen all the bass. He ran toward the barn hoping he would be able to stop them before they left.

———

Nate's first call was to the hotel in Houston. He was informed that Claudia and Robin had checked out early.

His second call was to the lead agent of his Houston security detachment. "Boss, according to my schedule, by this time, they must be headed toward the Houston international airport. Hang on, I'll call the security team traveling with them." When there was no response by the fourth ring of the cell phone, the agent in charge and Nate knew they had a problem.

Nate's third call was placed to Terry Flynn. Flynn didn't know whether to be alarmed or pleased that a joint American–Mexican drug enforcement task force had already been informed that a plane had disappeared off their radar screen over San Antonio and was presumably headed into the heart of rural Mexico. Drug enforcement agencies regularly requested an "eye in the sky" radar plane, and this time one had already been detached from the Marine air base at Yuma, Arizona. Their crews were experienced in spotting unidentified planes that had their transponders turned off and no filed flight plans. They knew where to look.

———

Charley's alert instincts began to kick in the minute he entered the barn and could see the four empty stalls. Glancing toward the tack room, he could see four saddles and their accompanying gear was missing. The "Old Charley" took command. Without hesitating, he walked over to the jeep parked just outside the rear entrance to the barn, climbed in, and was headed toward the river's trail head when he spotted Jeff emerging from the house.

Jeff didn't need to be told what was happening. He jumped into the moving jeep. The two old combat veterans were soon heading down the trail.

———

Identifying the plane hadn't been a problem. From their high altitude the crew was able to report the plane's location and follow its route to a seldom-used gravel airstrip near El Fuerte, the old colonial city situated at the base of the Sierra Madre mountains.

Interdicting the plane while it was on the ground was not an option. The trail of dust made it possible to trace the fast-departing car. With the aid of high-tech cameras capable of photographing a license plate from significant altitudes, real-time pictures identifying the exact house and its location where the car had stopped were immediately transmitted to Terry Flynn in San Francisco, and to the FBI and drug enforcement agencies in Washington, Phoenix, Houston, and Mexico City.

Terry Flynn was having difficulty making the nation's top drug enforcement officers understand what he was saying. "This is not a drug deal. Robin Cook and Claudia Roth have been kidnapped and are being held in that house. Any attempt to approach could get them killed. The sudden appearance of unfamiliar faces could get them killed. Tell your men to stand down until we can figure out how to safely rescue those two women."

———

Unfamiliar with the trail system, Charley and Jeff were forced to guess when they approached the first of several forks that followed the mesquite-lined arroyos. It took them three tries and fifteen minutes before they were able to find the secluded pond.

Andi and Meg, after suggesting the boys begin fishing, had unsaddled the four horses, removed their headstalls, and tethered them in a grassy meadow next to a shallow stream.

By the time the two emotionally drained men wandered onto the scene, the women were sitting on a blanket, enjoying a bottle of wine, and quietly chatting. Seeing the jeep approaching at a high speed and suddenly braking, their first instinct was concern over the tethered animals. Any unexpected or sudden motion could cause the animal to break. The leather thongs binding their front legs to within eighteen inches of each other could inflict a lot of damage.

Andi, confused by their sudden appearance and worried about the animals, was on her feet, walking toward the men, raising and lowering her arms, palms down, signaling for them to slow down.

Meg, having made her way over to the horses, was doing her best to settle them down.

The two boys, intent on their fishing, had wandered toward the far end of the pond and were hidden behind more than one thicket of mesquite bushes. They remained unaware of what was happening and couldn't they hear their mother calling. The noise of the breeze filtering through the bushes and trees was strong, and its downstream effect was adequate to drown out noises.

Already agitated by the sudden arrival of Charley and Jeff, both women, unable to see the boys or hear some response to their yelling, were beginning to panic. Jeff was thinking, *Have the boys just wandered off and all we have to do is stay calm and wait for them to return? As long as they remain next to the pond, they shouldn't get lost. Or has something happened? Men could be hidden in all that brush and we wouldn't know they were there.*

Charley and Jeff didn't need to be told to find the boys.

Instinctively one of them began to quietly circle around the pond and the bushes to the left, and the other circled to the right.

For Andi and Meg, the pain of waiting was becoming unbearable. The negative expectations of not knowing flooded their minds. Trying to listen for any little sound or looking for any signs of movement only added to their stress. Fear immobilized them.

At first Meg, didn't appear to react. The younger of the two boys came running around the last of the thick bushes. He was holding up the line of his fishing rod to show his mother his great catch. A twelve-inch bass was wiggling on the end.

―――――

In deference to Meg's two boys, the dinner conversation was devoted to work on the ranch, riding horses, catching fish, and playing baseball with their new friends. The subject of business didn't come up until they were halfway through dinner. While Jeff was opening a second bottle of wine, Charley, absentmindedly said, "I wonder what J.W.'s reaction to that report was."

"Report? What are you talking about?" Meg asked.

"The report that contains the names of all the people involved in the Chinese-Taiwanese transshipment tariff avoidance scheme," Jeff said. "The list starts with the names of the responsible Chinese manufacturers and the involved business executives. It includes the names of the Chinese government officials, the people who were involved in the transfer of the product from China to Taiwan to the United States, and the responsible Taiwanese government officials."

"And do you mind telling us just what you're going to do with all this information?"

Without thinking, Charley said, "We plan to present the

information, along with some other data we have been able to collect, to the Chinese government."

"Present information to the Chinese government? What are you two planning to do?" asked Andi.

Entering the conversation, Jeff said, "It's all part of our plan to convince the Chinese government to lift their Bamboo Barricade to allow Cheng Yee's company to manufacture electronic parts in this country and stop all these attacks."

"Blackmail the Chinese government! Bring Chinese manufacturing to America? Have you two lost your minds? Surely, you can't be serious!" Meg exclaimed.

"Oh, we don't have to be. By now I'm quite certain J.W. has already taken care of things."

Meg wouldn't let go. "Taken care of what? And just why do you think the chairman of the world's largest automobile manufacturer is prepared to do your bidding?"

"Because he is about to find out that at least four of his new directors also serve on the boards of some of his major suppliers who maintain ongoing relationships with their Chinese suppliers. If he isn't involved in their conspiracy, what other choice does he have?

"Once the Chinese government receives that information, we're hoping they will want to take advantage of the communication back channel we've established."

"Back channel! What is that?" Andi asked.

"Perhaps I'm the one who should answer the question," Charley said. "If J.W. doesn't have a direct relationship with the Chinese, I'm quite certain some of those directors who sit on the U.S. Motors board do. Once the Chinese government becomes aware that these illicit practices could be aired in the cold light of day, they may wish to settle all these problems and some others we have on our list on a back-channel negotiated basis."

"What do a couple of New Mexico cowboys and industrial management jockeys know about establishing back-channel communications with the Chinese government?" Meg asked.

Any possibility of further conversation was suddenly interrupted by dogs barking, the outside motion lights suddenly shining blindingly, and the presence of two "construction workers" suddenly entering the room announcing, "We are under attack. Women and children should go down into cellar and take cover. You men need to grab whatever weapons there are and join us on the roof."

The sound of two mortar shells hitting the house turned startled curiosity into undisguised fear. Andi and Meg and her two boys ran into the pantry, opened the door, and disappeared into the cellar below.

Unconsciously, Charley, the old warrior, was starting to take charge. After lifting one of the heavy wooden benches, he walked over to the locked closet door and with one mighty swing drove it off its frame. After motioning for Jeff to join him, the two men each selected a rifle and began to fill the shell bags with 30-caliber rifle rounds.

With arms in hand, the two men headed toward the rear outside porch and the stairs that led to the flat portion of the roof. Jeff followed. Kneeling behind the three-foot escarpment, each of them instinctively moved to opposing corners, joined the other agents, and, with the assistance of the night light telescopic sights mounted on the deer rifles, they began to study the surrounding terrain.

Nothing seemed to make any sense. Beyond the illuminated area, Charley could see the attacking force had been divided into three-man fire teams. Two of the three seemed intent on loading and firing the mortars. The third man appeared intent on firing into the dark away from the main lodge. Judging by the shots coming from the outer perimeter, the construction workers, White's security agents, had managed to spread out behind the attacking force and were trying to drive them toward the house into the illuminated inner perimeter.

From their vantage point, Jeff and Charley weren't having any trouble recognizing what had happened. "Charley, these people have been employed to kill us. If they hadn't been surprised by those construction workers, what would have stopped them from overrunning the lodge?"

Unprepared for such accurate incoming fire directed at them from a new direction, the "easy targets" became conscious of the punishing effect of the fire coming from both directions. Confused and disorganized, some of the survivors were forced to take shelter behind the few granite rocks that formed part of the desert landscape. Without any possibility of support or retreat, it didn't take the remaining operatives long to understand the seriousness of their predicament. After throwing down their weapons and raising their hands, they emerged out into the light from whatever protective shelter they may have found. The attack was over.

CHAPTER 37

FISHING AT LAKE HIDALGO

Terry Flynn knew from experience that finding where the captured victims were hidden could be the easy part; recovering them alive and unhurt could be a bit of a problem and take a while. Any direct assault could result in getting them killed. Flynn thought, *Things would be much easier if we were able to communicate with Claudia and Robin. How do we put one of our own people into that house?*

Flynn's job for the next few days was not being made any easier by all the publicity being released in every news center in the United States. Claudia's and Robin's disappearance warranted full press coverage. Knowledge of their mission, the surprising results of the road shows, and the growing public admiration for what they were attempting had already made the two ladies front-page celebrities. Their sudden and unexplained disappearance was rapidly becoming a subject of national anger. Pressure was growing for a timely conclusion.

Public concern was being translated into growing awareness of their mission and growing support for the pending legislation. The plan to remove Claudia and Robin was beginning to backfire.

Nate White's recovery team knew exactly where the ladies

were being held. The house was located on a dirt street in one of El Fuerte's poorest neighborhoods. It was not a place where vendors made deliveries. Local merchandise needs were filled from very small stores or from the stalls in the market. Any strange faces or unusual behavior would be immediately reported to the local police—law enforcement agents, some of whom were suspected of having a questionable set of loyalties.

An old mission-style hotel and the local fishing and hunting guides who catered to visiting American sportsmen provided the main employment. Older boys served as bird boys for the visiting dove hunters and deckhands worked for the visiting bass fishermen.

It was September. Dove season wouldn't open until November first, but it was the height of bass fishing season. No one paid any particular attention when American bass fishermen arrived in their private planes and landed at the El Fuerte airport. Vans from the hotel would be there to greet the visiting sportsmen and provide transportation back to the hotel.

Three days after Claudia and Robin had been kidnapped, Nate White and three of his men stepped from the privately chartered executive jet. Two members of the drug enforcement section of the national army met them. The older of the two was dressed to resemble one of the hunting outfitters and the other as a bellman from the hotel. After loading the tackle boxes, rods, reels, and baggage into the dust-covered, much dented Suburban with the cracked windshield and oxidized paint, they began to retrace the course back to the hotel.

Their route would take them through the old neighborhood and past the house of interest. Local occupants were given the opportunity to observe that new fishermen had arrived. The law enforcement agents identified the house where the two ladies were being held. The outfitter (drug enforcement officer) parked the old Suburban in the middle of the street.

One by one he began calling on each house on the left, while the hotel bellman (agent) began his quest on the right. They were searching for four boys to serve as deckhands for Mr. Casey Jones and party for the next three days.

After knocking on the side of the building next to the open front entrance, each of the two agents would say, "We are looking for four boys to help us as deckhands for Mr. Casey Jones for the next three days. If any boys are interested would you have them ready to go by 6:00 a.m. tomorrow morning?"

It had been three days following their arrival at the house. Claudia and Robin, unbound but carefully guarded, were able to roam around the house as long as they stayed out of sight. They were standing in the dark rear corner when the guide appeared. They didn't have to speak Spanish to understand the words "Casey Jones" and "Be ready at six o'clock tomorrow morning."

At 5:30 a.m., the guards could hear the start of a loud argument between Claudia and Robin. By 5:45 they were busy trying to break up the fight between the two ladies and to stop their screaming. At precisely 5:50 a.m. Nate White and company entered the house, subdued the engaged and surprised guards, and rushed Claudia and Robin to the waiting Suburban. At 6:15, they were on board the jet feeling its acceleration as it moved down the runway and away from El Fuerte.

CHAPTER 38

GREEN CEMENT

John Paul and Ivan had been fortunate. Once they were able to incorporate their new information into their chemical equations, they realized they were on the right track. With the benefit of their added confidence, each new experimental chemical cocktail was bringing them closer to a successful conclusion. Their progress was aided by the fact that the mixing capacity of all six trucks could be concentrated on just one set of parameters.

Anxious to take advantage of their good fortune, Ivan and John Paul had scheduled the arrival of the EPA administrator and her staff from Washington, DC, to occur within the next two weeks. Preliminary test results had been forwarded to her staff, and they were in receipt of the administrator's list of what she hoped to accomplish during her visit.

The first request was that the agency be allowed to select samples from six different locations, complete the subsequent testing, and evaluate the test results while they remained on-site.

On the appointed day, John Paul had arranged for six industrial front-loaders and heavy-duty dump trucks to be available to select samples from any of the random six locations the administrator cared to select.

The tests went well. The first tests involved the sampling of each of the different waste collection sites for the purpose of examining their chemical makeup. Once the high concentrations of heavy metals had been verified and quantified, the data could be used to establish a baseline for further testing of the resultant high-strength cement.

At the administrator's request, minor changes were made in the chemical formulas, and subsequent tests were repeated to test the sensitivity of the more refined formulas. By seven o'clock that night, the EPA team concluded the concentration of toxic materials exceeded industrial waste standards, the formula was correct, and the process could be used to economically produce high- strength, "green" cement in commercial quantities well within clean air and industrial waste standards and provide a cost-effective form of toxic waste disposal.

At nine o'clock that night, the EPA officials, Ivan, John Paul, and his staff had convened in a small local restaurant. It was late and they were the last remaining patrons. The local bourbon, branch water, and a surprisingly good steak served as a nice wrap-up to a stressful yet successful day. Everyone enjoyed the quiet satisfaction of sharing in accomplishing something of great value.

At ten o'clock p.m., the administrator said, "Ivan, John Paul, in case you didn't realize it, we had two reasons for visiting you today. Obviously, the first was to determine if your new chemical process can be used to produce the new revenue streams required to offset the higher cost of clean-burning coal. The second reason is a little more sensitive. Ever since the early tests on the Tennessee Valley coal-ash spill revealed those high lead and arsenic readings, we have been reluctant to proceed with further testing. Without a solution for dealing with hazardous waste, you can imagine the magnitude of the problem we could be causing if we proceeded with more extensive testing and it produced positive results. We could be faced with the impossible task of having to place costly burdens on the companies that produce 50 percent of our nation's electrical energy."

By eleven o'clock, all the test data had been loaded into the trunks of the EPA cars to be taken back to Washington for further examination.

By midnight, as they were preparing to leave, the EPA administrator asked Ivan if she could have a few minutes to speak with him alone. Standing in the privacy of a small banquet room, she said, "We understand why you want to have your license, approvals, and negative impact reports issued from Washington and circumvent the California regulatory process. We wish to be as helpful as possible.

"As you can imagine, we are receiving a tremendous amount of resistance from the western power companies. They have informed us that they are prepared to raise all kinds of local environmental issues to delay and possibly obstruct any possibility of your receiving the regulatory approval within your allotted time period. To put it as bluntly as I can, they are looking for any excuse to delay or stop your project."

Alarmed by what the administrator was telling him, Ivan almost missed hearing her next comment.

"Ivan, I am going to assist you in obtaining the approvals you need in Washington, but I need your assistance. We have been busy identifying any roadblocks that could delay your approvals. My people tell me you could be vulnerable in two areas.

"This coal-ash situation has presented us with a very difficult problem. Once you begin to move the coal ash, we have to be satisfied that its storage pending processing will conform to higher hazardous waste standards. In plain language, satisfaction of those requirements necessitates the transferring of it in its sludge form, in specially treated tanker rail cars, and storing it underground in specially designed concrete and steel-reinforced containers. We understand these vats are very expensive to build and install.

"The second problem requires that you design your plant to prevent any raw coal dust from contaminating the environment in the immediate vicinity of your plant. If your design called for the delivered coal to be stored underground in air-tight covered vaults, I think we can defend your plan from local environmental complaints."

After listening to her new stipulations, Ivan immediately recognized that he had just been subjected to the same kind of contingent requests that he had been forced to submit to so many times in all the different locales where he had previously developed industrial parks.

It was 1:00 a.m. After watching the taillights of the director's caravan of vehicles disappear, Ivan invited John Paul and the rest of the crew back into the restaurant for one final celebratory cocktail. An explosion, so strong that the concussion knocked Ivan, John Paul, and the members of their crew to the floor, interrupting their merriment. The sound of shattering windows, falling plates, and breaking furniture seemed to resonate for several seconds. "What the hell was that?!" John Paul yelled. "Is everybody all right?"

Ivan knew without looking that the blast came from the coal-ash dump where they had been conducting their experiments. The party, unharmed, drove out to the site but could see only that the damage was extensive. They retired for the night. The next morning, in the clear light of day, they discovered that there was nothing left of the six concrete mixing trucks, the front end loaders, the dump truck, or the big industrial crane. They looked like a scrap heap of twisted metal. The prefabricated metal building that housed all their testing equipment and working records had literally disappeared. The flatbed trucks lay in twisted shapes. The cargo of materials was pulverized by the blast and lay over the site like the ash frosting of a volcanic eruption.

Staring at the devastation, Ivan said, "Well, we may have been lucky. What are the chances that the administrator would ask to take our research records with her after the inspection? Let's hope she has all the information they will need!"

It was 2:00 a.m. in Washington, DC, when the director of the FBI, James A. Brumfield, placed a call to Terry Flynn. "What the hell has happened? Why weren't you able to warn us about the attack on the Tennessee coal-ash testing facility? We were lucky no one was killed!"

"Boss, we are as completely surprised as you. The two men involved in the kidnapping of Miss Taylor and Mrs. Mohr haven't provided us with any advance notice. Obviously, whoever is behind this used a different team."

"Maybe there is one thing we can do. Nate White is holding on the other line. He has a new theory. If we were able to make the connection between the men in Nevada to the multi-company-owned off-balance-sheet enterprise, maybe we could work the same system in reverse. If we could trace the money to whoever caused the explosion in Tennessee, we might be able to discover the identity of the new perpetrators. Give us a few hours and let's see what we can learn."

CHAPTER 39

A TIME FOR REFLECTION

Nate White was reporting to Terry Flynn. "Terry, thank God we established that construction job on the New Mexico ranch as an excuse to move my men into position. About a third of the enemy were killed, a third were wounded, and we have the rest in protective custody. This was no amateur operation. We've already been able to identify several of the attackers as members of a mercenary security company frequently employed by drug cartels to protect their drug shipments once they arrive north of the border. Believe me, they are no amateurs; you were dealing with a very bad lot."

———

Believing he was fully informed, Nate placed a conference call to Larry in London, Jeff in Palo Alto, Charley in Detroit, Aakil Chandakar in Mumbai, and former ambassador Tambour in New Delhi. "The Bureau, my organization, and I think I can speak for Larry—we have no choice but to interpret this last attack as China's decision to continue the pursuit of its secret war! Can it be that we haven't exerted enough pressure to persuade them to use the offered back channel to negotiate for a more constructive solution? How else can you explain the bombing of Institute's research lab, bombing in India at Chandakar's home, bombing at the temporary testing facility in Tennessee, the attempted kidnapping of Ms. Taylor, and the bombs planted on Mr. Hutson's and Mr. Mohr's planes?

"In reaching their conclusion, the Bureau has determined, to the satisfaction of the federal government, that American national interests have been violated. Clearly, a new proactive, invisible secret war strategy is indicated. The door is open for discussion."

Charley was the first to speak. "I don't know what bothers me the most: the threat by the Chinese government, or their influence inside the United States. In addition to all these attacks, the fact that China can use its influence over American subcontractors to manipulate the manufacturing policies of our country's largest car maker is a terrifying situation.

"There was a time when I thought about trying to find some way to separate Chinese companies from their government and restrict all contracts to be negotiated on a company-to-company basis. It has become apparent that the Chinese government is no longer willing to take advantage of the alternative offered by Mr. Tambour. We need to find a way to increase the pressure."

Jeff said, "When we had no choice, I think our options might have been different from what they may be today. I would like to believe the Employ American plan rebalanced the playing field. If we step back and look at what has happened, has almost everything they have done been the result of their trying to preserve and protect their manufacturing base?

"As one of the companies most directly involved, what prevents me from transferring all my Chinese production back to the United States? Add the offshore production of many of Employ American's potential charter members and I think we are capable of exerting a lot more leverage on this situation than we may realize!"

"It sounds to me as though we need to send Mr. Tambour back to China, armed with new information," observed Aakil. "If we accomplish nothing else, at least we will learn we have no other option than to directly confront them over the production of goods for American managed companies.

"If I might be allowed to continue, I would like to ask Jeff and Charley a question. What would you think of organizing a two-pronged attack? Charley, from everything I hear, you and your colleagues are far enough along in finding solutions for your problems that you are entitled to start formalizing the fulfillment of that 80,000-job stipulation.

"If Mr. Tambour is armed with the information of your intentions, and can be leveraged by the threat of so many other companies arriving at the same conclusion, why shouldn't we assume Mr. Tambour can force the Chinese government into reconsidering what their bottom-line policy needs to be?"

CHAPTER 40

TEA IN CHINA

Forty-eight hours later, Jeff was sitting in Cheng Yee's private office in Taen Jen. The two men were enjoying their ceremonial cup of tea. Jeff was concerned about his host's decision not to participate in Employ American. "I can understand how my questions during my previous trip may have confused and upset you and your government. With your indulgence, I would appreciate your giving me a second chance to arrive at a more constructive understanding.

"The progress of the Employ American plan so far indicates that as long as we recruit a sufficient volume of new employees, it will become a reality. It's important that you understand there are overriding reasons why Mohr Electronics and several other consumer electronics companies, given access to lower effective direct labor costs, must repatriate, at a minimum, 50 percent of our production. It's more than a dollars-and-cents problem, it's an issue of preserving and enhancing market share. It is an alternative that companies like mine can't afford to pass up."

Choosing to sit quietly rather than respond to Jeff's words, Cheng Yee was thinking about the three calls he had already received from his other American customers. *Over the years, I have developed a great respect for Jeff. He has always been an*

honest, reliable, and forthright business associate. He has already
offered to work with me and my company in the future.

I may not like what I am hearing, but at least I have had the
opportunity to hear, firsthand, from someone I can trust. Perhaps,
my government and I need to understand if we are to retain our
relationship with important American consumer products compa-
nies, we need to revisit the rigidity of our "Make It Here" policies.

Jeff was talking. "Cheng, the main question is how to best
implement the change. Which companies do we invite to continue
our relationship? What role do we ask them to play? On my previous trip, I asked all those open-ended questions in an attempt to
learn which companies were concerned about helping us succeed
and which companies were primarily concerned about maximiz-
ing their own self-interests and the needs of the Chinese government, independent of any of our concerns.

"As a consequence, I learned that your company and Aakil
Chandakar's company appear to be able to think about the future
on a broader spectrum basis. When I began to think of limiting
our offshore relationships to just your two companies, I realized
it has taken years for you to learn our products and our special
needs and for us to learn each other's cultures, and develop and
maintain such a good working relationship.

"Changing the location of production is one thing. Changing
production management is quite different. When I thought about
having to introduce and train an entirely new management organization, I started to worry about all the new problems that could
emerge. That's when I concluded that our interests are best served
by preserving your management and allowing you to take advantage of the opportunities being offered to occupants of our Employ
American campus. I hope such a move can make it possible for us
to improve the future potential for both our companies.

"We would prefer to retain your management and operational

skills here and encourage you to re-create them in the United States. Should we be in agreement, we would leave your current production undisturbed and shift the remaining Chinese production of our three other affiliates to the United States. We are prepared to make the same offer to Mr. Chandakar and divide the remaining Chinese volume between your two companies."

Cheng considered for a moment what Jeff had said and asked, "Are you aware of the sensitivity of what you are asking? Historically, when we succeed in relocating a foreign manufacturer to China, our country receives both the profits from our production efforts and the revenue from greater consumer consumption. If we agree to shift a portion of our manufacturing operations to the United States, we will still be able to participate in the value-added profits, but China will be forced to abandon the employment benefits. You do understand that your decision will require the Chinese government to rethink its entire national manufacturing policy."

"Cheng, it's absolutely imperative that you and your government appreciate that as long as we could use the American consumers' balance sheet to fund increased consumption, we didn't require the stimulating effect of added manufacturing employment. Now that we have found a way to reduce our costs, it only makes sense that the American industrialist be allowed to make whatever decision is in his best interests. Rather than preventing an American company from repatriating a portion of employment, why shouldn't the policy of the Chinese government remain to assist your American partners to reach optimal success?

"How long do you think it will take before restrictive production policies will move American companies from thinking *some here, some there to all here*? If we aren't very careful, we could initiate the mother of all trade wars."

"Jeff, believe me when I say I fully appreciate the logic of your argument and the generosity of your offer, but I don't think it would be a practical idea for either one of us to assume my government will react favorably to your proposal. A strategy shift from China's quest of world dominance to one of competitive national coexistence would require an enormous modification of a decades-long policy. I will pass along your offer and suggestions, but I seriously doubt whether it's realistic to expect the government to react positively, particularly within the time frame we are working."

The next morning, Jeff found a letter that had been slipped under his hotel room door.

Mr. Mohr,

We respectively suggest that you rethink your proposal. For years, my company and my colleagues have depended on the steady increase in employment your company has been kind enough to provide. If we have failed in any way to satisfy your expectations or to remain a cost competitive supplier, please inform us of what we need to do to retain your business. Any suggestions you might have would be greatly appreciated.

Cheng Yee, President

Immediately, Jeff was aware of the letter's significance. *The formal nature of the reply is not my friend talking; it reflects the influence of the Chinese central government. Regardless of the offer's merits, the Chinese government only saw one thing, loss of Chinese jobs. Unless we are prepared to introduce a great deal of pressure, it looks like there is little hope of resolving our trading differences. I assume the best thing I can do is to avoid burning any bridges and provide Mr. Tambour with the opportunity to make our case.*

After taking his time to carefully consider his reply, Jeff wrote:

Mr. Cheng Yee,

When I return to California, I'm expected to report to my board of directors. May I inquire if you are rejecting our offer to continue to manufacture for us if we repatriate a portion of your production to the United States?

I will be delivering your final word on this subject to my board of directors.

Jeff Mohr

CHAPTER 41

THE STRENGTH OF NUMBERS

Jeff couldn't remember when he had been more upset. His thoughts were racing, *If that is their last word, I don't know whether I should be pleased or disappointed. The one thing I know for sure is that I need to make some decisions. Maybe I should wait until I reach the American embassy in New Delhi before calling Charley.*

———

"Charley, the more I think about my conversations with Cheng Yee and your recent conversation with J.W., the more convinced I am that all his suggestions might represent a carefully designed mirage to mask China's true agenda. There's absolutely no question that the Chinese are threatened by the prospect of repatriating employment to the United States. If they're prepared to jeopardize four large manufacturing contracts in their attempt to dissuade us, should we be thinking about what else they might be prepared to do? Blocking U.S. Motors' interest could be one of those things. Is there some way you can find out?"

Jeff had barely finished his call with Charley when Aakil and Mr. Tambour entered the small conference room. Secure in the American embassy's inner sanctum, Jeff began the meeting. "Before we discuss our Chinese problems, I want to let you know that I analyzed our future manufacturing needs. Although Mohr has agreements with multiple offshore organizations, I hope we can reduce our relationships and concentrate more of our production in fewer hands. We assume two organizations should be able to provide all the offshore manufacturing Mohr Electronics will require. I am proposing that we leave our current production agreements with your company undisturbed and ask you to absorb whatever portion of our Chinese production you would be comfortable producing in the United States."

Aakil responded immediately. "As you Americans say, that's a deal I can't refuse."

Shifting his attention to Mr. Tambour, Jeff asked, "Have you had an opportunity to talk to your friends in Beijing?"

"According to them, the Chinese government was already in possession of your report on the Chinese-Taiwanese transshipment problem before we met. Consistent with traditional custom, the Chinese government was not willing to disclose the source of their information. But my friends have reported that it would be difficult to overestimate how upset they are.

"After listening to their comments regarding their embarrassment and concern about how the possible implications of transshipment might adversely affect their international trading reputation, I am convinced that left to their own devices we can assume they will deal with the problem in a very aggressive manner."

Jeff listened to Mr. Tambour's report and then said, "Despite their good intentions, we still have some unresolved issues. Are they still planning to use their influence over U.S. Motors suppliers to prevent America's largest car maker from participating in Employ American and refusing to issue Yee, Inc. a license to manufacture in the United States? And there is the matter of these continued attacks."

"For openers, why don't they inform their American suppliers of their wish to withdraw their opposition to Mohr Electronics and U.S. Motors' participation in the plan and provide Yee, Inc. with the license it needs to manufacture in the United States?"

"Mr. Mohr, before we can expect the Chinese government to respond to your suggestion, we need to add some other threat or compromise to the equation. It's been my experience that to save face they will need to believe they have received something in return for their offer to compromise."

"Mr. Tambour, how do you think they might react if they understood it was no longer a question of dealing with Mohr Electronics and U.S. Motors but with a broad cross section of American industry that is prepared to announce their support of the Employ American plan?

"Do you really believe the Chinese government is willing to extend their Bamboo Barricade policy to include a diversified group of 80 to 100 American employers who control more than 100,000 jobs?"

Amused by the suggestion, Mr. Tambour asked, "Is there some way you can verify such a claim?"

"Would signed affidavits suffice?"

CHAPTER 42

NO, I DON'T THINK SO

It was late. Andi and Charley had just returned from the theater when Charley said, "Andi, why don't you fix us a couple of single malts while I turn on the music."

They were quietly sitting close to each other at his bar. The lights of Detroit and Lake St. Claire could only be vaguely seen through the snowstorm that was beginning to form. With their old-fashioned glasses half filled with fifteen-year-old Macallan single malt scotch, the music of *La Bohème* playing in the background, they were content to sit quietly together, and enjoy the moment.

Andi felt secure and safe sitting next to Charley. She mused, *How things have changed since that night when he left me half clothed to answer a call from his boss.*

Charley, too, was engaged in his thoughts about her. His mind had drifted back to the late-night walk they had taken along the lake in front of the Royal Wolf Lodge. *I'm still not certain what happened. All I know is my life will never seem the same if Andi isn't part of it.*

Charley turned to face Andi. To say what he wanted to say, he needed to face her and look into her violet eyes. "Andi, I've been thinking—"

Charley's cell phone began to chime. Andi said, "If that's J.W. calling, tell him you will call him back. This time, I want to hear the rest of what you were about to say."

The familiar voice said, "Charley, can you be in my office at ten o'clock tomorrow morning?"

Turning to Andi, with any thought of his previous statement forgotten, he said, "I wonder what that call was all about. It's been several weeks since J.W. and I had that curious conversation at the airport in Cimarron; now he wants me to be in his office at ten o'clock tomorrow morning. Could things be coming to a head? Is U.S. Motors prepared to commit to Employ American? Do I need to prepare for what I suspect could be a very serious meeting?"

"Charley, I'm warning you, the last time you accepted a late night call from J.W. you allowed it to ruin a perfectly good evening. Both your good friend and your wanton woman are telling you, not this time. Just to make certain there will be no misunderstanding, I am planning to take off my blouse and bra. If that doesn't give you any ideas, I will be severely disappointed!"

The next morning, the sky was overcast and chilly air blew through the streets bordering Lake St. Claire. Charley, with a big smile, was hurrying along on his six-block walk from his apartment house to the U.S. Motors building. He couldn't help but think, *Andi has an interesting way of making sure I am late leaving.*

Charley's secretary was waiting for him as he approached his office. "You should probably go right up. J.W. left word he wants to see you the minute you arrive."

Charley's sixth sense alerted him that things were about to become very serious. As he entered J.W.'s palatial office, Charley was not surprised to see the company's chief legal counsel and several of his "kitchen directors" sitting around the executive conference table. The first thing to cross his mind was, *Is J.W. about to reveal his true agenda?*

J.W. began talking before Charley had a chance to pull his chair up to the table. "Who authorized you to hire those investigative firms and gather all that information? What the hell do you think you were doing? Do you realize how much trouble those reports could cause some of our suppliers?"

Charley said, "I'm quite certain if the information contained in those reports was ever to become public record it could cause U.S. Motors and the subject suppliers more trouble than you can possibly comprehend. Conflict of interest and unnecessary export of American jobs could become a very interesting subject of debate. Do you think, for one minute, an already agitated American public isn't going to vehemently react to this kind of news?"

Looking directly into Charley's brown eyes, J.W. said, "If you think for one moment you can come waltzing in here and try to blackmail us into making a positive decision about joining the Employ American plan, you are sadly mistaken. The board of directors believes we can't risk the future performance of U.S. Motors on an untested and yet-to-be-completed plan. They believe there are too many problems to solve and too little time to solve them. Consequently, they have voted to provide me with the authorization I need to execute the Chinese option!"

Rather than debate J.W.'s suggestion, Charley decided to pursue a different approach. "Mr. Chairman, do you agree with the conclusion of your board, or are you just reacting to the will of some of your directors who serve on your board and on the boards of companies who enjoy substantial relationships with Chinese manufacturers?"

"That's a strange question for you to be asking."

"J.W., by now, I am sure you must be aware that the Chinese government has been attempting to use its influence over their American affiliates to prevent U.S. Motors and other companies from participating in Employ American. Their threatened

Bamboo Barricade is just one example of the many things they have attempted. By now you must have questioned who has been responsible for the attacks on me and my colleagues."

"Charley, that's a pretty tall statement, even for you to make. Do you mind sharing, for the benefit of the rest of us, why you think it is necessary for me to respond to your question?"

Before he trusted himself to respond, Charley asked, "J.W., could I borrow your pen? I would like to write out my resignation. I don't want there to be any confusion over what I am about to say. It's more important that you appreciate the sensitivity of the situation and don't regard my comments as an effort to salvage my job!"

After handing J.W. his one-paragraph, effective-immediately resignation, Charley continued. "There is only one possible explanation for how you knew about the results of British Securities' investigations of the transshipment problem. You had to have someone monitoring the calls we made from the in-flight telephone on our return trip from China. It is important that you understand we have been following the instructions of the FBI and Homeland Security. It was their suggestion that we give you a copy of that report. It was our way of testing whether you or any of your directors were collaborating with the Chinese.

"When the information showed up in Beijing, we had no alternative except to conclude that either you or your supply companies had passed copies of the report I gave you in Cimarron along to your Chinese subcontractors."

J.W. was noticeably upset. His flared nostrils were starting to turn white. "Under the instructions of the FBI, Homeland Security, knowledge of information arriving in Beijing—what the hell have you gotten us into?"

Unmoved by the ferocity of J.W.'s response, Charley responded in his coolest and calmest manner. "As far as the FBI is concerned,

they have been deeply involved in this case ever since the laboratory bombings and the failed attempts on Jeff's life and mine. It
would appear they have reasons of their own for wanting to be
involved. I suspect their investigations reflect a much deeper interest than just anything I might have 'gotten us into.'"

"Charley, the record will show I gave copies of the report with
a personal note attached to each of the directors of the aforemen-
tioned companies. I fail to see how my actions could have broken
any laws or knowingly caused any of the problems you are suggesting. I thought and still consider my actions to be an appropriate effort to warn my directors of possible improprieties that
may being practiced by the other companies they represent. By
the way, how can you possibly know if the Chinese government
has received or not received that report?"

"You might be interested in knowing that India's former
ambassador to China, Mr. Tambour, happened to be a guest of
Mr. Chandakar's the night his house was bombed. According to
Jeff, as a result of the threat made against them, his old friend
decided to change his involvement from one of interest to his using
his relationship with the Chinese government to establish back-
channel communications. As a part of his efforts, Mr. Tambour
keeps us informed."

J.W. paused thoughtfully to consider what he had just been
told. Gathering his thoughts, he said, "Charley, it seems to me
you should be less concerned about what I have done and become
more worried by all the things you need to accomplish to finish
your assignment."

Now Charley was confused. *Why would J.W. say they are preparing to exercise the Chinese option in one breath and in the
next admonish me for not finishing my assignment? Is there something going on here that I don't understand?*

"Why are you questioning my ability to complete my original

assignment after you have informed me that you have exercised the Chinese option?"

"Who said anything about exercising the Chinese option? The board of directors' decision only provides me with the authority to execute the agreement. It doesn't require me to complete it. There are a lot of fine-print matters that remain to be resolved. We are a long way from having a finished agreement."

Charley took a few seconds to process what he had just heard. "Just one more question. Would the cancellation of the Bamboo Barricade influence your decision to execute the agreement?"

"Charley, you understand better than most how U.S. Motors' sales in China affect our bottom line. Of course it would."

A verbal explosion from the far side of the conference table succeeded in capturing everyone's attention. Five of the directors were on their feet. Their acknowledged spokesman loudly announced, "Not only have we approved a 'done deal,' but in case you haven't noticed, we have the votes to approve any last-minute changes."

Interrupting the exchange, Charley said, "No, gentlemen. I don't think so. That is not going to happen." He reached into his briefcase and extracted a file that had the FBI official seal prominently printed on its cover. "In light of this information I am about to provide you with, you may also wish to reconsider some of your recent policy decisions. Conflict of interest can be a very serious charge!"

CHAPTER 43

GENTLEMEN, WE NEED TO REACH AN UNDERSTANDING

Within two weeks of Employ American's filing its environmental impact report at the federal level, a western coalition of regional power-generating utility companies filed injunctions for relief. Even if they were unsuccessful, the time required to complete a long and complicated legal process could cause catastrophic delay. A new battle line was about to be drawn.

Within days, the CEOs of three large public utility companies received a similar phone call from James A. Brumfield, Director of the FBI. With only the briefest of explanations, he invited each man to join him and Terry Flynn for a sensitive meeting of the utmost importance. To avoid any concerns about the confidential nature of the meeting, a closed luncheon had been arranged at the French Club, an exclusive San Francisco private dining club.

Shocked by the personal call from the director of the FBI, each bewildered man tried to learn more about the nature of his request. "Jim, what's this all about? Do I need to include the company's chief legal counsel?"

All they learned was that it would not be necessary to bring an attorney. "I suspect we will be able to reach an agreement without the services or advice of counsel."

Each CEO instinctively knew not to further question the director or refuse his invitation. Arriving within five minutes of each other, the men instructed their drivers to remain with their cars, whether it was for ten minutes or three hours.

Terrance Flynn was waiting at the entrance to the club to introduce himself. "Thank you for joining us on such short notice. If you will follow me, the director is waiting to meet you."

Once they were all seated around the small conference table, the director came right to the point. "In case you are wondering, your counsels will tell you the information I am about to hand you is more than adequate for the Justice Department to appoint a special prosecutor and impanel a grand jury to criminally charge each of your companies with two counts of destruction of private property, involuntary manslaughter, and attempted kidnapping."

Without taking an extra breath, the director continued. "Gentlemen, I have asked you to join me here today not to advise you of pending litigation but to inform you of a course of action with which we would appreciate your active support and cooperation. I am here to ask you for your assistance in solving certain public issues that will, hopefully, take precedence over your companies' serious lapses in judgment.

"Today, our government finds itself committed to improving employment in the United States and preparing to convert its coal-fired energy industry into a more environmentally compatible source of coal- and natural-gas–generated electricity.

"In considering what we are going to propose, you should be concerned as to whether we are going to require all coal-fired generating plants to conform to pending EPA regulations regarding clean air emissions or just the new plants that are expected to come on line in the future. With regard to coal-ash toxic waste, you will be expected to comply with current standards if the anticipated testing of your industrial waste reservoirs demonstrates concentrations of heavy metals, and any other carcinogenic materials that no longer conform to prevailing EPA industrial waste standards.

"You can fight us in the courts or you can help us set the precedent of requiring new plants to conform to current carbon dioxide clean-air emission standards, take your choice. There will, however, be no exceptions granted for dealing with toxic coal-ash reservoir waste. Should the presence of unacceptable levels of dangerous materials be found, both local and federal laws clearly dictate it must be eradicated."

Rising from his chair, the powerful chairman of the largest utility asked, "If I may respectfully interrupt, I think you owe us an explanation. Mr. Director, since this is an industry-wide issue, why have you singled out our three companies?"

"Since your companies have seen fit to impede important progress, we thought it only appropriate that we provide you with an opportunity to help us formulate new and precedent-setting coal-burning policies."

"Wait just a minute, Mr. Director! What you are suggesting represents your use of government influence to threaten us into doing certain things that in the ordinary course of business we wouldn't necessarily care to do. Do you really believe you are entitled to use the power of your office to threaten us into adopting your suggested course of action?"

All eyes shifted to the director. His authority had just been challenged.

Anticipating the question, Terry stood up, walked over to a side table, and picked up three copies of the same file. Once he had handed a copy to each of the three utility executives, the director said, "If you would be so kind to review the evidence contained in these files, I think you might conclude that there is enough documented evidence to support the empanelling of a grand jury and that it is more than adequate to obtain criminal indictments of your companies."

The three utility chairmen scanned the summary portion of the document. Their expressions began to indicate their growing concern over what they were reading.

Using his most direct manner, the director calmly said, "You might wish to modify your accusation. You were quite accurate in suggesting that I'm going to use that file's contents, and the FBI's influence, to encourage you to do what I want. But you were wrong in suggesting that I would threaten you. Have you considered what might happen if we choose to stand aside and allow the government to pursue its case against you in the courts and in the press? Please understand, we're proposing to use our considerable influence to help you, not hurt you, by providing you with a choice."

CHAPTER 44

IT'S TIME TO TAKE OUR
BILL TO THE FLOOR

The jet carrying the Claudia and Robin landed at the Scottsdale Airport and taxied to a stop in front of the private jet terminal. Three highly polished black Suburbans carrying the four secret service agents had parked on the tarmac nearby. With a minimum of conversation, the agents greeted the two ladies, still suffering from shock, and motioned for them to get into the middle vehicle of the three-car caravan.

Ten minutes later, they pulled to a stop in front of the celebrated, Frank Lloyd Wright–designed Sonora Desert Arizona Biltmore Hotel. Special arrangements had been made for them to stay in the Wrigley's private mansion. Originally constructed as the private home of the hotel's founder, the elegant structure was located atop a hill, overlooking the golf course, just a short distance from the main hotel. Its separation and vistas made it a convenient location for guests needing tight security.

Unaware of all the publicity their abduction had caused, and the unusual reaction from members of Congress, the financial community, and the administration of the United States government, all Robin and Claudia could think about was hot showers, cool sheets, and air-conditioned rooms. Left undisturbed, for the first time in their lives, the two high-energy women slept around the clock.

———

Relieved by news of their rescue, Congressman Sam Walcott and his bill's cosponsors were smiling. Mr. Sam suggested, "Don't you think it's time we take our bill to the floor for a vote?"

———

In New York, Claudia's partners were also smiling. For several weeks they had been receiving field reports, "Thanks for sending us two remarkable ladies with such an exciting investment opportunity. When you are ready, we are prepared to proceed to market!"

———

Refreshed, showered, and wearing the new clothes that had been left in their rooms, Robin and Claudia decided to explore their new residence. They were sitting on one of the mansion's outdoor terraces when a waiter approached with a breakfast menu. Giving it only a quick glance, Claudia said, "Would you mind first bringing a pitcher of your best Bloody Marys, a pot of black coffee, and a copy of every newspaper sold in the hotel? Later we'll take a platter of fresh fruit, two orders of huevos rancheros, a side order of well-cooked bacon, and a basket of dry rye toast. We have a lot of catching up to do!"

Two envelopes were resting on the tray holding the drinks and the pot of coffee. They had both finished their first Bloody Mary when Robin could no longer resist the temptation of opening the note with her name on it.

Dr. Cook,

Congratulations on your game-changing national tour. We have been told the passage of the "new employment" legislation is assured. Speaking for all your friends in Organized Labor, we thank you for a job well done and look forward to working with you on our national labor recruitment and training programs.

After reading Robin's note, Claudia said, "Robin, I couldn't be happier. Now, there is a compliment you deserve! I couldn't be more proud if that note had been sent to me."

Leaning forward, Claudia embraced her dear friend in a long, strong hug and kissed her right on her lips. Not feeling Robin recoil, Claudia held her a little bit longer and allowed her kiss to progress from that of a congratulatory friend into an invitation for much more.

Slowly withdrawing from Claudia's embrace, Robin, in an effort to mask any surprise she might have been feeling, said, "Don't forget there is a second note with your name on it."

Making a show of slowly filling both their glasses with a second helping from the tall pitcher, Claudia waited as long as she could before picking up the second note. It was from her partners in New York.

Congratulations on a fine tour. We've been receiving nothing but glowing reports from our people and all the representatives of the different groups you've addressed. These reports and the results we are hearing from Washington are what we've needed before we can proceed to market. Please inform Dr. Cook that it is no longer necessary for you to complete the balance of your tour. On behalf of your friends and partners at Lazarus & Co., we tip our collective hats to you on the dawn of what could be a new generation of private sector industrial financings! Good job, thank you!

After reading the letter for a second and third time, with a sly grin appearing on her face Claudia asked Robin, "Want to play the cocktail napkin game?"

Robin took Claudia's hand and said, "Who needs a cocktail napkin?"

CHAPTER 45

A DIFFERENT KIND OF TROUBLE

When it was time to leave Arizona, Robin and Claudia were tan, happy, and well rested. They were also in love. Leaving each other in the airport was going to be difficult. Almost as if she could read Claudia's mind, Robin suggested, "Why don't I walk you to your gate. Who knows, maybe your flight will be delayed, and we will have some extra time to spend together."

Robin walked back to her own gate to await departure, thinking, *Watching Claudia leave on her plane for New York has to be one of the most difficult things I have ever experienced, at least since Isaac died! Just the thought of sex with another woman would be very upsetting. Have I been a lesbian all these years and not realized it or been unwilling to admit it? How am I going to feel about telling others of my love for Claudia? Am I really ready to come out of the closet?*

Claudia's flight eastward had leveled off and the first round of drinks had been served. She was slouched down in the roomy first-class seat. Her shoes had long since disappeared beneath the seat in front of her. She was sipping ice cold vodka from a frosted glass, feeling totally relaxed. For the last ten minutes she had been lost inside her mind. *What the hell has happened? How can it be that after all these years I have fallen in love with another woman? Could this be why I've burned through three marriages and all those affairs?*

———

In Robin's absence, things hadn't been going well at the Institute. Robin picked up a memo that was lying in the center of her desk. It read, "Response to job fairs unsatisfactory, we need to talk." Within twenty minutes of her arrival, a conference call had been arranged with the presidents of the four sponsoring labor unions.

Robin was having a difficult time getting the telephonic meeting under control. Each of the separate unions had organized and promoted job fairs in areas where they had historically enjoyed their greatest support. From more than one union rep, she heard, "The attendance was less than half of what we had expected. It seems there are a lot of unemployed people who are not very motivated to go back to work."

Another added, "Even worse, a lot of them are no longer willing to trust employers, their labor unions, or the government."

The leader from Michigan said, "Say what you want, but how can we expect people who've been exposed to the adversities they have experienced to not have enormous issues of trust? There is a valuable lesson to be learned here."

The fourth executive added, "Or maybe they are losing their appreciation for the value of a good job and the dignity of work. We have a big problem, and we need to find a way to solve it!"

Robin said, "If you are interested, I know of a person who has her doctoral degree in this exact field, and she has been successfully practicing employment selection processing in the greater Detroit area for some time. It might be interesting to learn what she might suggest. Her name is Dr. Andi Taylor, and she can be found in the psych department at Detroit University."

———

Charley's first stop had taken him to Cleveland, Ohio, to call on one of the city's more important manufacturers of industrial motors, generators, and pumps, the Jenkins Motor Works. The company manufactured some of its parts and subcontracted the production of the balance to independent, small, family-owned companies scattered throughout Ohio, Michigan, Pennsylvania, Illinois, and Indiana.

Dan Jenkins had served as the leader of the family's privately owned business for more than fifteen years. The company's suppliers trusted him and believed him when he said, "We are like the arms and legs all connected to the same body. You depend on us to generate the orders and we depend on you to fill them."

Over the last ten years, the Jenkins' family loyalty to its suppliers had been regularly tested. Chinese parts purveyors had, on regular occasions, submitted bids so that the company could access lower-cost offshore markets. Competing companies regularly bid against Jenkins Motor Works for major contracts. To remain competitive, Dan had lowered prices and narrowed his margins to prevent losing the business volume on which his suppliers depended.

Sharing his dilemma with his suppliers, Dan was encouraged when they all suggested that they would do whatever was necessary to keep Jenkins Motor Works from going offshore. Although cooperation was forthcoming, the realization they were fighting a losing battle was becoming increasingly apparent. Profit margins were squeezed and plans for expansion had been postponed more than once. The capital required to retool had long since disappeared.

Dan was running out of options. The day was approaching when he would be forced to make a decision to either close down the company or accept the offer of the Chinese government. Either choice would cause him to abandon his domestic suppliers.

Recalling the impressive presentation by Dr. Cook and Ms. Roth, he had placed a call to his old friend, Charley Hutson. *Could Charley's program represent the reprieve I have been seeking?* Dan wondered.

Dan Jenkins was another man with whom Charley had served in Iraq. Friends of respect and affection for more than twenty years, both men had been very careful to preserve their wartime friendship. They communicated on a regular basis, keeping track of each other's career progress and any life changes. They trusted each other.

"Charley, before we get started, I need to tell you, when all this Employ American business began to boil to the surface, our board of directors gave me one year to find an alternative solution to transferring our manufacturing to China. If lower direct labor costs represented the only source of our problems, I would like to think my suppliers and I could have found some alternative. When Dr. Cook and Ms. Roth started to discuss the other problems needing solving before their plan could be initiated, they caught my attention. At least three of them represent problems we haven't been able to solve by ourselves.

"Our facilities are old and getting older. We really need to modernize our production lines, introduce new technology, separate ourselves from these high, fixed-cost labor contracts, and find some way to lock in longer-term more affordable energy costs."

"Dan, if I may, I would like to tell you about the situations at U.S. Motors and Jeff's company, Mohr Electronics. Many of the problems they are trying to solve appear to be similar to yours. Explaining this is going to take a while. Is there any possibility a man could get a cup of coffee?"

Once Dan and his team began to understand how the cost-savings features of the Employ American plan could result in their offering their suppliers a different system of choices, the emotional atmosphere in the room started to change. Hope was beginning to replace disillusionment.

When Charley finished, Dan said, "What a fascinating story. I'd be lying if I didn't say we failed to give as much thought to some of the other issues we should have considered before making our decision. Of course, we didn't have the alternative you are suggesting."

"Give me the word, Dan, and I can have a team here tomorrow to assist your people in completing a feasibility study."

"Wait a minute, Charley. I thought applications for the tax credit program were to be limited to new employment, not the redeployment of existing jobs. We don't have any plans to increase the number of people we employ. Quite the opposite; by adding state-of-the-art equipment, we would expect to eliminate jobs and increase productivity."

"Originally that was the case. Once it was pointed out that by preventing a company from moving offshore and having to absorb a corresponding amount of unemployment, we concluded, conceptually, there was no difference in the economic effect between creating new jobs or preventing the loss of old jobs.

"Our problem quickly became one of developing diagnostic proof that an employer was sincerely planning to move offshore if it became known that employers were making false threats to qualify for employee tax credits. Actually, it was one of the employers we had chosen for admission to our program who suggested it. He asked, 'Why not require a no-growth employer to move onto your campus as a means of demonstrating diagnostic proof of his sincerity? It's a whole lot easier than moving to China.'"

Dan immediately asked, "If we were to relocate our operations, is there any reason my suppliers wouldn't have the same choice?"

"We have deliberately set up the campus structure to encourage supportive parts and sub-assembly suppliers to participate in our program. They are the ones who are the most vulnerable to offshore competition. I wouldn't be surprised, someday, to learn that they are the ones encouraging their customers to participate in Employ American."

"Charley, how quickly can one of your support teams arrive and help us better understand what's involved, and if appropriate, assist us in submitting our application?"

CHAPTER 46

BOLD MOVES

The ink was barely dry on the Chandakar agreements when word of Mohr Electronics' decision to shift a portion of its foreign manufacturing operations to the United States was announced. It was a bold move. People were trying to understand why a global electronics company would enter into working agreements with an India-based manufacturer to produce its consumer products in the United States.

A press conference had been organized to allow Jeff and Aakil to announce their decision. One reporter asked, "Mr. Mohr, why would you want to employ an Indian manufacturer to produce your products here in the United States?"

Smiling, Jeff said, "Maybe I should answer your question with a question. Why would I want to replace the management of a tested and loyal partner with a new and unproven production management organization?"

The same question was directed to Mr. Chandakar, who replied, "For more than ten years, I have had the privilege of working with Mr. Mohr and his company. Why would I want to jeopardize the support of such an excellent customer? In addition,

I believe that the establishment of a new production facility on the Employ American campus will provide my company with the ability to better supply Mohr and his company's future growth, and it will be in a better position to compete for new manufacturing orders."

A third reporter asked, "Mr. Mohr, why haven't you extended a similar invitation to any of your Chinese suppliers?"

Jeff answered, "Oh, but we have."

"Would you care to elaborate?"

"Not at this time!"

"Why aren't you prepared to answer my question?" the same reporter asked.

Thinking twice, Jeff said, "If you study the details of our contract with Mr. Chandakar's company, you will learn that we have a two-part agreement. One part deals with our decision to leave our present Indian production undisturbed. The second part provides us with the capacity to replace any production we decide to repatriate from other offshore suppliers. Before any Chinese manufacturer can renew expiring contracts with Mohr Electronics, we require them to transfer a substantial proportion of their production to the United States. This transfer would require the consent of the Chinese government. So far, we have yet to see any modification in their position."

"Point of clarification? Mr. Mohr, are you suggesting that you are offering the Chinese the choice of losing all or half of an American customer's production? Are the rumors true about your and Mr. Hutson's efforts to recruit other American companies, currently active in China?"

"Let me answer your question this way. From the outset, we understood there are at least four other reasons beyond the effective reduction of direct labor costs that motivated Mohr

Electronics to participate in Employ American. For some time, I have been traveling around the country, discussing this topic with my friends. I have been pleasantly surprised by how many of them are looking forward to enjoying the same advantages should the opportunity became available in this country."

CHAPTER 47

PRODUCT BRANDING

Charley was in the express elevator ascending to the 84th floor of the Sears Tower in Chicago. The increased pressure on his feet and the slight pain in his ears made him conscious of the car's speed. At the invitation of one of the country's largest wholesale home appliance distributors, Allied Appliance, International, he was heading to a meeting that, if successful, could result in enormous implications for the Employ American plan. Intuitively he understood how so many of the changes in the manufacturing venue had been originally predicated on the appearance of lower offshore labor costs. Any reconsideration of those decisions would be based on other developments.

Anticipating a wide range of questions, he had invited a representative of the national union leaders and an investment partner from Lazarus & Co. to accompany him.

The meeting opened on a surprising note. A marketing consultant was there to present the results of a consumer survey his client had recently commissioned. The part of the presentation that resonated most with Charley was the consultant's statement: "The majority of the consumers polled said they would opt to buy products that were certified 'Employ American made' over foreign-made products. Based on our distillation of the test results, we have concluded that it is reasonable for any company producing products from an Employ American campus to anticipate improving its market share.

The Allied Appliance executive said, "Once we became aware of our ability to reduce our virtual direct labor costs, we revisited our quality-control problems, the disruption of failed delivery of critical parts, and research-laboratory-to-retail-shelf timing issues. When we totaled the cost savings and the potential increase in revenues associated with improving market share, we have concluded that our decision to join Employ American may be a very easy one to make. I'm hoping we can take advantage of this meeting to discuss any other problems that need to be solved before we can move ahead."

Charley couldn't wait to respond. "I have to admit we overlooked your product branding suggestion. When I think about the comparative consumer response to labels saying "Made in China" and those that read "Made by Employ American" I could become very excited, particularly, if we add differentiable product quality and customer service."

Pausing, to give him the opportunity to change the subject, the Allied Appliance CEO said, "Let's talk about the union situation. How are you planning to deal with the high fixed cost and upward pressure on wages and benefits should organized labor become involved?"

"Why don't we allow labor's representative to speak for himself? Ken, if you please?"

For weeks, Ken Fraser had been following the progress of Claudia and Robin's road show, preparing to answer that exact question. "In our minds, there is absolutely no doubt we are operating in a different environment than existed when the labor movement originated in this country. Different times require different attitudes. If we expect the American manufacturer to compete on a global basis, we understand the preservation and generation of jobs will depend, among other things, on our collective ability to assist management in generating orders.

"And, finally, we recognize that energizing this new program is going to require national recruitment and training of a lot of people. Programs of this magnitude are expensive and most likely will exceed most companies' budget limits. In reviewing the Employ American plan, we were particularly impressed with the idea that these costs can be absorbed by the same cooperative organization, responsible for operating all of the on-site facilities, and invoiced to each of the participating employers as a surcharge on their energy bills."

"Wait a minute," the Allied Appliance CEO said, "you are talking about one hell of a change! I've been hearing reports about your decision, but I guess I wanted to hear it from you before I am asked to make a recommendation."

CHAPTER 48

A MORE FORMIDABLE COMPETITOR

After the Mohr Electronics press conference announcing the company's intention to enter into working agreements with an Indian company to manufacture electrical consumer products in the United States, the CEO of Orion Electronics told his board, "Once Mohr succeeds in implementing his new plan, we can look forward to his competing with us on a new product level. He will be able to solve his lab-to-retailer-shelf timing problem and become independent of the transshipment mess that has been unearthed in Taiwan and China. Unless we are prepared to deal with these consequences, I recommend we consider either buying or merging with his firm."

In Berlin, the managers of an international electronics and switch-gear company were talking about Mohr Electronics. "Now Mohr is about to solve his manufacturing problems, why shouldn't we consider buying his company? Ownership would provide us with the toehold inside the American market we have been seeking for a long time."

In Palo Alto, Jeff's phone was ringing more often. Each day, more of his friends called to learn more about the solving of each of the major problems. The friends he had previously visited were calling him back. Other friends were inviting him to visit them. Some were offering to come to California. They made no secret of the fact they were rethinking their own manufacturing situations.

For decades, the eyes and ears of Wall Street had enjoyed an extraordinary ability to see in the dark and around corners. Early access to accurate information represented the magic sauce of the private investment community. Fortunes have been made and lost, betting on what many have perceived as proprietary information.

For no apparent reason, the price of Mohr Electronics stock began to improve. Whoever was accumulating the stock knew what they were doing. Their buying pattern was irregular. The volume varied. There were no major blocks being traded.

During all the excitement, Claudia gave Jeff a call. "I think you need to come to New York and talk to me and one of my partners. Two different companies of substance have approached Lazarus to inquire if you would be interested in selling to or merging with their company."

Three days later, Jeff, his president, and his CFO were aboard the company plane headed to New York. The plane had barely leveled off when Jeff suggested, "Why don't we pretend that one of you is the lead negotiator for the acquiring company and the other is the lead negotiator for the selling company. Whoever is playing the role of the responsible officer of the selling company could start by making a range of projections estimating the change in our profitability should we repatriate our manufacturing, and accordingly, begin to increase our market share. Once you have completed those projections, you should be able to calculate what the company's current value range should be if we decided to retain ownership.

"Whoever plays the role of the acquiring company should make a different set of projections. You should assume there is an added opportunity to take advantage of cost savings and sales expansion that invariably occur as part of the merger process. Once you plug those factors into your calculations, you should be able to determine what the acquisition value range of Mohr Electronics would represent.

"The object of the exercise will be to determine if there is an area of overlap between each of your value computations. Once we determine what that value is, we will be able to discover if either of these companies is serious or if they are on a bottom-fishing expedition."

They were over St. Louis when the two men completed the last of their calculations. Jeff said, "If you are prepared to proceed, each of should consider your information as proprietary information, known only to you."

They were over Indianapolis when the "selling negotiator" said, "Excuse me, but at the values you are proposing, our shareholders' interest would be better served by retaining ownership. Unless you are prepared to discuss a significant premium, I doubt that my shareholders would be interested in your offer."

They were over Pittsburgh when the "acquiring negotiator" finally suggested, "If you are prepared to talk in terms of a leveraged buyout, not a merger, I think we would consider a higher price for your stock."

They were on their final approach to New York's Kennedy Airport when the two men agreed on price, terms, and conditions.

Jeff, who had been taking notes, said, "Good job, I think we all gained a valuable insight into what we may be exposed to over the next two days. Now if I may, I would like each of you to make copies of your projections, the critical assumptions, and the key criteria you used in arriving at your final positions and give me a copy. I think we are ready to proceed."

CHAPTER **49**

HELIX MOTORS

Within twenty-four hours of making his call, Charley was sitting in front of Bart Corbin, chairman and CEO of Helix Motors. The two men knew each other by reputation, but they had never met.

"Charley, if Jeff hadn't called me, I would have called you. I'll come right to the point. We have a new product line that needs to be built on your Employ American campus. We need a real rainmaker to make it happen. We are talking about someone who knows how to solve issues, who can smooth our first-time production problems, who knows how to recruit and motivate a management team, and who is someone on whom we can rely to tell the rest of us what we need to know. We need a man who understands our business conceptually but isn't bogged down with all the worries of a traditional car guy.

"Jeff has been telling me you are that man. Independent of what he has told me, I have been following you and your career path for a long time. I've talked with people who are familiar with your work, and everything they've told me indicates that you have touched all the bases and appear ready to take charge of a big and complicated operation.

"When you resigned from U.S. Motors, you sent an interesting message to the rest of us. I interpreted it to mean that not only were you not willing to work in an environment of conflicted interests, but if you couldn't play a significant role in making important things happen, you needed to move on. Your resignation convinced me that you are the person I want telling me what I need to know."

Caught by surprise, Charley momentarily became lost in his own thoughts. *How could Bart possibly know about the contents of that meeting? Discussions of possible conflicts of interest shouldn't be part of a casual conversation, at least not one involving any of the directors who happened to be present. That only leaves J.W.*

Finally, Charley responded, "I wasn't thinking in terms of a job. I am still committed to doing whatever is necessary to ensure that the Employ American plan becomes a reality. If the opportunity is still open when I'm finished, I can't think of anything that I would like more than talk to you about your offer.

"Now, if you wouldn't mind, I would prefer to shift our discussion back to why I am here."

"Charley, I've been closely following what you and Jeff are trying to accomplish. You'd be surprised to learn how many parallels there are between the discussions you had with Dan Jenkins and our own situation. We may be regarded as a car-making company, but in reality we are an assembler of parts and merchandisers of the finished product. We generate the orders and our suppliers fill them.

"I regard Employ American as a program that has to happen. In my opinion, once you and Jeff have everything organized, the best possible thing that can happen is for the two of you to be turned loose to manage two leading companies capable of exploring the plan's full potential. But that topic of discussion should probably be reserved for another day.

"In supporting Employ American, I have to anticipate that my board will ask about U.S. Motors' decision to withdraw. 'Too many problems, too little time' is a pretty serious charge. If you would be so kind as to explain what is involved in solving any remaining problems, I'm quite certain we at Helix Motors can make up our own minds."

Choosing his words very carefully, Charley finally responded. "I'm not aware of any remaining problems that have been left unsolved. Based on Jeff's and my most recent estimate, our concern has shifted from meeting the minimum job stipulation to having sufficient capacity to service the demands of future interests. It may be that we have uncovered certain Chinese policies and practices that could cause any potential Employ American candidate to reconsider the future practicality of remaining interdependent with the policies of the Chinese government."

"Charley, is there still enough capacity to fulfill a Helix order of 10,000 jobs *and* U.S. Motors' 10,000-job requirement? I know you have discounted their wanting to participate, but I wouldn't give up on U.S. Motors. You might be surprised. Not only have I been receiving a surprising number of calls from many of our suppliers, but I'm also receiving calls from U.S. Motors' suppliers as well. Apparently, they are learning how the improvements offered by Employ American can improve their future and the future of the final assembler. Collectively, they think if both Helix and U.S. Motors were to relocate a portion of company manufacturing operations to the same campus, the advantages offered to our common suppliers would be very impressive.

"When the more responsible members of the company's board of directors come to their senses, it's entirely possible they might choose to resubmit their application."

"If that possibility were to occur, how would Helix Motors react?"

"I would expect Helix Motors to do whatever is practically

possible to encourage U.S. Motors' or any other car maker's interest in the plan. For decades we have all been located in Detroit. Why shouldn't we operate from some other common location? We may think we compete against each other, but in reality, American car manufacturers are engaged in a serious battle of mutual survival with their offshore competitors."

CHAPTER 50

NEW YORK RULES

New York investment banking protocol governing the conduct of meetings between acquiring and selling companies has evolved over a long period of time. Historically, all business points are negotiated between members of the investment banking team and representatives of the acquiring team or the selling organization, but never in the same room at the same time.

Partners and junior members of the investment banking company, lead lawyers and their backup attorneys, and partners of national accounting firms and their supporting staff were seated around the large, highly polished conference table, waiting to meet Jeff Mohr and the other members of his team. Two days had been scheduled to allow morning and afternoon sessions to discuss the interests of each of the acquiring companies.

The first day's meeting started smoothly enough. Jeff and his two senior officers found themselves being barraged with questions about their company. Ignoring the fact that most of the information had already been sent prior to their arrival, Jeff was patiently answering each of their questions. More than once he would consider, *I wonder if they keep asking the same question to determine if there are inconsistencies in our answers.*

In the middle of a conversation, the young analyst would excuse himself, gather his notes and work sheets, and leave the room. A few minutes later, he would return with new computer printout and insist on showing his work to the lead negotiator.

After watching the charade for a few hours, Jeff couldn't decide if he was supposed to be impressed, intimidated, or annoyed.

During the afternoon sessions, the investment bankers' questions were directed toward learning more about Jeff's motivation for selling his company. The question, "What do you hope to accomplish by selling your company?" was asked in so many different ways that Jeff lost track. What was obvious, however, was that their questions represented an attempt to develop the kind of leverage they could use at a later time to negotiate the best possible deal for their acquiring client.

Jeff had become confused. *Why are they trying to develop a prenegotiated term sheet when I thought we were being invited to hear what kind of a value the interested companies would place on our firm? Perhaps, we need to approach this process from a different direction.*

Annoyed by their cat-and-mouse game, Jeff finally said, "Gentlemen, I think you have misconstrued my intention in accepting your invitation. We are not here to sell you our company or negotiate terms and conditions. Having been apprised of your clients' interests, my directors have asked me to sit down with you fellows and do whatever I can to assist you in determining a price you would be willing to pay us for our company.

"Should you be willing to express a serious interest and present us with a proposal, I would be happy to present it along with my recommendations to my board of directors and promptly provide you with our response."

"Are you telling me we can't talk about price, discuss the

different unresolved issues, and develop a terms sheet?" the lead negotiator for the acquiring company asked.

When Jeff failed to respond, his silence shocked everybody in the room. Finally, the lead negotiator said, "Goddamn it, Jeff, that's not the way we do things in New York! Didn't anybody explain the customary procedures and conventions we use in meetings of this type?"

Misunderstanding Jeff's hesitation as a continued demonstration of arrogance, the lead negotiator picked up his papers and signaled to his colleagues to stand, and together they filed out of the room. Jeff, his two officers, the Lazarus partner, and his assistant were left sitting at the table.

Not certain what he should be doing, the Lazarus partner finally asked, "Jeff, do you want me to cancel tomorrow's meeting?"

"Before we decide, why don't you call the other company and describe what has happened here today. Maybe when they learn what occurred, they won't want to meet with us. We are staying at the St. Regis Hotel. Let us know what you would like us to do."

A Lazarus limousine was waiting for them when they exited the building. Half an hour later, Jeff and his officers were sitting at the bar in the St. Regis's King Cole room. They were on their second drink, engaged in serious debate, trying to determine what the hidden message was in the mural hanging on the wall behind the bar. Out of the blue, Mohr Electronics' CFO said, "Boss, aren't you concerned you might have insulted the people gathered around the other side of the table?"

Jeff laughed and said, "Are you under the impression you *can* insult New York dealmakers and their attorneys? Relax, we've only finished round one. They want us to play by New York rules. Once they are convinced we are ambivalent about selling our company, the burden of keeping the ball in play shifts to them. They should understand we are not prepared to come to the negotiating table until they make us a satisfactory minimum offer."

"Okay, Boss, I'll bite. How do we determine what a satisfactory minimum offer is?" the company president asked.

"The same way you did yesterday. A satisfactory offer represents a price that is good enough to eliminate the risk in our having to produce more future value than what we have been offered. It's not a question of how much we might improve the deal, it's an issue of what we believe is enough."

A note informing them that the other buyer wished to meet was waiting at the front desk.

The next morning's meeting started quite differently. Files containing price and suggested terms were lying in front of each place around the table when Jeff and his team arrived. The Lazarus partner opened the meeting. "Mr. Mohr, the folder sitting in front of you contains an offer you may wish to present to your board of directors. We have been apprised of your concern of not wishing to negotiate price at this time. If you are convinced that our client's interest is sincere, you may wish to examine some of the more relevant terms and conditions of the offer. We are prepared to answer any questions of clarification you and your team may wish to ask."

Jeff was impressed. "If you don't mind, I would appreciate it if you would allow my president and CFO to ask their questions. I would prefer to wait until last to determine if I have any unanswered questions."

Any sense of contentiousness was immediately replaced by concerned people who now wanted to identify any possible problems that needed to be solved before a deal could be reached. A positive problem-solving environment became the norm. All questions were asked and answered in a way that would not disturb the positive working atmosphere. They finished their work in time to have a leisurely lunch and still have time to arrive at the airport in accordance with their previously filed flight plan.

Jeff was not too surprised to learn that a manila envelope was waiting for him. Resisting the temptation to immediately open it, Jeff said, "Let's not spoil our luck. Why don't we wait until we are at altitude and having that first well-deserved drink?"

The plane had leveled off and the first round of cocktails had been served when Jeff suggested, "Why don't I open the envelope and place its contents along with the other offer and compare them side by side with your earlier calculations?"

After making the comparison, Jeff sat back in his chair, and smiled. "Well, gentlemen, it appears we have two motivated buyers!"

CHAPTER 51

PENDING LAUNCH

Long before the first factory brick had been laid, the first manufacturing employee hired, or construction on the new coal-burning plant started, news teams were reporting daily on the preconstruction progress of the new campus. Rough-graded roads were beginning to appear, transforming what had once been productive farming land into a quilt-like tapestry of forty-three construction sites. Overhead temporary power lines were extended on poles to what would become individual construction supply yards. Prebuilt, temporary construction offices were being erected. Cyclone fences were installed around future construction-material storage yards. Tank farms were being installed to provide storage of water, a variety of lubricants, gasoline, and diesel fuels.

Railroad construction crews were busy grading in the on-site rail service spurs. They were closely followed by a serpentine of gravel and rock trucks delivering roadbed materials. Next in line were the trucks carrying the creosoted railroad ties. The last of the procession consisted of the trucks carrying the heavy steel rails and the cranes required to unload and spot the ties and rails.

Surveying crews, wearing their yellow construction hats and vests, were clearly visible as they used their transits and measuring rods to set the multitude of survey stakes. Different colors of spray paint, ribbons, and felt-pen-applied labels were added to each of the stakes marking boundaries, providing grading cut and fill information, and delineating future utility line locations.

"Q" school–tested applicants would be arriving from destinations scattered all over the United States. The composition of the applicants would be diverse. Army vets, high school dropouts, former automotive production workers, men, women, people of different ages, races, and nationalities would be arriving within the next thirty days. Tent cities were being erected to house the flood of incoming qualified trainees. In former times, these early tent cities could have been described as being similar to World War II field military barracks or what in the Depression years could have been CCC tent camps.

Andi and local union personnel were busy organizing temporary quarters in local firehouses, movie theaters, and empty retail space, anyplace where tools and equipment could be installed and specific instruction could be taught. Space in local hotels, apartment houses, and vacant houses was being rented in anticipation of the arrival of instructors, teachers, and administrative staff. Defunct restaurants were being refitted.

Adjacent land had been reserved for specially designed living quarters. Each building was designed to house eight people. Qualifying applicants, in order of arrival, independent of age, gender, or background, were organized into teams of eight. They were assigned a parcel and a mentor. Together, they were expected to design their house, obtain all permits and regulatory approvals, and learn each of the trades. During the day, they would work on their house. At night they attended construction school. Union representatives of each of the building trades were on site to conduct the classes.

Students were tested on a pass-or-fail basis. Those who passed continued on. Those who didn't pass were sent home. Team building was progressing. Applicants were learning the meaning of trust. Andi's concepts were working.

The local economy was undergoing a twenty-first-century economic renaissance. The underemployed were going back to work. Local demand for goods and services was rapidly expanding. The citizens of the older and more traditional city were watching how the new waves of recent arrivals were beginning to re-energize their community.

Historically a racially mixed community, Stockton and its environs were accustomed to eclectic and diverse groups of people arriving in their town in search of work. For decades, recent arrivals had been attracted to Stockton in search of work and their desire to educate and raise their children in America.

Appreciative of the economic revival, welcome groups were organized to meet and greet the new arrivals. The seamless absorption of the new arrivals wasn't going unnoticed. Articles describing the unusual process first appeared in the local press. Stories reporting the social phenomena were beginning to appear in the national press. In a short period of time, Stockton was being transformed from its recent role as the foreclosure capital of America to a well-publicized national center of reemployment.

Exhausted but excited, each night Andi called Charley to give him a report. "When are you coming out here? You can't spend all your time calling on potential customers. I can't wait for you to see what we're doing. It doesn't look like much, but you need to know, whatever it is we're doing is creating one hell of a personal rush. Talk about people sharing a dream, I've never seen anything quite like it. Everybody is revved up. I'm not sure if it's the interdependence involved in team building, the growing sense of positive self-esteem, or the sharing of dreams, but some combination of those things is making a huge difference. Something of importance is happening."

CHAPTER 52

DIFFICULT DECISIONS

Less than a week had passed since Jeff and his team had returned from New York when he received a call from Claudia. "Jeff, your suitors are getting nervous. They have been asking if you've had a change of heart. Is it a question of price? Are there terms or conditions that are bothering you? What can we tell them?"

"My lawyers have been advising me that I need to call a legally announced and noticed board meeting and obtain the board's consent before I can proceed. Now that we have two serious indications of interest, there isn't much I can do without their approval and authorization. Knowing they are expecting me to make a recommendation, I've been delaying the process to have more time to think about how I feel about the "sell, don't sell" decision. Strangely enough, the issue isn't about money, it's a question of how the interests of the company, its employees, and shareholders will be best served. Selling a company is a big decision and we only have one chance to get it right."

"Jeff, believe me when I say I understand what a complicated decision this must be for you. Not ever having children, I can only assume selling what has been your 'baby' for so many years and putting it in the hands of someone else to complete its raising must require a great deal of complex thought.

"How does Meg feel about your selling your company?"

"That's just it, you would think with all the money that is involved, the prospect of financial security, and my getting rid of what has been the equivalent of a twenty-five-year 'mistress,' she would be ecstatic. But I'm not so sure that is how she feels. Consistently, she has continued to remark, 'Jeff, this has to be your decision, I am prepared to support whatever you do.' She has only asked one favor. She wants me to accompany her while she inspects a big Colorado–New Mexico cattle ranch that may be coming on the market."

"Jeff, trust another woman's instinct. While you are trying to decide what to do, I advise you pay very careful attention to Meg's ranch idea; there may be a lot more involved that she is prepared to reveal!"

"Duly noted! Why don't you tell our friends that I am scheduling a short vacation with my wife, and when I return I will convene my board and provide them with my recommendation?"

Understanding Charley had his own life-defining career decision to make, Jeff asked his old friend, "How would you and Andi like to join Meg and me for what I suspect will not be such a 'small' ranch inspection trip?"

———

As the four friends were boarding Jeff's plan, Meg announced, "Do you mind if Andi and I sit in the back? We would like to be able to have a good old-fashioned girl talk. With the two of us out the way, you men can discuss all the business you want."

Not wanting to waste a single minute of the flight, both women immediately became engaged in deep conversation. They had a lot to talk about. Andi asked, "Have you recently noticed how many times the words 'freedom' and 'independence' keep appearing in our vocabularies? What are we thinking? What are we trying say?"

Meg replied, "I keep thinking about what must be going through Jeff's mind. What does a man do, when after years of dedicated work, he is offered such an unusual opportunity? He has an interesting choice. He can sit back and enjoy a life, or he can accept a challenge of taking his company to the next level. How many men are offered such an opportunity?"

Andi responded, "Charley's choices are different. Regardless of what he chooses to do, I plan to convince him that whatever the challenge, he can do a better job and enjoy himself more, if he makes room for a loving and supportive companion. Life without his buddy is not an alternative!"

"Andi, be serious for a moment. You've known Charley for less than a year. You have no idea how it can be, once a high-achieving performer becomes totally absorbed with his work. Very few women have the ability to entertain themselves and not become convinced they have to compete with their husband's career in order to survive. Believe me it's not always so easy to be married to one of these 'rainmakers.'"

"Meg, you've been lucky. You've been in love with Jeff ever since you were in college. How many years has it been since you and Jeff started facing the challenges of life together? That's what I am hoping to do. There may be a lot of nice, sensitive men out there, but how many are there like Jeff and Charley? Give me a man who knows how to 'make things happen,' and I'll make the rest of it work!"

After noticing the copilot standing next to them holding a wine bottle and two glasses, Andi paused and said, "Don't mind if I do."

Meg responded to the copilot, "Ray, you might as well leave the bottle and save yourself another trip."

Ten minutes later when Meg reached forward to pour them a second glass of wine, she said, "I've never met another woman who possesses your range of interests, your intelligence, your talent, and your energy. Ever since you became involved with this recruitment and training program, I've been closely watching you. I think I'm beginning to see a different woman. You have that same look of pride and excitement I'm used to seeing in Jeff's and Charley's eyes."

"Meg, I might want to keep working. The role I have been asked to play has completely captured my attention. It's not the idea of creating some test or conducting interviews that interests me. It's the idea of trying to identify the nature of people's deficiencies and creating individual programs designed to help them remove their personal roadblocks.

"My role at Employ American provides me with a great opportunity to test the barriers of my behavioral psychology training and hopefully help a lot of people improve their lives. It's what I've been educated and trained to do."

"I wish things were that simple for Jeff. Andi, ever since this interest in purchasing his company has come to light, I've started worrying about Jeff. I know there's a lot of money involved, but that doesn't seem to impress him. What does a man do when he has a pocketful of money, no new business challenge, and is forced to trust people he doesn't know to take his 'baby' to the next level?

"Despite all that, how do I know there isn't some new challenge he would rather pursue?"

After pausing to think about it, Andi said, "I don't think Jeff is the only one who's thinking about the future. In the short time I've known you, I've watched you learn to relax and enjoy yourself when you were on your family's ranch. You seemed like a completely different person. It even occurred to me, during that horrible attack, as long as Jeff was there to protect you and the children, you weren't as upset as you might have been. There must be a kind of primal thing that occurs when a man and a woman are forced to defend themselves and their children in a frontier atmosphere.

"Could it be that there is a 'ranch girl' buried in the 'urban woman'? I am beginning to believe this ranch expedition is a more serious subject than I may have originally perceived."

———

Sitting in the forward arrangement of club seating, Jeff had been discussing Charley's invitation to join Helix Motors. Finally Jeff asked, "Charley, tell me something. How satisfied are you with Bart's mission statement and being interdependent with Helix Motors?"

"I have no problem working with Bart. With the possible exception of working with you, I can't think of anyone with whom I'd rather work. And I don't have a problem with the mission statement. I couldn't have written it better myself. I guess if I have a reservation it's my not knowing who the other 50 percent partner is going to be. The wrong cook in the kitchen could spoil the broth."

"Charley, if you knew who the second partner was going to be and you had no reservations, would you take the job?"

"It's been a different question that has been bothering me. I'm not sure whether our work with Employ American will be finished or just beginning once we satisfy the last of our stipulations. Knowing we have to complete the launch of our first campus, deal with individual employer problems, and help organize the next campus, I'm not certain where I can make the biggest contribution.

"Jeff, what's more important? Does the country need a new car company or would it benefit more from the proper introduction of a program specifically designed to restore the competitiveness of the American manufacturer?"

"Listen very carefully to what I am about to say. The answer to your question is 'both.' What greater contribution can you expect to make than creating a successful auto manufacturing company that can stand 'toe to toe' and profitably slug it out with foreign competition?"

Smiling at the earnestness of Jeff's response, Charley asked, "Are you sure we're talking about my problem and not yours?"

———

Preoccupied with their individual conversations, no one paid much attention to the plane's landing or its taxiing toward the small private plane terminal and the waiting rental Suburban.

Standing in front of the vehicle, Jeff said, "Charley, what do you suppose is running through a woman's mind when she insists on dragging a man and her friends out to inspect a ranch in the middle of nowhere? Meg, if I could be so bold, may I ask why, all of a sudden, you have so much interest in buying a big ranch? I'm quite certain that your aunt would enjoy having us as guests any time. That is, if we can assure her our 'friends' aren't planning to blow up the place."

"Jeff, this is a serious subject and not one I care to discuss when we are standing at an airport in a twenty-five-mile-per-hour wind, no shade, and ninety-degree heat."

After they had traveled a hundred miles, Meg noticed a roadside sign, "Stop at Stella's, two miles up the road, Home of the World's

Greatest Chili Cheese Burger." As they got closer, they could see that Stella's was a well-maintained, cottage-style restaurant. It was painted white and had red shutters and a mudded-in mission tile roof. A white picket fence surrounded a lush, neatly mowed green lawn. A combination of ironwood and blue paloverde trees were planted at irregular intervals around the house. Rows of colorful flowers had been planted next to the house and along the inner portion of the white picket fence. A latched gate that swung inward to a wooden-bordered red-brick path marked the entrance. A parking lot large enough to accommodate big trucks was located on both sides and behind the homelike restaurant.

Andi said, "Why don't we stop there, it looks much nicer than those other 'greasy spoons' we passed further back. I don't know about the rest of you, but a hamburger sounds pretty good to me."

As they entered Stella's, a pleasant-looking, middle-aged woman greeted them. "Welcome to my restaurant. My name is Stella. May I show you to a table?"

Once they were seated, she placed a large basket of tortilla chips, a smaller bowl of salsa, and four glasses of iced water on the table and took their drink orders. Returning with four diet cokes, she said, "May I suggest our Ortega Chile Cheese Burger? It's our house specialty."

Once their orders were taken, wanting to continue her earlier conversation, Meg finally said, "I don't suppose either of you men has any interest in talking about some of the ideas Andi and I might have."

Without giving the men a chance to respond, she said, "Where does it say that only you men are allowed to chase your dreams? Don't forget the reason we are here is to look at a ranch. Jeff, before you say anything, it's important you understand what I am about to say. You have to believe me when I tell you that nothing has changed about the way I feel about you and our life together. I still love you more than life itself and want to be your strongest and most enthusiastic companion in whatever course you choose.

"What I am about to explain won't change any of those things. It may, however, allow me to add another dimension to my personal life, one that can help fill the void that will be created when the children leave home and you are pursuing your next goal."

After, pausing to take another sip of her coke and grab a few more chips, Meg continued. "Given the choice of living in an urban environment or on a large working cattle ranch, I would prefer the latter. But it is more than just a matter of personal preference. I want to start learning how big ranches operate.

"When you're not working, I want to have you all to myself and know that your mind isn't still focused on your work. I don't know if you realized it, but when you and Charley joined us on the Davis ranch, more of your attention was focused on us and the things we were interested in than I have been able to recall for a very long time."

Pausing to put up her hand, she continued, "No, it doesn't mean you will have to close the windows and sing 'Good Morning Mary Sunshine.'"

"If I could be serious for a moment; someday, I look forward to exchanging my mother and household-manager roles for ranch management responsibilities. Don't forget, I have a business degree! Also, I have been around you most of my life, and I would like to believe that I have earned a graduate degree in home management. Given the opportunity, why can't I learn to manage a ranch?"

CHAPTER 53

ORGANIZED CHAOS

When the last of the contingent stipulations were removed and construction loans were closed, the shovel-ready construction projects were immediately begun. Overnight, the 5,000-acre site was being transformed into one magnificent demonstration of organized chaos.

Mammoth earth-moving equipment had been transported from the oil sand fields of Alberta, Canada, and Montana and North Dakota. The giant machines could be seen moving in the kind of unison that resembled a long conga line of grain harvesters operating on the giant cotton and grain ranches of California's Southern San Joaquin Valley.

Enormous amounts of earth were being extracted from what a few short weeks ago had been crop-producing land. Working in unison with the long line of water-filled trucks and the big self-propelled compaction equipment, the giant carryalls spread their heavy cargoes into thin layers. They were immediately followed by water-trucks spraying a carefully measured quantity of their liquid cargo over each new layer. Self-propelled heavy rolling machines came next, compacting the moistened surface into the next laminated layer.

Repeating the sequence over and over, the continuing procession of strange-looking machines, layer by layer, were building up what would ultimately become the carefully engineered, above-ground protective banks required to support the steel-reinforced concrete walls of the underground raw coal storage facility. More than a mile long, the project began to look like the early pictures taken when excavation for the Panama Canal was first begun.

The scale of the individual projects was exciting. Large cranes, stockpiles of steel beams, lumber, sheet rock, and pipe and electrical conduits were beginning to arrive. Long lines of transit concrete mixers and trucks carrying sand, gravel, rock, and hot asphalt were beginning to form.

Survey stakes with their markings and various colors of attached ribbon were beginning to resemble seas of wildflowers. Men dressed in orange, yellow, and lime green vests and hard hats could be seen in every direction. Circular metal wheels, armed with steel-toothed buckets, could be seen digging the trenches for the water, sewer, electrical, and telephone underground utilities.

The steel structure of the clean-coal generation plant was beginning to appear. The scale of the structure appeared to be much larger than anticipated from the plans. Drilling rigs were preparing to dig the wells that would inject the liquefied carbon dioxide into abandoned gas fields and extract the natural gas.

To encourage and control public interest in the many different on-site activities, visitor parking lots and viewing stands had been installed at a variety of locations. Drink and hot dog vending trailers magically materialized. With so many different things to watch, increasing numbers of visitors were regularly appearing, wishing to watch the progress of their favorite projects and continue their conversations with the ever-present job superintendent.

Television reporting was starting to resemble the broadcasting of a professional sports event. Commentators were quick to recognize the public interest involved in following daily progress and the comments and explanations of enthusiastic job foremen. The visual excitement of watching construction progress was becoming a regular-viewing habit for many people.

In a world of economic uncertainty, and the daily reporting of one serious problem after another, access to positive news was becoming infectious. Optimistic job superintendents were being interviewed regularly. Their growing public recognition along with their expert explanations of what audiences were witnessing, elevated construction watching into another much-viewed sporting event.

The press was having a field day. Employ American was being observed as a bright light in a sea of economic depression and despair. The public's growing sense of excitement was becoming contagious. Local broadcasts were being picked up on nationwide feeds in other cities.

CHAPTER 54

STELLA'S PLACE

The sounds of a busy kitchen and the smells of cooking hamburgers and French fries could be heard and smelled from the kitchen. Despite the appetizing sounds and the intriguing aromas, everybody was waiting for Meg to resume her earlier conversation.

Any further discussion was interrupted by the appearance of four magnificent Ortega Chile Cheese Burger plates. Each of the three-quarter-inch thick, mesquite-grilled hamburgers had been formed into a rectangular shape and served on the bottom half of a specially baked English muffin, shaped like a hot dog bun. An Ortega chile had been laid along its length. The hamburger and the chile were covered with melted cheddar cheese. Served on an oval-shaped dinner platter, together with the other half of the toasted bun, an assortment of lettuce, sliced tomatoes, pickles, and red onions and accompanied by a small mountain of freshly cooked, golden brown French fries. The combination created a remarkable vision. Small condiment dishes of mayonnaise, catsup, mustard, and relish were placed alongside each of the platters. Refills of Diet Coke were immediately offered.

Expecting much less, the four of them, who moments before had been engaged in serious conversation, fell strangely silent.

Their appetites had returned. Making the final arrangements of America's favorite meal to fit their personal tastes took precedence over discussions of a more serious nature.

———

The route to the headquarters of Springer Cattle Company branched off the main highway and led in the direction of the imposingly high and rugged Sangre de Cristo Mountains. Jeff was forced to drive slowly over the rutted, curvy, corduroyed, dirt road as he tried to avoid the potholes and any large rocks. The distractions created by the sight of the steep, granite-sided canyons, the rushing stream paralleling the road, the high mountain vistas, and the growing sense of curiosity of what lay beyond dominated their attention.

When they emerged from the steep-sided canyon, Meg was totally unprepared for the view that was unfolding before her. For years, Meg had heard different members of the Davis family describe the marvelous Springer ranch. At the heart of the ranch stretched a five-mile-wide meadow. It served as the winter range for the company's registered Black Angus breeding herd.

The 13,000-acre winter grazing pasture extended from a very large reservoir to the base of the surrounding mountains. Thousands of black cows with their newborn calves at their sides made an interesting contrast with the brown color of the winter range grasses. Live and California oak trees were sprinkled around the giant pasture. They provided winter shelter and protection from the sun during the summer.

Flatbed trucks with their cargoes of baled hay slowly moved through the cattle. Ranch hands, standing on the truck beds, separated the wafers of hay from the bales before throwing the daily supplement of feed to the waiting cattle trailing after the truck.

A fenced lane separating the different pastures led to ranch headquarters. The original two-story main house, ringed by its freshly painted white balconies, had served as a residence for five generations of Russells and a guest sanctuary for visiting friends, cattle buyers, and vacationing relatives.

The exterior of the buildings had been religiously maintained and painted to preserve its original Southwestern territorial character. Restored many times, the building's interiors were a model of modern luxury and comfort.

Located on top of the bluff overlooking the big reservoir, the majestic homestead represented a Southwestern version of what might have been a medieval European castle strategically located to protect its feudal estate.

Clayton Russell, his wife, and two of their younger children were waiting on the porch of the main house to greet the arriving guests. So were the two faxed messages. Familiar with the long hours and the duress of travel that visitors to their ranch were required to endure, after the introductions were complete, Clayton suggested, "Why don't you unpack, relax, and we'll meet at 7:00 p.m. It's an arriving night custom that you'll have to join your host for one of his famous 'Southwestern old-fashioneds.'" I hope you like bourbon!"

After giving his staff the guest room assignment instructions, he handed the two men their messages. "Why don't you use my office? It's fully equipped with computers, printers, and fax equipment. It also has two separate telephone lines."

CHAPTER 55

RIO DE JANEIRO

With their work on the Employ American committee completed and the last of the details required to fund the development bonds finished, Robin and Claudia were at last headed for their long-anticipated and much delayed vacation to Rio de Janeiro.

Arriving late at night, a thoroughly exhausted Robin and Claudia had been up for forty-eight hours. The complexities of having to arrive and depart from three different airports, and having to stand for long hours in lines and endure three security inspections and two customs inspection stations, materially added to the regular stress and strain of travel.

When they were finally shown to their penthouse suite, they didn't take the time to unpack, open the curtains of their room, or turn on the television set. With the last of their remaining energy, they opened their cosmetic cases, extracted what they needed, and collapsed into bed.

A habitual early riser, Robin was the first to awake the next morning. Not wanting to disturb Claudia, she quietly climbed out of bed, wandered over to the floor-to-ceiling windows, and carefully parted the heavy curtains by a few inches, just far enough to be able to see the view.

On the 34th floor, their suite overlooked Sugarloaf and the rest of Rio de Janeiro's bay and coastline. Mesmerized by the view, Robin was fully absorbed, when she heard, "Robin, you have to see what's on television. It's in Portuguese and I can't tell what they are saying, but they're talking about us."

Borrowing the remote, Robin began looking for English. "Look, CNN has an English-speaking channel." It was Sunday, and the talk show hosts were discussing the California governor's Employ American press conference. Glued to the television, they watched one news program report after another. Any further inspection of Sugarloaf would have to wait.

The sun was at its zenith when Claudia finally turned off the TV and opened the curtains. "We didn't come all the way down here to sit inside watching television. Besides, we've seen the show and know how it ends. How long do you think it will take us to put on those almost bathing suits we brought, walk down to the beach, and order our first drink?"

They were sitting in deck chairs, admiring the magnificent vista, listening to the sound of the breaking waves and the faint sounds of a marimba band playing somewhere behind them. They were enjoying their first cocktail when Claudia said, "Robin, you naughty woman, when was the last time you had a drink before breakfast? I guess I'm going to have to keep an eye on you!"

Not to be intimidated, Robin responded, "Isn't it strange to watch your work being discussed on international television? I can't get over how different our work appears when it's reported on television and the way it felt when we were actually doing it. To me, it seemed like someone had handed us a large stack of bricks. From Monday to Friday we worked as hard as we could to shrink the pile, only to find on the following Monday that more bricks had been added. There were times when I thought we would never be able to complete our work!"

"How many separate presentations do you think we made on our tour? By the time we left Houston, I had lost count," Claudia said. "In retrospect, I always thought my part was the easiest. Talking about the financial issues always seemed so much simpler than having to respond to all those labor-related issues. Every time someone would drag you out on thin ice, I found myself holding my breath. The pressure you were under was incredible. Not once did I ever see you flinch or complain."

"Claudia, dear friend, if you could manage to catch the eye of that waiter walking up and down the beach, I'll let you in on another one of my secrets."

Waiting for Claudia to order another drink, Robin couldn't help thinking, *Don't forget your partner can drink like she has two hollow legs and both of them are a lot longer than mine.*

After accepting the tall frosted glass from the waiter, Robin made sure she placed her second swizzle stick in the warm sand next to the first one. Taking more than a polite sip from the large balloon-shaped glass, Robin let the delicious mixture of rum and fruit juices swirl around in her mouth until she had extracted the last bit of taste, before letting the cool liquid slide down her throat.

Robin said, "Long before we arrived in Hawaii, I was discovering it was your presence that was making the difference. When I would find myself in unexplored and strange territory, I wasn't sure how to react or what to say. I was never certain what to think about all those vicious remarks. I would wonder, were those reporters seeing something we didn't understand? All I know is with each meeting, each new town, and each new day my appreciation of you was rapidly growing beyond the bonds that customarily form the relationship between professional colleagues. My feelings about you were becoming clearer to me. No matter how difficult things became, I knew that my loyal, unconditional, and caring friend would always be there for me."

Totally surprised by Robin's directness and candor, for one of the few times in her life, Claudia found herself speechless. Finally she said, "If you felt that way, why didn't you say something or a least make some kind of signal? You have no idea how complicated you were making my life. Try to imagine what it was like for me. There I was, a thrice-married, tall, athletic woman with all this sensuous female equipment, confused by her feelings for another woman, and not sure what to do or, more important, what not to do. You have no idea how difficult it was to break the ice and express my feelings that afternoon in the bar at the Wrigley mansion."

Reaching over to grasp Claudia's hand in hers, Robin said, "Well, here we are 5,000 miles away from our companies, Employ American, and anybody who can interfere."

"Maybe for a little while, but all I see is a lot of hard work waiting for us when we return."

"Who said anything about going home? I'd like to think we have solved the big problems and it's time for the real people trapped inside our bodies to take control of our lives."

"What an interesting suggestion!"

―――

A week later, the Lazarus partners were sitting around the circular dining room table that was strategically placed in front of the large picture windows overlooking the East River. There were watching the early signs of a nor'easter beginning to settle over Manhattan. A somber mood enveloped the group. Claudia's unopened letter, postmarked Rio de Janeiro, conspicuously lay in the center of the table.

The senior partner present said, "Will somebody tell me why I don't want to open that letter? Why do I think I am not going to like what's inside?"

They were enjoying their coffees when one of the younger partners said, "I can't stand the suspense. I'm going to open Claudia's letter."

After he slit the envelope and slid the paper out, he said "It's a one-sentence letter; let me read it to you."

> In accordance with the terms and conditions of our partnership agreement, I hereby inform you of my wish to take my one-year sabbatical leave, effective immediately.
>
> Claudia

In Robin's absence, Charley Hutson was chairing the regular directors' meeting of the Sentinel Trust. Public reference was beginning to refer to the group as the "New Sentinels." Ivan said, "Before we open the meeting, it might be appropriate if I read a letter I have recently received.

> Under separate cover, I have informed the Sentinel Institute of my intention to take a long overdue one-year sabbatical, effective immediately. Claudia and I have decided to devote our time and our lives to each other. We plan to spend the next year traveling. Wish me luck on my new adventure.
>
> Robin

CHAPTER 56

THE PENDULUM SWINGS IN BOTH DIRECTIONS

Meg had Jeff and Charley visiting a ranch somewhere in Colorado when Ivan Stone was asked if he would join a conference call with Nate White, Larry Wilshire, and Terry Flynn. Entering the conversation, he listened to Larry Wilshire, who was saying, "Aakil Chandakar is trying to reach Jeff. Apparently he has received word from Mr. Tambour that Mr. Cheng Yee and Yee, Inc. have received a license from the Chinese government approving their request to conduct business in the United States. Yee is anxious to talk to Jeff and determine if his submitting an acceptance of his earlier offer, before Mohr's next board meeting, is still appropriate.

"Chandakar and Mr. Tambour believe China's issuance of the business license is intended to transmit a much bigger message placed in context with its decision to remove the "Chinese barricade" affecting U.S. Motors and Mohr Electronics. They are of the opinion, on a case-by-case basis, the Chinese are signaling a change in their national manufacturing policy. I think their exact words were, 'Tell Jeff, when he introduces Yee's offer to his board, to make certain they clearly understand that Mohr's response could represent an important first step in a new era of industrial Chinese–American diplomacy!'"

―――――

A number of important things were rapidly occurring in U.S. Motors' executive suite. The repercussions of Charley's revelations and the contents of his most recent files were quickly spreading. Overnight, the company's full board of directors, the directorships of the five American–Chinese parts supply companies, the Justice Department, and the White House administrative staff had become involved. The possible appearance of high-level conflict of interest was being taken very seriously.

Resignations of the five overlapping directors were immediately accepted at U.S. Motors and at the five supply companies.

Efforts were being made to fill the absent board seats.

Special federal investigative units were activated to reanalyze Employ American and make appropriate recommendations.

Charley's assistance was needed. A message requesting he contact J.W. at his earliest convenience was sent to Hacienda España Nueva headquarters.

―――――

Following short naps and hot showers, and dressed in fresh ranch clothes, Meg and company rejoined their hosts for their pre-dinner cocktail. Clayton Russell, always the congenial host, was standing behind the long, highly polished and preserved, heavy, planked frontier bar. He was preparing to make his famous Southwestern old-fashioned. A member of the household staff had placed all the ingredients he would require on top of the bar. A bucket of ice, a small bottle containing the bitters, a bowl of granulated sugar, a bottle of carbonated soda water, slices of orange, a bottle of maraschino cherries, a bottle of Irish whiskey, and a bottle of Southern Comfort had been arranged in the order that Clayton would use them.

With his family and guests gathered around, Clayton began his nightly ritual. Once his task was complete, he handed each of his guests their drinks and proposed a toast welcoming them to Hacienda España Nueva. It was also obvious he was waiting for their drink comments.

With the ice broken, the members of the Russell family and their guests wasted no time opening up conversation that would help them become better acquainted.

Later that evening when the gracious hosts had retired, Meg made her way over to the green, velvet-covered gaming table situated in front of the big picture window that overlooked the reservoir. It was a crystal clear night, the stars seemed a bit close, and a reflection of the full moon was shining off the reservoir.

She motioned for the rest of them to join her before she asked, "In case you're interested, Andi has some very exciting ideas of her own. With all that has happened today, she hasn't had the opportunity to say anything about them. Andi, why don't you tell them what you were telling me on the plane."

Charley didn't have to be told that he better pay very close attention to whatever Andi was about to say. *We may be in Colorado, but I think I'm about to hear the other half of our Alaskan discussion.*

"Charley, I understand you're under the gun to make some very important career-defining decisions. How would you feel about taking up residence with your 'best friend,' part-time wanton woman, a challenged career professional, and a full-time girl who loves you very much and wants to begin sharing all the experiences that lie before us?"

After listening to Andi express her feelings, Charley said, "I think two people who really love each other and are also good friends shouldn't feel guilty about maintaining an active professional life. Have you ever noticed how good friends invariably think about the other's needs first and try to do what is necessary to make that person feel better? Now I understand why becoming good friends is so important."

Knowing all eyes were focused on him in expectation of how he was planning to respond to Andi's invitation, yet resisting the temptation to provide an immediate answer, Charley took his time before responding. He needed time to think.

I've been waiting all my life for this moment. Have I finally found somebody to love who I want to share the rest of my life with and who won't require I push back from the big table of my work life?

After taking both her hands in his, he said, "How can a man refuse such an offer, particularly if he is in love with his best friend, wants to share an adventurous life, and plans to turn a wanton woman into an honest woman and the mother of a bunch of rug rats?"

———

Life on Hacienda España Nueva was turning out to be more vigorous than anyone expected. Clayton and his wife were intent on showing their guests every inch of the ranch they could reach by car, horseback, or hiking. Their exploring also included using snowshoes to climb the snow-covered elevations leading to the highest peaks and the best views.

The exhausted travelers would pause near the crest of the slope, break out their picnic lunch, and enjoy the magnificent vista of the southernmost extension of the Rocky Mountains. They talked about whatever people want to discuss when they feel as if they have departed the real world.

The next day, when it was time to hike a new terrain, Jeff suggested, "Meg, why don't we take a separate route? There is something we need to discuss!"

Reaching the crest, Jeff said, "Maybe we can sit on that old tree stump over there. I think I am about to reach a decision. I need to discuss it with you. It's complicated and I need your support.

"Believe it or not, before we came on this trip, I thought I had made up my mind to sell the company. It's been a long journey, I could use a break, and it's important to me that I become as supportive of you as you have been of me. Now, I'm not so sure that is what I want to do.

"It was this 'good friend' subject Charley and Andi were discussing and you talking about your dreams when I realized my decision won't affect how I feel about you and how supportive I want to be. If you can say one thing about our twenty-five-year relationship, it must include what good friends we've always been.

"When we are finished looking at this ranch, if you want to buy it and live here, then that is exactly what we will do! Give me the word and I will tell Clayton."

Meg was relieved. She had made up her mind the minute she saw the magnificent meadow surrounded by the rugged peaks of the southern Rockies. Worrying about Jeff's reaction had been such a dominating thought that she wasn't prepared for his response.

Without thinking, she walked up to him, put her arms around him, looked directly into his eyes, and said, "Not so fast! There was one part of Andi and Jeff's talk you haven't mentioned. Can I be your wanton woman?"

The shadows were beginning to lengthen by the time they started down the mountain. Walking down a steep slope, in soft deep snow, wearing snowshoes, doesn't encourage conversation. It wasn't until they were sitting on a rock about halfway down, removing their snowshoes, when Meg asked, "You mentioned there was something else that has caused you to rethink your decision? Would walking down the rest of the mountain be a good time to discuss it?"

They were within visual range of the main house when Jeff finished explaining. He had been talking for more than twenty minutes, when Meg said, "Well, I can tell you one thing, I've never been so impressed by anything. I couldn't be more excited. I have to be frank, in all the time I have been studying your decision, it never occurred to me that you weren't prepared to allow some owner, over whom you have no control, to lead our company to the next plateau. I don't believe I have ever been as impressed with you as I am right now. Count me in!"

———

By the time Jeff and Clayton emerged from his office, the others were already gathered around the bar. During the mixing of the cocktails, Meg formally signed the option agreement. The combination of the excitement, copious amounts of champagne, old-fashioneds, wine over dinner, French cognac, and the high altitude finally took its toll. It was one o'clock in the morning when they concluded their final toast of the evening and straggled off to bed.

At 8:30 the next morning, aware someone was moving around the room, Charley finally woke up. Lying motionless in the warmth of his bed, he was secretly praying that whatever had been planned for the next morning had been canceled.

Noticing Charley was awake, Andi sat on the edge of the bed, handed him a glass of orange juice, and began to rub his back. An hour later they were sitting by themselves in the deserted breakfast room enjoying a limited fare of coffee, toast, and Charley's favorite marmalade.

After finishing her second cup of coffee, Andi announced it was time to start their day. Before she could stand up, Charley reached over and gently took hold of her arm.

"Andi, in all the excitement, I haven't had an opportunity to tell you about my own situation. Yesterday morning I wired Bart Corbin at Helix Motors to thank him for his very flattering invitation and explained I have been considering another position."

Andi was confused. "Another position, I wasn't aware that you were talking to another company."

"I haven't been, at least not until I returned J.W.'s call shortly after I arrived."

"After your last meeting, I thought we had seen the last of Mr. Porter and U.S. Motors. What could possibly have changed your mind?"

"After what J.W. said, I am having a difficult time believing so many important changes could have occurred in such a short time. U.S. Motors' newly elected board has requested J.W. to continue as chairman; they have resubmitted their application for 10,000 jobs to Employ American and asked for the remaining 8,000 jobs to be reserved for their major suppliers who appear to have had a very interesting last-minute change of heart.

"J.W., on behalf of the board, has formally extended an invitation to me to become the first president and CEO of the newly formed U.S. Motors of California."

Temporarily stunned by this, Andi finally asked, "What could J.W. possibly have said to influence you to accept?"

"Eleven words. 'Would you like to have the opportunity to finish your job?'

"Come on, Charley, there has to be more!"

"As usual, you are correct. After many hours of careful

thought, I have decided that helping to contribute to the success of Employ American has to take priority. What could be more challenging than working alongside Jeff? Can you imagine what we might be able to accomplish if we're able to help a major electrical consumer products company and a new generation car maker become shining examples of what can be accomplished in a rejuvenated American industrial environment?"

An obviously delighted Andi said, "Congratulations! One day you agree to live with me and the next day you make a life-defining decision. Charley, my man, I am really beginning to think there is hope for you!"

CHAPTER 57

A CALIFORNIA TSUNAMI

The governor of California, anxious to draw national attention to all the progress taking place in his state, made full use of the publicity afforded his position. He was to host a press conference at the Roth-Demaureux Auditorium on the Sentinel Institute campus. Invitations to join him on the podium were extended to General Benjamin Wells, Congressman Sam Walcott, and Ivan Stone.

Members of the working press, particularly the ones who had been the most active in reporting the Employ American progress, were invited and encouraged to ask the tough questions.

After approaching the lectern, Ivan Stone, the newly elected Employ American Sentinel Institute managing partner, said, "Before I introduce the other speakers, I have several announcements of importance I would like to share with you.

"Employ American is proud to announce the formation of Global Motors, a new, privately funded affiliate of Helix Motors and a consortium of New York private equity funds. This company has been specifically organized to develop a new generation of cars and will employ 10,000 workers in the first phase of our Employ American campus. Their commitment allowed us to satisfy the last of our contingent stipulations and to proceed with the active phase of construction."

After pausing to allow the applause to subside, Ivan continued. "You might be asking what our plans are for the remaining first-phase capacity of 17,000 jobs. I have recently received a formal application from U.S. Motors and its principal suppliers for the remaining capacity."

One of the reporters reporter asked, "Mr. Stone, it was previously reported that Chandakar Industries of Mumbai, India, has committed to building a new plant on your campus to facilitate the repatriating of more than 10,000 jobs from China. Does their commitment represent part of your first-phase efforts? What has been the Chinese reaction?"

"Some time ago, Mohr Electronics made an offer to Yee, Inc., a proud and distinguished manufacturer of electronic parts. For more than ten years, Mr. Cheng Yee and his company have been admirably serving Mohr's lower-cost manufacturing needs. Although, on a company-to-company basis, there were no difficult unresolved issues, China's granting of a U.S.-domiciled manufacturing license involved a great number of very complicated national issues.

"If it hadn't been for Jeff Mohr's remarkable vision, Yee's participation may not have happened and an unfortunate hardening of Chinese–American trade relations might have occurred. I credit Jeff Mohr's belief that existing conflicting national political agendas might be best resolved through the continuing growth of the two countries' economic interdependency."

As soon as the applause began to abate, Congressman Sam rose from his chair and proceeded to the lectern. Standing next to his proud friend, he began to speak. "None of the progress reported here today could have occurred without the support of the American Congress. In an environment of big government and concentrated wealth and influence, the achievement of the enabling legislation could not have happened without a bottom-up, old-fashioned political battle.

"As the result of the tireless efforts of two very remarkable women, Dr. Robin Cook and Ms. Claudia Roth, the Employ American plan was presented to many different audiences in our country's major population centers. Because of their brave, skilled, and indefatigable efforts, these ladies have provided us with a perfect example of why it is so important that 'we the people' need to be involved in establishing public policy and legislative agendas."

The audience was standing, clapping, whistling, and shouting its appreciation and approval. General Benjamin Wells emerged from stage right. Holding up his hand, he quickly walked toward his two friends. After shaking their hands, the iconic military leader turned to the audience and said, "Ladies and gentlemen, twelve months ago, on this very same stage, I told you that our military men and women are committed to protecting 'America and all that it stands for.' At the time, I expressed my concern that I wasn't certain, in our current environment, what those words really meant. Now, twelve months later, having had the opportunity to witness what these people have been able to accomplish, I hope you agree with me that we have just observed an extraordinary example of what those words 'America and all that it stands for' really mean!"

The governor of California was clapping his approval as he approached the dais. Flanked by the three outstanding men, he said, "Ladies and gentlemen, citizens of California, members of the press and the great American public, I want to assure you, for somebody with my political ego, I had no idea that I would have to follow three men with such inspiring and important messages.

"In my capacity as governor of the host state of Employ American, I would like to talk about the significance this plan is having on our state and on our nation.

"Mr. Stone, if you wouldn't mind stepping forward, I would like to compliment you and your team on solving such an important lower-cost, cleaner energy problem. I think I'm safe in saying, not only will your on-site coal- and natural-gas–generation system solve important manufacturing cost problems, but it will lead to significant improvement in reducing America's dependency on foreign oil. Nice job, thank you."

Pausing to allow the standing ovation to abate, the governor continued. "Like so many of you, I have been glued to my television set watching our national press report the daily construction progress. When have we ever seen a face put on construction jobs? At first, I thought the excitement of the new progress was limited to the directly affected areas in California's great valley. Early surveys indicated while the first construction-site visitors lived within fifty miles, later surveys indicate that visitors are coming from all over California and other western states.

"Focus group testing clearly indicates that people are becoming excited. Some have said the emergence of Employ America reminds them of what it must have been like when we mobilized for World War II.

"At the local level it has been reported, in the last sixty days, preconstruction and start-up construction activities have provided more than 10,000 jobs. Open office space has been leased. Vacant apartments and unsold homes are being rented. The local economy is beginning to respond. Public attitude is rapidly changing. California sales tax revenues are reflecting higher levels of commercial activity.

"When completed, the two-phase Stockton project it is programmed to create 200,000 on-site manufacturing jobs, and introduce an additional 600,000 service jobs off-site for a total increase of 800,000 jobs. When you consider that this revenue-and-employment-enhancing program can be accomplished without requiring the government to make an out-of-pocket investment, even this old politician recognizes that's a pretty good deal.

"Historically, California has enjoyed a certain reputation for being one of our country's most progressive states. I feel extremely flattered that our state has been selected as the host state for this remarkable experiment. How often is a state offered the opportunity to help itself and contribute a working example of what can be done across our great country?

"Ladies and gentlemen, I would like to make a prediction. The Employ American program could very well create an economic tsunami, a new wave of prosperity, that could begin in our Pacific Coast state and cascade over our entire country and not stop until it reaches our eastern seaboard!"

ACKNOWLEDGMENTS

To John Heinz, my friend, who opened my eyes to the influence of corporate lobbying. To Allen Druery, who encouraged me to tell my stories. To Shankar Bajpai, whose introduction to the world diplomatic community helped make this story possible. My thanks to Hank Paulson, Jeb Bush, and Pete Wilson for their interest and encouragement. My gratitude to University of the Pacific President Pam Eibeck, and Lou Gale, Dean, Eberhardt School of Business for their interest and support. To my lifelong friend, Mike Berolzheimer, whose encouragement and introduction to interesting people and events have contributed to the formation of the "Matter of Importance." To my many friends whose entrepreneurial leadership has created the model after whom the principal characters have been modeled. And last but not least, to my wife Anne of fifty-one years; without her support and love, the writing of this book would not have been possible.

APPENDIX

TIME PERIOD	Age of Economic Equilibrium			Age of Consumer Products		
	1960	1970	Change	1970	2000	Change
GDP (billions)	517	1,012	495	1,012	9,709	8,697
Average rate of growth			6.5%			5.4%
Employable Population*	117	137	20	137	215	78
Available Civilian Labor Force	74	87	13	87	136	49
% Population Employable	63.2%	63.5%		63.5%	63.3%	
Total Non-Farm Employed*	54	71	17	71	129	58
% Employed	73.0%	82%		82%	95%	
% Unemployed	27.0%	18%		18%	5%	
Total Earned Income*	279	546	267	546	4,885	7,584
Per Employed	$ 5,167	$ 7,694	$ 2,527	$ 7,690	$37,868	$30,178
% GDP	54.0%	54.0%		54.0%	50.3%	
Fixed Living Expense*	$ 155	$ 267	$ 112	$ 267	$ 2,091	$ 1,824
% Earned Income	55.6%	48.9%		48.9%	42.8%	
Personal Income Taxes*	$ 56	$ 109	$ 53	$ 109	$ 939	$ 830
% GDP	10%	10.8%		10.8%	9.7%	
% Earned Income	20%	20%		20%	19.2%	
Discretionary Income*	68	170	102	170	1,855	1,685
Per Employed	$ 1,259	$ 2,394	$ 1,135	$ 2,394	$14,380	11,985
% Earned income	24.4%	31%		31%	38%	
Discretionary Spending*	84.3	190.3	106.0	190.3	2,264.0	2,074
% GDP	16.38%	18.8%	21.4%	18.8%	23.3%	23.8%
Per Employed	$ 1,561	$ 2,672	$ 1,111	$ 2,672	$17,550	$14,878
% Earned Income	30.2%	34.9%	39.7%	34.9%	46.3%	27.3%
Total Consumer Debt*	207	455	248	455	7,379	6,924
Per Employed	$ 3,833	$ 6,408	$ 2,575	$ 6,408	$57,202	$50,793
% Earned Income	75%	82%	102%	82%	151%	168%

* in millions

APPENDIX

TIME PERIOD	Age of Real Estate			The Bubble Bursts		
	2000	2007	Change	2007	2010	Change
GDP (billions)	9,709	13,668	3,959	13,668	13,026	(642)
Average rate of growth			4.8%			−1.6%
Employable Population*	215	232	17	232	238	6.000
Available Civilian Labor Force	136	146	10	146	150	4.0
% Population Employable	63.3%	62.9%		62.9%	63.0%	
Total Non-Farm Employed*	130	138	8	137.6	130.1	(7.50)
% Employed	95%	95%		95%	87%	
% Unemployed	5%	5%		5%	10.2%	
Total Earned Income*	4,885	7,584	2,699	7,584	6,947	(637)
Per Employed	$37,868	$51,945	$14,077	$51,945	$51,080	$ (865)
% GDP	50.3%	55.5%		55.5%	53.3%	
Fixed Living Expense*	$ 2,091	$ 3,056	$ 965	$ 3,056	$ 3,152	$ 96
% Earned Income	42.8%	40.3%		40.3%	45.4%	
Personal Income Taxes*	$ 939	$ 1,157	$ 218	$ 1,157	$ 1,034	$ (123)
% GDP	9.7%	8.5%		8.5%	8%	
% Earned Income	19.2%	15.3%		15.3%	14.9%	
Discretionary Income*	1,855	3,371	1,516	3,371	2,761	(610)
Per Employed	$14,380	$24,430	$10,050	$24,430	$21,238	$ (3,192)
% Earned income	38%	44%		44%	39.7%	
Discretionary Spending*	2,264	4,227	1,963	4,227	3,498	(729)
% GDP	23.3%	30.1%	49.6%	31%	27%	100%
Per Employed	$17,550	$30,630	$13,080	$30,630	$26,901	$ (3,729)
% Earned Income	46.3%	55.7%	72.7%	55.7%	50.4%	(12%)
Total Consumer Debt*	7,379	13,668	6,289	13,668	13,062	$ (606)
Per Employed	$57,202	$99,766	$42,565	99,766	100.4	0.6
% Earned Income	151%	180%	243%	180%	188%	8.0%

* in millions

QUESTIONS AND TOPICS
FOR DISCUSSION

As the novel opens, it's 2010—just four years after the collapse of the great consumer debt bubble. The United States economy is dangerously overleveraged and people are underemployed. The resurrection of the American economy depends on the restoration of the competitiveness of the American manufacturer and goods-producing jobs.

Only one of the original Six Sentinels is still alive: Madam Cecilia Chang Stone, the venerable founder of the Sentinel Institute. Her daughter, Robin Chang Cook, and her son, Ivan Chang Stone, along with five other equally accomplished entre-preneurial leaders, learn of the Sentinel Institute's doctoral thesis "Employ American: A Matter of Importance."

Carefully researched, *A Matter of Importance* attempts to connect the dots of contemporary history. The story takes place over three continents and exposes the inner workings of sovereign governments, offshore manufacturers, foreign oil producers, and domestic power-generating utilities threatened by the possible realization of the Employ American plan. The book tells of the main characters' quest to solve each of the required problems, to avoid the danger of the secret war, and the drama of their evolving lives.

1. The composition of this thriller has required the author
    to identify, investigate, and write about what he considers
    "subjects of current interest." Do you share his concern,
    and what do you think should be done about it?

2. If we fail to restore "goods-producing" employment,
    what other means could we hope to utilize to restore our
    economy to full employment?

3. Should the manufacturer of globally purchased consumer
    goods be required to absorb the total social cost of
    advanced-nation employment?

4. If you agree the government receives a net increase in tax
    revenues of $2.00 for every dollar paid the "new goods-
    producing worker," should the government share 35
    percent with the responsible employer?

5. In addition to reducing direct labor costs to internationally
    competitive levels, how would you rank the remaining
    aspects of the graduate students' Employ American plan?
    (5 = high; 1 = low)?

    - Development of coal and natural gas into affordable,
      green energy;
    - Affordable installation of state-of-the-art production
      retooling;
    - National recruitment and training programs;
    - Programs to reinstate pride of employment and
      dignity of work;
    - Installation of mega industrial campuses;
    - Creation of private sources of investment funding,
      independent of government support; and
    - The restoration of public awareness and
      participation in congressional legislation.

6. If you were present at one of the town hall meetings that
    Robin and Claudia led, what question(s) would you have

posed to those finance/economics experts?

7. Were the efforts by Robin Chang Cook and Claudia Demaureux Roth to garner the cooperation of unions, bankers, and government officials plausible?

8. Did you agree with Charley Hutson's "third option" to prevent his employer, U.S. Motors, from having to choose between accepting high American production costs or outsourcing its manufacturing to China?

9. Did you think that Jeff Mohr's and Charley Hutson's efforts to sell the Employ American plan to their colleagues were realistic?

10. How do you interpret Jeff Mohr's business philosophy, "Beware of yesterday's success; it can be the source of tomorrow's roadblock to opportunity"? Do you agree/disagree with it?

11. Do you believe the American consumer would develop brand preference for "Made in America" products?

12. Were behavioral psychologist Andi Taylor's ideas about "removing the barriers of personal growth among America's unemployed" conveyed adequately?

13. Were you interested to learn, as Ivan Chang Stone put it, "the EPA is hesitant to continue its testing of coal-ash reservoirs until they are convinced of the existence of an affordable means for disposing of the reclassified toxic material"? Can coal be burned in an environmentally sensitive and affordable manner? Should Americans pursue making "green cement"?

14. If individual entrepreneurial leaders and problem solvers don't combine their efforts to solve goods-producing employment, where else can we look? Who do you think will step forward in our modern world in the way the Sentinels and their supporters do in *A Matter of Importance*?

ABOUT THE AUTHOR

Gordon Zuckerman writes his works of historical financial fiction with the informed eyes and ears of an international businessman who has a penchant for history. "As a history buff all my life, with a financial-entrepreneurial career that led me to deal with Congress, bankers, and the Treasury Department, and a broad cross section of American enterprise, I became aware of just how a few powerful individuals can seal the fate of the world, often out of greed masked by political ideals," says Gordon.

"Early on, I discovered I wanted to tell the story of some of the major historical events behind not just World War II, but of other wars, coups, revolutions, and national economic events that became such an important influence in our lives.

"By connecting the dots of history, I believe it is possible to learn more about what the real story behind the story might have been. Not content to limit my efforts to illustrating what might have represented a more complete story, I decided to describe what accomplished entrepreneurial leaders might have done to oppose the misdirected efforts."

The first three of the author's Six Sentinels series have been published. Zuckerman's books are historical thrillers, written for the college-educated reader of both genders, over the age of forty—the reader who enjoys a well-told story about a well-known event that keeps you informed and on the edge of your seat.

The author has been an active participant in the promotion and marketing of his books. He has engaged in more than eighty radio talk show interviews. Articles have been published in local newspapers that have reached more than two million readers. He is a regular participant in commercial and charitable book signing parties. More recently, he was asked to speak on the topic of "Entrepreneurial Leadership" at the University of Pacific's Winter Business Forum.

Born and raised in a long-time asparagus and potato farming family in Stockton, California, he earned a BS in Mechanical Engineering from the University of California and an MBA from Harvard Business School.

Mr. Zuckerman, early in his business career, worked for an international real-estate development company. A charter officer, he created a nationwide joint-venture development division and provided the interfacing between some of our country's more entrepreneurial developers and New York's investment community.

In 1985, he organized Resort Suites of Scottsdale, a nationally recognized golf-resort hotel company, and in 2005, sold his company to a New York investment fund and retired.

He currently serves as a director of The Brubeck Institute and several private companies. He resides with his wife, Anne, of fifty-one years, on their ranch in Northern Nevada. They have two children, four grandchildren, two Irish setters, and two horses.